I0601600

Other books by Alex Acks/Alex Wells

*Murder on the Titania
and Other Steam-Powered Adventures*

Hunger Makes the Wolf (Angry Robot Books)

Blood Binds the Pack (Angry Robot Books)

WIRELESS

and More Steam-Powered Adventures

Alex Acks

This book is a work of fiction. Names, characters, places and incidents are products
of the author's imagination. Any resemblance to real people or current events is
purely coincidental.

Contents

Blood in Elk Creek

THE SKY HAD GONE upside down, and her mouth tasted of blood.

Through a brain fogged with viscous, roiling smoke, Captain Marta Ramos thought that perhaps she really ought to do something to correct these problems. Neither development could be classified as anything but bad.

Black fluid oozed over one eye. She tried to wipe the sticky muck away, but her left arm seemed to be trapped under something soft, but heavy, and her right arm…

—bleeding hell, nerves screaming is supposed to just be a metaphor—

Her right arm let her know emphatically that they were no longer on speaking terms.

She seemed to be hanging over something solid, like a rug draped over a fence, out to dry in the noonday sun. An apt comparison, since beyond the unending stream of complaints from muscles and bones slowly registering with her mind, she felt as if the skin under her chin was starting to crisp a bit.

The world under her swayed. There was a crack like a gunshot, and she fell about four inches, though the surge of adrenaline that hit her system made it feel more like forty feet. Debris shivered down around her, glass and twists of metal winking hotly in the sun, flutters of cloth.

That likely wasn't a good sign either.

Another crack, this one even louder, and she fell.

Darkness.

Colonel Geoffrey Douglas heartily wished he was at his aunt's funeral. A funeral, with its grief, awkward conversation, and incongruously delicate food, would have been immeasurably more pleasant than crawling up a low hillside that seemed to have been used as the public toilet for every buffalo in the area. Far less pleasant was his sense of self-preservation, well-honed on the Canadian Front, insisted he'd hear a moan and feel blunt teeth tear into the back of his neck at any moment.

Something so ordinary as a funeral was unlikely, as all six of his aunts were alive and well, and none of them lived anywhere near the Dead Plains. They were all safely ensconced in well-appointed, middle-class homes in various duchies along the Atlantic coast. Which was technically where he was supposed to be himself, at the aforementioned impossible funeral.

Or at least that was the story he had told his employer, the Grand Duke of Denver. Geoff was not a man comfortable with lying. Years spent as a decorated soldier in Her Royal Highness's Expeditionary Forces prior to his career-ending injury had instilled in him an unbending code of honor that at times clashed uncomfortably with his current career as Chief of Security. He spent all of his time trying to hunt down very sneaky people, and in turn had been forced, disconcertingly, into becoming a significantly sneakier person himself.

He found it immeasurably more disconcerting now that one of those very sneaky people he felt the need to pursue came from within the ranks of the Grand Duke's own men. From *high* in those ranks.

Geoff tucked his cane, incongruously heavy due to the blade concealed inside, securely underneath his body as he crested the hill. It wouldn't do to lose that; while the cane didn't hold sentimental value, the improperly set break in his leg that had ejected him from the service meant that he wouldn't be able to move at all swiftly without it.

To his dismay, the rolling valley below him was neither empty, nor even populated by manure-producing buffalo. Instead, a small military camp, white canvas tents in neat rows, spread out across the flattened, dried grass.

This was what he'd come looking for and the very last thing he'd actually wanted to see. He had held on to his vain hope that this was a regiment of someone else's army that just so happened to have decided to camp in the same location to which a series of intercepted telegrams had led him.

Geoff pulled a small set of binoculars from a leather pocket on his belt. The soldiers still wore the colors of the Grand Duke, of all cheeky things, the familiar forest green uniforms almost black against the pale backdrop of dried grass and canvas. The presence of the Grand Duke's own forces did raise the disquieting question again: *Did* the Grand Duke know about this? *Was* this an official expedition into the Dead Plains, which had, by common agreement of the surrounding duchies, been abandoned only a few years into the Infection?

And if so, *why* had Geoff been cut so neatly from the information loop?

That was the thing that grated most as he scanned over the camp. He was the Chief of Security, the Grand Duke's left hand, supposedly. Only he was beginning to think he'd lost the Grand Duke's trust after that sordid affair with the tin orrery, and succeeding months of exemplary service and an all-new low in the crime rate had done nothing to repair it. Well, it had been unreasonable for the Grand Duke and that mad fool Del Toro to expect his support when it came to an unprovoked war—

Del Toro.

In the camp below, Geoff caught sight of one of the soldiers lounging against a water barrel. The regimental crest on his sleeve was that of the Black Bulls, General Del Toro's regiment.

That tore it. Geoff hissed a foul word under his breath. He'd known the general was up to something when he had departed from the Grand Duchy of Denver under the claim that he intended to visit family in the Grand Duchy of Phoenix, then conspicuously departed on a north-bound train. And then he had discovered that the day before Del Toro's departure, the Black Bulls had been dispatched for field exercises in Berthoud—and they had never actually reached that destination.

But what was he about? And did the Grand Duke know? The Grand Duke had repeated the cover story to Geoff, that this was all for a training exercise with new armaments. Perhaps the Grand Duke believed a lie Del Toro had told him, or perhaps he was manufacturing the untruth himself.

The latter thought made Geoff feel deeply discomfited. He respected his employer and even liked him at times, those times being when he wasn't engaged in some sort of political strategizing. Such as when he was asleep. He didn't at all like the thought that the Grand Duke would baldly lie to him. There had to be some sort of trust there.

Never mind that he'd lied to his employer in order to make his way to this hillside.

A thorough examination of the camp through binoculars did nothing to answer any of his stomach-churning doubts. The camp was orderly, precisely regulation, and dishearteningly devoid of any clues as to what their purpose might be. They had their horses picketed near four empty caissons and two more carrying Gatling guns. The other caissons were loaded with more standard rifle ammunition and rounds for the Gatling guns.

Several supply tents at the center of the little camp or the command tent might hold more specific clues, but all of those had their flaps buttoned tightly shut.

Really, he thought in near petulant frustration, would it be too much to ask for them to leave a handy battle plan tacked to the outside wall of a tent? Perhaps a stray map sitting on a water barrel? Well-disciplined troops were all well and good, up until the moment one faced them.

His best course of action seemed to be to enter the camp himself and have a look around. A uniform would be necessary. While the regiment was small enough that all of the soldiers were no doubt at least passingly acquainted, Geoff was a nondescript enough sort—reasonably tall, built neither all that broad or short, light brown hair, and the common pale skin—that he'd be able to pass at a distance if he was dressed properly. He hadn't let himself run to fat despite his desk job and was still in proper military trim; he'd even kept his officer's mustache in a proper cut.

As to where to acquire a uniform, he did see a few drying by the tents of their owners. That had the obvious problem of requiring an approach to the camp. His best bet really seemed to be one of the sentries. He turned his attention and vision to picking them out as they patrolled slowly around the perimeter.

Across the little valley from him, a creek flowed down from the dark hills in the distance, with a few straggling trees growing around it. Likely, the camp was using the creek as their water source. The trees and shrubs near the creek afforded the best cover of any location around the camp. He'd have to take the man near it and perhaps wait until close to dark to do so.

He found the sentry for that area through his binoculars and stifled a groan. While the man looked about the right size for stealing a uniform, a stroke of luck there, he was also quite young. And enlisted. Geoff's pride and joy would have to be sacrificed on the altar of looking a bit more believable in the part.

Geoff sighed. Well, the mustache would grow back eventually. His fictional aunt's funeral would just have to be an unusually long and ornate affair in the telling.

Satisfied that he had the lay of the land, he squirmed his way back down the hill and stood, doing his best to ignore the myriad of new brown stains—some of them definitely not common soil—that dotted his field clothes. He made his way slowly back to where he'd left his horse, an ugly roan with an even temper and a smooth gait, acquired not long after he'd arrived in the Grand Duchy, since Geoff had always had a weakness for the large beasts. Together, they rode a large circle around the camp to meet up with the creek. He brought the horse as close as he dared, planning for a swift retreat if necessary, then took out his soap and the sharpest of his pocket knives. He stared into the rippling water of the creek and worked up the nerve to shave, fearing the consequences of inferior tools and no good reflective surface on his face.

Duty called, and he—and his mustache—must obey. He took a deep breath, brought the knife carefully to his face, and set to work.

A few minutes later, his upper lip burning like a brand, but not bleeding if his fingers, now decorated with light brown bristles, could be trusted, Geoff followed the creek in toward the camp.

Some skills, once learned, never atrophied. Geoff had been educated in the arts of silence and woodcraft on the Canadian Front, where it had stood between him and death on more than one occasion. It served him well here, allowing him to creep up, if painfully thanks to his bad leg, within striking distance of the sentry, using the sparse cover of the trees to his best advantage.

It was a warm day, and the man was sleepy, showing in the way his walk wavered a bit. This seemed an excellent opportunity, really. Geoff waited for a few minutes, charting the course the man walked, considering the timing of when he would be closest, when his back would be turned. He began to ease forward toward him, cane held at the ready—

The sound of hooves pounding against the hard-baked earth made him freeze, then slip back into the better cover of a low—if unfortunately prickly—evergreen bush.

The sentry quickly straightened, all sleepiness brushed aside as he hailed the approaching men with a friendly, "Good to see you back, sir! Was starting to wonder if they'd be sending out another patrol to look for you."

More men of the regiment, then.

Geoff leaned out to catch a glimpse of five horses and four men. The extra horse was dragging—aha—another Gatling gun on a caisson. They all looked a bit sweaty and disgruntled.

The captain in the lead drew up next to the sentry. "Wasn't easy to drag that thing"—he jerked his thumb back at the Gatling gun—"up and down the bloody hills."

"Did you at least get the spy?"

"Shot him down neat as you please," the captain answered, sounding a bit more cheered by that. Though, then his annoyance returned full force. "Spent the rest of the bleeding morning trying to search the wreckage out in the hills. Couldn't find whatever god-forsaken canyon he crashed in. Finally gave it up, since I didn't see a point in being out there until dark."

"Not in those hills, I should think," the sentry agreed. "Not now."

"Yes, too close to the test site for my own liking."

The sentry grimaced, hesitated, then asked, "Did you see…it?"

"No." The captain made a motion with his hands. Oh, he was crossing himself. "But that was another reason to get out of there. The aeroplane was a light flyer. There wasn't going to be much left of it to look through at any rate. And only a miracle would save the idiot piloting it."

"Save him just long enough for—"

"Don't even say it. I don't want to think about it. Nasty business." The captain waved a hand. "Anything to report?"

"Haven't seen a soul, sir."

"You never know when the savages will come springing from the grass." Another hand wave. "As you were, chap. Dinner's not too long off."

The sentry snapped a pretty enough salute and stood at attention as the party rode by. Interesting, the mix of familiarity and nervousness in the conversation. This man was new; Geoff recalled seeing in the regimental paperwork several recent transfer orders, an unusual number, one more thing that had tipped him off. That made the chances of success for this rather trite plan just a bit higher, as the entire regiment wouldn't necessarily be best mates by now.

Though, Geoff also knew well the easy camaraderie of camp life. He rather missed it. And the attitude of the captain felt as if the camp had been established for quite some time, enough for a routine to be established and danger, while not forgotten, no longer quite so pressing to keep every man on the knife's edge. The regiment must have come straight up here after leaving the Grand Duchy of Denver.

But to do *what*?

The answer to that wasn't forthcoming. Geoff sighed internally as he watched the now wide-awake sentry return to his patrol, and he settled down into the prickly bush to wait for his next opportunity.

THIS TIME, THE SKY was in the right place, at least according to her inner ear. Marta winked up at the cloudless blue, by necessity rather than any sort of existential coquettishness. Her left eye seemed to be glued shut.

The good news seemed to be that her left arm was no longer trapped. The bad news—

—oh, what a curious sensation. She'd never really given credence to the idea of whiting out, rather than blacking out—

—was that the right arm situation had not improved in the slightest. Marta used her left hand, a trifle awkwardly, to clear away the muck from the left eye. Her fingers came back black and gummy. Partially dried blood, then. She scraped her curly, deep brown hair back from her forehead and thus could finally see properly. Her sinuses felt as if they'd been scrubbed with a wire test-tube brush, the remnants of smoke acrid on her tongue.

Her concerns had become legion now, ranging from the breadth of what had happened, to the throbbing pain of her arm. But survival dictated the first and most important problem was the combination of blood and smoke. Whatever had occurred—

—she remembered now, fighting with the aeroplane's stick, which stubbornly refused to move because the tail of her lovely machine had been reduced to tattered ribbons—

—was currently not so important as the fact that unwanted attention was likely turned her way. The Infected could scent blood at great distances, and most still had the basic mental acuity to react to visual and aural disturbances, such as an aeroplane crashing in flames. She needed to move, despite all the shrieks of protest and alarm being reported to her brain by her body.

The body was ultimately a tool for the mind and subservient to it. Pain was a construct that could be put aside when necessary. Those statements were rendered hollow as she reached across her body to grab her right wrist and tug it onto her stomach.

After a presumably spectacular crash, there didn't seem to be much purpose in worrying about noise at the site. She didn't bother trying to hold back the visceral scream that forced itself from her throat. Then she stayed still and panted for a solid minute before she felt at all prepared to embark on the next step of her plan.

She sat up.

This wasn't nearly as painful as it could have been, with her arm already propped in her lap. The movement ended with her swallowing back bile, rather than a scream. She wasn't certain if that was at all preferable, come to think of it. She allowed herself another minute of much more controlled breathing, the pain in her arm settling into a dull ache that terminated with a worrying tingle at her fingers, before she opened her eyes and looked around.

What stood—though perhaps at this point *leaned* was a much more accurate verb—before her had once been a very stately tree, cinnamon-colored bark indicating it was a Ponderosa Pine. Well, cinnamon-colored in the places it had not been scorched by the small fires still burning sullenly around it. It seemed by a turn of luck that there'd been rain recently, or she would have been nothing but a charred skeleton by now. The tree leaned at an unhealthy angle, propped against a smaller, nearby pine tree, a few of its roots popping up from the earth of the grassy hill.

Perhaps she should have found it obliquely comforting that her tiny aeroplane had still been solidly built enough to do that sort of damage to an undeniably tough organism. Parts of the aeroplane were littered as far as she could see: shreds of metal, glass, and cloth; large sections of pipe and bent frame struts; oh, and there was the tiny boiler, sitting in an impressive furrow in the ground.

Ragged, regular holes had been punched through the larger pieces—bullet holes, her mind identified them automatically: .58 caliber. Gatling gun.

It was comforting that she was in far fewer pieces than the unfortunate aeroplane. Marta finally hazarded a look at herself. A multitude of little cuts and burns, along with quite a bit of bruised brown skin, peeped through tears in her clothing; those were easy to dismiss. The unnatural angle of her upper right arm and the enormous, swollen knot not far from her elbow could not be ignored. "Hell," she hissed under her breath. That she'd broken her arm badly was obvious. That it was her right—dominant—arm quite literally added insult to injury.

Marta cast around for cloth of some sort. She caught sight of a flutter of scarlet in the branches of another pine tree—her frock coat, the gleeful trademark of her professional piracy. It would do. She carefully tucked her hand into her belt and began the unpleasant and thoroughly humiliating process of standing. In comparison, babies made the effort look thoroughly easy.

This time, it did involve vomiting. A patch of wildflowers that had somehow escaped the falling debris would never be quite the same.

Well, it wasn't as if anyone was around who would mind. Simms would—right, Meriwether Octavian Simms, ginger giant and her right-hand man, wouldn't *anything* at the moment. He was safely back in the Grand Duchy of Denver, seeing to a veritable laundry list of simple assignments she'd left to him. That was something of a relief, all things considered. The only way the current situation could be more ghastly was if she'd had to pick bits of his brain from her hair in the process.

Without even a hint of sentimental hesitation, she tore the scarlet frock coat down from the tree, then used her left hand and her boot knife to dissect it into usable sections. There would always be other coats to wear, though if she didn't remove herself from this situation quickly, she wouldn't even have a funeral at which to be so nicely dressed.

Much more fumbling than she liked ensued as she tried to knot the thick fabric one-handed. Obviously, there was a bit of practice she'd need to add to her routine after she escaped this situation and made it back home. How silly of her, to not consider the possibility of having to do everything one-handed, and with only her left hand at use.

Too late to worry about that now. She added it to her mental checklist for later.

A brightly colored sling now holding her right arm as immobile as possible, Marta cast around the crash site, looking for anything that might be of use before she departed with all haste. She turned up her machete, then found her goggles under a bit of the aeroplane's frame. Half the lenses were shattered beyond use, but the goggles as a whole still seemed functional enough. She set them on her head and continued hunting around for her pistols. Of the three she normally carried, she found only one, and the barrel of it had bent at a nearly thirty-degree angle.

In a clump of bushes nearby she found her leather satchel, smoldering foully. Hastily, she stomped the small fire out with her foot. Her compass and maps were ruined, and the collapsible water skin as well. Only the oilcloth-wrapped packet of pemmican had survived, though it smelled of acrid smoke. She stuffed the food into her sling. It would have to do; all of her other belongings were scattered and broken.

Marta struck a path away from the wreckage as quickly as she could; the climb up the grassy hill was far harder than it had any right to be. Brown-tinged sweat dripped from her hair, and her mouth began to feel like dry, cracked leather, even with the frequent shade of tall pines. At long last, she reached the ridge, pausing to take in the territory that surrounded her: sharp hills dark with pine trees like the one she had murdered with her aeroplane, outcrops of gray rock protruding from them as far as the eye could see.

While the details of the crash were still hazy, Marta knew where she'd been headed as she departed the Grand Duchy of Denver: into the heart of what was not-so-whimsically called the Dead Plains. The Dead Plains made a great swathe across the western plains and the northern Rocky Mountains of the North American continent, territory too vast, too rugged, too resource poor to justify the cost of the war it would take to clear out the Infected. The lands had been effectively abandoned as people had retreated into the cities, ceded to the dead. At least that was the common story the people of the duchies told themselves from behind their electrified fences.

Marta had traveled into the Dead Plains before, and indeed she knew that packs and even hordes of Infected survived in the wild reaches. But she also knew that this plague, somehow more foul than the ones brought to this continent by Imperial settlers, had delivered some of the lands back to the stewardship of their native tribes.

She also knew, from the lay of the land, where she was in a general sense: the Black Hills. Well, she supposed, it could be worse. She no longer needed to worry about the descent of a ravening horde of the undead at any moment. The Black Hills were not the hunting grounds of the Infected, but rather that of the Oglala Lakota. And as far as she could recall, she hadn't thoroughly annoyed any of them recently.

A promising glimmer of water caught her eye, vitreous flashes between the trunks of the pine trees far down the hill. Water. A stream. And a stream could lead her to a hunting camp, perhaps. More importantly, a stream would let her clean out her wounds and enable her to peel her tongue from the roof of her mouth.

Her legs felt loose and unsteady as she made her way down the hill, though her head simultaneously felt strangely clear. This, Marta realized, was not a good thing at all. She had to keep her steps slow, pausing to clutch at tree trunks; even so, she almost barreled over a small outcrop of rock. An undignified scramble saved her from a potential broken ankle or worse, though she then had the strange impression that the two squirrels she caught sight of overhead were laughing at her clumsiness. Well, let them laugh.

After a time that subjectively felt like a century at least, she dropped to her knees on the rocky little bank of the stream. She leaned over the water, greedily shoveling handfuls of liquid into her mouth. She forced herself to stop, breathing hard, as her stomach twisted in a small, warning cramp. There was a strange, heavy scent to the air that she couldn't quite identify, her nose still ruined with smoke. Marta looked into the water, seeking the sleek shapes of fish—a little snack right now wouldn't be unwelcome, and the need to escape the area felt less urgent now.

Indeed, she did catch the silver, sinuous lines of a fish moving through the water, but the image seemed strangely blurred in a steam that should be nothing but fresh rain runoff. Marta squinted, refocusing on the odd cloudiness, reddish-brown threads quickly shredding to nothing in the running water.

Her stomach cramped again. This time, it had nothing to do with the chill of the water.

She looked upstream, but the view was occluded by rocks and more pine trees. There was a loud splash, followed a moment later by another surge of clouded water.

Marta levered herself to her feet, then drew her machete. The heavy blade felt strange and clumsy in her left hand. Feeling a bit drunk on adrenaline, she made her way around the rock with exaggerated care.

The stream took a sharp turn on the other side of the rocks, widening. Two corpses were laid neatly out in the shallow water. A coyote stood over one, worrying at its arm—the source of the splashes and the gouts of old, coagulated blood.

Blood.

Hand still clutching the machete, Marta bent over and retched, forcibly ejecting all of the water she'd just drunk from her stomach. She wiped her mouth with a handful of grass and looked up to find the coyote now staring at her, a profoundly unimpressed look on its face and a forearm and hand dangling from its jaws.

Marta's stomach cramped again. *Stop that*, she mentally commanded herself. It was a reaction entirely in her mind, nothing but fear.

Tail at a cocky angle, the coyote trotted off with its prize, though the animal did give her a wide berth.

Marta approached the bodies with more trepidation than she had ever felt when faced with any number of corpses. Neither of the corpses had heads; each simply had a stump blackened with blood and rot. She recognized the look of the cuts; she'd made similar wounds herself, more times than she cared to remember.

Each head had been removed with two or three strikes from a machete. The corpses still wore the tattered remnants of leather trousers, feet yet covered with moccasins. A few decorations partially obscured with muck and blood were made from colored porcupine quills; this was not the clothing of those who resided in the duchies.

All of these small details, building readily into a disturbing picture in Marta's mind, felt curiously beside the point. Her left hand shook as she raised it to her goggles again, flipping through the loupes until she found those of treated calcite. The delicate lenses had cracked and crazed into a thousand tiny rhombic shapes, but even through that, she saw the telltale glow that oozed from the bodies, that swirled through the water that touched them and confirmed her worst terror.

The corpses and stream, the stream she'd so greedily drunk from, were alive with Infection. Bright flecks showed on her left hand, which she'd used to scoop water to her mouth. A horrible sort of laugh squeezed from her throat.

She'd survived the most impressive aeroplane crash of her career just long enough to kill herself.

A bead of sweat hung from the end of Geoff's nose and stubbornly refused to fall. If anything, it seemed more interested in being sucked into one of his nostrils. Of course, that was perhaps preferable to having another stinging drop roll slowly over the highly displeased skin that had once housed his mustache. His bad leg ached and burned, a cramp threatening in his calf. It took all of the remembered discipline from his Expeditionary Forces days, coupled with the far more cunning patience he'd developed as security chief, to keep utterly still and continue to wait.

The return of the patrol unfortunately *had* livened the sleepy sentry back up. That made creeping away from him now a far more dangerous prospect than moving in had been. Geoff had done his best to wait it out in a sort of meditative haze, which was unfortunately interrupted often by the intrusion of bugs, wayward gusts of breeze causing the bush in which he hid to prick at him with thorns, and the sentry's absolutely foul habit of smoking. He had to hold his breath more than once as the man passed close by, disreputable hand-rolled cigarette dangling from his lips.

When he'd been in the Expeditionary Forces, Geoff would not have tolerated that sort of slovenly behavior from a man on duty, no matter how boring the duty. The very thought threatened to push his annoyance into something like outrage. He'd have a word or two to put in the Grand Duke's ear, yes indeed—

Well, no, he wouldn't. He had no excuse to know of the bad habits of the Black Bulls when they were out in the field, more the pity there. But perhaps he could talk the Duke into a few surprise inspections all the same.

The sentry exhaled one more smoky sigh and then tossed the butt of his cigarette toward the creek, nearly hitting the bush in which Geoff crouched. Geoff froze, not even daring to breathe as the man approached even closer so he could nudge the still-glowing stub away from the brush and into the water.

"Can't imagine the storm o' shit if I set a fire," the man muttered.

Of course, he by all rights should have kept the extinguished butt in his pocket until he could bury it or at the least put it in with the rest of the camp's refuse, Geoff thought with annoyance. That was what one did in enemy territory, rather than letting evidence of their presence wash through the camp and out into the wild.

Not that anyone had asked his opinion.

The sentry moved even closer to Geoff's position, toward the tree next to him. For a moment, Geoff recoiled in alarm, thinking perhaps he'd been spotted; his grip tightened on his cane—

No. The sentry fiddled with the buttons of his trousers and then proceeded to paint the roots of the tree down with urine, humming to himself as he did.

Well, this seemed like the best opportunity he might get, though it meant he couldn't avert his eyes. He'd seen far worse things on the Canadian Front anyway. Geoff waited until the man seemed to have finished his business—he didn't want to steal a uniform that had been graced with an unfortunate liquid decoration—then surged up out of the brush and swung his cane like a cricket bat.

The sentry, his hands occupied with his trouser fastenings, had only managed to open his mouth to shout when the cane's head hit him on the left temple with laudable precision. The blow landed with a meaty crack, the man reeling and then falling solidly onto his side. Leg and knee screaming, Geoff still dove for him, cane falling to the ground, and covered the man's mouth and nose with his hands. There was a brief, undignified struggle—but when had combat been anything but undignified? Geoff had learned that particular truth very early on—during which time Geoff managed to plant one knee on the unfortunate sentry's chest to hold the partially stunned man in place. Smothering him into unconsciousness took time, but the outcome was inevitable.

Grunting with pain, Geoff clambered back to his feet. His bad leg was a misery of creaking complaints, but there was little he could do about that. He focused on undressing the limp sentry, then binding him with some cord and gagging him with a handkerchief. Geoff made certain the man was still breathing all right, then left him tucked under the prickly bush that had until recently served as his own hiding place.

The stolen uniform was not the best fitting of garments; the trousers were actually a bit too long, as were the sleeves. Better too long than too short, however; this way was much easier to hide. And Geoffrey reassured himself that the tightness across the chest and shoulders of the jacket was entirely due to the young enlisted man's rather spare frame and had nothing to do with any potential softness of his own middle. Despite the ill fit, he found himself standing a bit straighter in the uniform, feeling rather smart indeed. He'd missed the feel of the high, stiff collar.

Geoff took the time to stow his own clothing safely with his horse before venturing into the camp. He tried to walk with nonchalant confidence, though he'd been forced to retrieve his walking stick and use its aide. A pronounced limp would be far more visible and a much more obvious indication something was amiss than the plain black cane. Thankfully, the unadorned wooden sheath, scuffed and pitted from hard use in the field, gave no indication of the well-cared-for blade beneath. From a distance, it might look enough like an ordinary stick to pass, though he did his best to keep it concealed as much as possible with the line of his body as he walked.

On his way into the camp, one of the other sentries hailed him. "Chow time already?"

Geoff only half-looked over his shoulder. The most important thing now was to act naturally. "'Fraid not," he said, doing his best to mimic the tone and accent of the man he'd rendered unconscious. "My relief came early. Think he wanted a little time to himself."

Let the man make of that what he would. "Lucky you, then. Save some soup for me."

Geoff flipped an easy salute and continued on, a swing in his step completely at odds with the churning worry in his stomach.

Of all the times to be without a pistol, Marta reflected grimly, this was the absolute worst. By all rights, she should be preparing to put a carefully placed bullet into her brain. Unfortunately, all she had was a machete. While she could think of several easily engineered setups that would allow her to remove her own head with the weapon, she didn't relish the thought of trying any of them.

For some strange reason.

But then what would be the end game? She refused the idea of becoming a mindless, ravening beast, searching through the Black Hills for human flesh and blood to consume. A painful death was preferable to hideous unlife.

She still had time. Infection of this sort took far longer to overtake a person's body than that transmitted by bite. Perhaps she would be one of the astronomically rare few to fight it off. Such things were possible. At least, that was what she had read, had been told. She had always dismissed those anecdotes as hogwash before, but her mind clung to the laughable hope.

If she began to show symptoms beyond stomach cramps, which could just as easily be caused by fear of her impending death, she would no longer hesitate. If the beds of her fingernails began to turn black, that would be the incontrovertible proof. She was not in the habit of lying to herself and had no pity for those who did.

Until then, at least there was the question of the pair of corpses that lay in the stream.

The question of anything but this new and pressing death sentence.

Marta approached the bodies with caution, not wanting to slip on the stream bank and risk exposing herself to even more Infection. Why invite death with even more haste? She set that thought aside, taking refuge in the clinical cool of observation and logical deduction. The bodies of the Infected did not rot normally, but had their own, more alien states of decay defined by their consumption by opportunistic organisms and desiccation if the environment was dry enough.

Using a stick, she gently lifted the shreds of leather clothing that still decorated the lower halves of the corpses, noting all of the wounds were caused by animal teeth. The corpses were both those of tribesmen, so logic dictated they were most likely of the Lakota, who lived in the area. What was left of their clothing was consistent with that. Both had taken numerous rifle shots to chest and abdomen. Neat cut marks still remained in their tattered clothing, where small decorations had been removed, the flesh beneath scored. That gave her a sense of the dimensions of the knives, far too long and wide for what should have been delicate work. The bodies were not otherwise fouled, no trophies taken by anything but coyotes.

Grimacing, she crouched down to take up the remaining hand of the nearest corpse. The flesh was bloated with water and blackened by Infection, but she could still read the pattern of callouses there, the story of the living man's profession. An archer; not surprising, that. She had seen men from this tribe use both bows and rifles proficiently. He had the speckled remains of powder burns on his hand as well. The observations added up to the picture of a warrior, a hunter, not long into adulthood. The other corpse was much the same.

Marta pulled her goggles down and found the least cracked of the magnifying loupes. Crouched as low to the ground as she could without completely destroying her thought processes with pain, she crawled slowly along, reading the churned-up earth. The depredations of scavengers had done little to obscure this story: Here, the prints of feet wearing boots, not moccasins, four different sets going back and forth from the creek. Farther away, depressions in the soil and torn plants indicating the passage of a cart, one with only two wheels. Horses, their hooves shod.

The corpses had been brought from elsewhere to be dumped into the creek; the two Lakota men hadn't met their end in this place. And the architects of this little scene had been men of the duchies; the boots, the shod horses, the presence of a cart were indication of that. But which duchy, and to what end?

Marta straightened dizzily, pushing her goggles up, then pressed her hand against her middle. The ache there, she told herself, was entirely psychosomatic. The ground covered as thoroughly as currently possible, Marta returned to the creek and laboriously dragged the corpses from it. She didn't have the strength or hands to do anything else, even produce fire. But at least they would no longer be directly tainting the water supply for this area.

The water supply.

The bodies had been deliberately placed to taint the water. That fact alone was disturbing to the point of being nauseating; humanity had spent much blood, treasure, and time trying to eradicate Infection. What sane person would seek to spread it? If she hunted this line of questioning to its conclusion, all would be revealed as a matter of course. Revulsion, while natural, was not a useful reaction when she needed to think through a head ringing with pain.

Animals were unaffected by Infection; it was purely a disease of humans, and a good thing, that. Marta didn't want to contemplate the idea of an Infected bear, or even an Infected cow. But that meant there was no point at all in tainting a water supply unless there were humans around to drink it and be Infected by it. Therefore, whoever had placed the bodies had expected or known there to be humans downstream.

Outbreaks of Infection lived on an exponential curve, exploding outward to consume every human not lucky enough to be either very swift or cowering behind an electrified fence. This could be the start of a new epidemic if it wasn't dealt with swiftly, sweeping across the Dead Plains like fire. And someone had tried to light it off on purpose.

"Hell," Marta muttered. "*Hell.*" There was no word in her vocabulary suitable for this situation, the anger and fear that she felt. She turned her feet downstream and began to walk as quickly as she could. The bodies had been there for days. If it was too late for her, it was likely doubly, triply so for anyone else who had drunk that water. But she had to try.

THE CLUSTER OF TENTS near those of the commanding officers was relatively unoccupied as the sun began to sink toward the horizon. Geoff slipped into the first, expecting to find supplies and getting just that—ammunition, spare rifles, and sabers. More interesting were the barrels upon barrels of machetes, square and menacing blades black and unpolished. Why would so many be necessary unless they were expecting to deal with a large force of Infected?

That thought sent a shiver down his spine. He had seen no Infected since his entry into the Dead Plains, but that did not mean packs did not still roam. Perhaps they had been sent to covertly clean up a large concentration? But why? This was the sort of activity in which all duchies would participate, since it was for the common good, and it would only make the Grand Duke look good to advertise such an endeavor.

He frowned, shaking his head and carefully shutting another barrel that proved to contain only gunpowder. There had to be more to it than that.

The next tent, he nearly walked into, assuming that it was empty. Only at the last moment did he hear the sound of abstract humming. He moved to the shadowed side of the door flap and flattened himself there, waiting.

A moment later, a short, rather rotund man emerged. Nothing about him, from his impressive beard and obvious age—white hair and wrinkles; he had to be nearly seventy—to his ratty tweed were at all military. Geoff watched him with interest as he paused to check his watch, frowned, and walked away. For effect, Geoff saluted the man with the respect befitting his age at least, but the gentleman didn't even seem to notice his presence.

Even more curious.

Geoff watched him go, considering the wisdom of following him. Obvious oddities were perhaps the best places to start trying to unravel this puzzle, and he had limited time. But he paused to peer into the tent the man had just vacated. Another caisson sat in the tent, its tongue propped up on a stack of crates. On the caisson sat a strange device of wood paneling and brass. For the most part, it looked like only a large box with a few dials on the side and a hand crank waiting at the ready. Antennae bristled from it, and seven flasks with different colored liquids were in a holder in front of it, a small box with the label *FRAGILE: GLASS TUBING* next to those. But most interesting was the polished brass horn that emerged from the box's top, flaring out at the end like a morning glory flower. Like a giant's ear trumpet, Geoff thought.

Or a gramophone. But a large, ugly, and ungainly one.

He did not think that he would be able to read its purpose through studying its parts; he'd never been an engineer of which to speak. And there were no papers near the device, no handy book of instructions proclaiming its name. The best bet, then, seemed to be following the man who had just been in its company.

The man who was now out of sight. *Blast.*

Geoff turned, affecting the air of a man who has just remembered he left something in his tent, and headed in the same direction as the round, shabby man. The tweedy man hadn't been walking all that fast; even with a limp he had to covertly disguise, Geoff ought to be able to catch up.

He'd only made it two tents over when the sound of conversation caught his attention, coming from one of the command tents. Geoff carefully drew closer, angling so that he would not be visible either through the partially opened flap or as a shadow against the wall. That was the problem with these camps; the privacy of a tent was a complete illusion, one that only became reality if everyone in the area agreed to pretend that they heard nothing.

"—finished replacing the secondary tube. Your men were far too rough with the device," said a man. His voice had that indescribable blur that made it sound old—the man in ratty tweed, perhaps?

The answering voice was all too familiar, from meeting after meeting filled with arguments as the Grand Duke of Denver simply watched on in obvious amusement: General Del Toro. "The terrain here is difficult, Professor Nielson. Even if they handle it carefully, the caisson will knock it about. You must take that into account. Modify the design if you need."

"I hardly have the proper materials." Professor Nielson, then, the older man.

"All the resources of the camp will be at your disposal, Professor," Del Toro said, sounding almost bored. "If that's not enough, I may have to call your genius into question."

"There is also the factor of time," Professor Nielson answered stiffly.

"There is still plenty of that as well," Del Toro said. "We haven't yet picked the next site. Cheswick?"

"What? Oh!" A third man's voice, this one sounding much younger. Presumably the "Cheswick" in question.

The man sounded, Geoff noted, entirely nervous enough to be a Cheswick. Geoff had gone to school with someone of that name, and the poor boy had spent most of his time playing toast rack and practice target for the other boys in the dormitory common room; in school on a scholarship himself, Geoff had never wanted to draw attention by defending poor Cheswick. He was still a bit ashamed of that, even now.

"Sorry, I was miles away."

Geoff heard Del Toro's annoyed sigh, even through the thick canvas of the tent. His own lips twitched in response, just imagining the look on the man's face, something rather like indigestion. Geoff was familiar with that expression; he caused it with increasing frequency these days.

"Show me that site again."

"Ah, right." There was a bit of muttering, not distinct enough for Geoff to unravel. "This, the original one. I know we've already been there, but the samples look very promising. I need to have another look at it for comparisons."

"I want to have you check the other locations near there that we haven't gotten to yet; that'll take a day or two before we get that far," Del Toro said, his tone indicating the topic had closed. "Which ought to be more than enough time for *you* to get the primary device ready to be moved again, Professor. If the site looks likely, the next step is making certain the area is clear."

Again? Geoff frowned. What did it do, and where had it been used before? He reached up to smooth his fingers over his mustache, grimacing when he encountered only skin that felt far too raw and gave it an unintended smearing of sweat.

"But—" the older man said.

"Professor," Del Toro cut him off. "You have all the hands you could need here. I will leave orders that your work is to be given priority, and my men will obey. I am growing very tired of your excuses." There was an edge of temper to his voice that Geoff recognized well. He'd heard that once, right before the man had thrown a soup tureen on the floor during a lunch meeting and stormed out. He could only hope that if there were any tureens concealed in that tent, they would be aimed at a wall other than the one at which he listened.

Perhaps the Professor finally realized the line he had begun to tread. "Right. Well, I will do my utmost. Of course. It's just a matter of the tools—"

"Professor." Del Toro hissed the third syllable like an angry snake.

The man laughed nervously. "I'll hammer something together. I wasn't named inventor of the year for nothing."

"Don't disappoint me, Professor. This project and the lives of my personal regiment depend upon it. You wouldn't want all of that on your conscience, I'm sure. Not when I'll collect any debts personally."

"Yes, General. Of course. I'm sorry to have made you doubt. Well, look at the time! I'll just go fetch dinner, shall I…"

And then the Professor, his tweed somehow a bit more ratty, as if Del Toro had physically chewed on him instead of just bombarding him with chilling words, emerged from the tent. Geoff hastily ducked back and watched the round man disappear into the camp with commendable speed.

Geoff only considered following him for a bare moment. No, much better to stay close to Del Toro. That was where the meat of this mystery would be. As he concentrated on the conversation between Del Toro and Cheswick, however, he found that Cheswick had launched himself into a rambling discussion of the geography of the Black Hills, and a bit about the rock types, about folds and…vents…and…

Geoff liked to think of himself as an educated man, but the natural sciences had never been his strongest area. He was much more inclined toward the investigatory arts. Still, he did his best to fix key words of the discussion in his mind—hydrothermal? Fault lines? Washout?—for later consideration. He wished he'd brought something upon which to write.

Right, and that wouldn't look suspicious at all.

"Yes, very good, Cheswick. Enough." Del Toro finally cut the man off. "We'll leave at first light tomorrow. I trust you'll be ready."

"I'll make certain all my equipment is packed tonight, General." Somewhere during his geological dissertation, Cheswick had become more animated and less nervous; he sounded something dangerously close to confident now.

"Excellent. Dinner is calling, then."

A bit of rustling, and Geoff ducked back again as the two men emerged from the tent. Dark, appropriately bullish Del Toro, Geoff was unsurprised to see. But the other man, his sleeves rolled up and his black waistcoat dusty…

Lanky, closely shorn hair, skin so dark that it was nearly black. He had that same dreamy, far-off look to his expression as well, Geoff noted with consternation. This man wasn't *a* Cheswick. He was *the* Cheswick, the one with whom Geoff had shared his hideous first-form years.

Well, this had just gone and gotten a bit weird. Though even as he skirted the side of the tent to keep solidly out of their immediate line of sight, Geoff was forced to wonder if perhaps this would work out to be useful. He had a personal connection, no matter how awkward, with the man. That might be enough to get him to talk. If he could be separated from Del Toro.

Rather than follow the two men, Geoff gave them a few minutes to move away into the dim dusk, then ducked into the tent himself. There was a chest, saddlebags, a cot and bedroll. The normal stuff of camp life. But there was also a folding table at the center of the canvas structure, covered with maps.

He must have mistimed his move. Outside, he heard a startled, "Oy! What do you think you're doing?"

Geoff cursed under his breath and quickly turned to face the doorway as another soldier, an enlisted man, came into view.

"All right, boyo," the man said. "You know you're not allowed in here."

"Got a bit lost, I'm afraid," Geoff said, moving forward. "Don't report me. It was a mistake, sergeant, honest."

For a moment, the sergeant seemed about to accept the excuse and wave him on, and then his gaze flicked down to the cane in Geoff's left hand. There was no way to conceal it at this angle. As the man opened his mouth, Geoff hastily raised his cane and hit the trigger for the spring-loaded release in the cane's head. The sheath sprang away and hit the man squarely in the chest, momentarily stunning him, then Geoff had the blade up and at his throat.

"Quiet now, if you please," Geoff hissed. "Wouldn't want to make a mess in the general's tent, would we?"

The sergeant tensed, but hesitated; having a blade at one's throat tended to do that. Geoff used the moment he'd bought himself to move in and strike the man squarely in the jaw with nearly bone-cracking force. With a blow so well-considered and aimed, it had the intended effect: the sergeant dropped, stunned.

For a moment, Geoff considered the possibility of tying him up and continuing his search of the tent, only to have that train of thought cut short by a shout ringing out from the west side of the camp, the creek side. He could only surmise that the sentry had been found, or at the very least missed. Better to make his escape now.

Geoff turned back to snatch up the top map from the table, hopefully the one Cheswick and Del Toro had been perusing, and stuffed it into his jacket, cringing at the sounding of crackling paper. Then he retrieved the sheath, reuniting the two pieces of his cane, and hurried from the tent.

There was enough motion in the camp, with the possibility of an attack having been raised, that he was able to reach the perimeter unmolested. Soldiers had gathered there, preparing to look for the still-missing sentry—a relief, that—so Geoff was able to slip away into the growing night.

On his way down the creek, he paused at the bushes where he'd hidden the man, who was now thrashing as best he could and moaning quite piteously. Geoff bent to yank the gag down— no need to make the man suffer needlessly, after all—though before the soldier had a chance to shout, Geoff tapped him lightly on the shoulder with the tip of his cane. "I trust you shan't tell the general you were bested by a cripple?" he asked.

The man, eyes reflected wide in the moonlight, nodded dumbly.

"There's a good fellow," Geoff said. "You can start shouting now if you like."

That offer seemed to stun the soldier enough that Geoff was nearly fifty feet away before the man began to roar like a wounded bear. It was all the head start Geoff needed to reach his horse and escape.

THE BANK OF THE little creek at least provided fairly level ground to follow. Marta had reason to appreciate that as the hills on either side steepened to become a canyon. Knowing that there might be Infected around, the hemmed-in terrain left her feeling uneasy.

But this would also, she thought, be an ideal place for a camp if one *wasn't* worried about a pack of Infected.

Her nose was still feeling rather ill-used after the crash, but the air smelled heavier, something strong enough to overpower the normal earthy smells one associated with a creek. There was a sour, choking tang to the air. It made her stomach cramp again, out of sick anticipation rather than simple nauseated reaction.

It gave her the terrible feeling that she must be too late.

Marta rounded a small copse of pine trees to come into a clearing. There she paused, regarding the blackened, churned-up ground before her. She allowed herself a single, jolting moment of primal terror before ruthlessly cutting the feeling away and retreating into the detached routine of observation.

There had been a camp in the clearing. The tattered remnants of it were testament to that fact: torn streamers of leather, fallen tipi poles, broken pots and flattened baskets, the burnt circle where a fire had once been. Drying frames had been smashed across the ground, braided ropes of white vegetables—prairie turnips, Marta's memory informed her dispassionately—ground into the earth.

The area had probably been quite solid before, nicely softened with grass from the look of it. There was nothing left but green shreds now, the soils churned and gone black with blood and effluvia, the source of the rotting smell. The corpses of several dogs lay twisted and still, already picked over by birds and other scavengers. She was days too late.

But there were no human bodies. Not even pieces.

That fact chilled her more than anything. There was no way the camp had been empty, not with the amount of blood that had soaked into the ground. But the Infected had not stopped to feed; they had attacked and moved on. That was unheard of. In attacks, a few people might only be wounded and thus taken by the Infection themselves, but always, at least a few people were eaten. The Infected were called the Hungry Dead in rougher company for a reason.

And yet. What could have driven the Infected to move so swiftly? Their hunger was never satisfied.

Marta eased her goggles down over her eyes, flipping the calcite loupes into place once more. As one might expect, the ground where some blood had not completely degraded still glimmered with Infection. As did the stream.

What if, then, the Infected did not pause to feed because their victims had already been in the throes of the disease? Perhaps the taste of the very disease that powered them proved unpalatable. It was as good a hypothesis as the next, but she had no way to test it.

Better, then, to concentrate on the cold, hard facts. And swiftly; there was no way of knowing how far from here the Infected had ranged. She switched the loupes in her goggles over to magnification and began to quarter the area as quickly as possible.

For the most part, the sticky, blackened earth was far too torn to tell a true story, though what she found fleshed out the detail of her initial assessment. The number of tipi poles added up to four of the large tents; a small band, then, probably using the stream as a home base while they harvested the surrounding land for wild vegetables. She found scraps of fine bead and quillwork, a torn leather ball, shattered arrows, shreds of broken fingernails.

They had fought. But if already ill, they would have been far overmatched. She read the lines of individual struggles pressed into the dirt and then moved on.

More interesting was the story told by the surrounding ground, that not so thoroughly destroyed.

The Infected had approached from the west, their path not very far removed from where she had walked. She followed the trail a little back into the woods, finding a few long, black hairs tangled on a twig. So these Infected had been tribesmen, the even less fortunate brethren of those left decapitated on the stream bank. The bark was slightly damaged on several of the trees, as if the Infected had run into them and continued on. It was unheard of for the Infected to walk with such purpose.

And this was not the way they left. The tracks she found only led toward the camp.

Frowning in concentration, Marta backtracked to the destroyed camp and circled around it until she found another trail. There were more footprints, more varied in size. All of the Infected, from the old to the fresh, had departed in this direction. Perhaps not unusual; they tended to form loose packs.

Quite some distance from the camp, nearly far enough that she almost turned back, she found the ruts left by the wheels of a caisson. Smashed into the grass were several cigarette butts, a brand common to both the Grand Duchies of Denver and Salt Lake.

Marta frowned, following the trail a bit farther. It loosely followed that of the caisson. Perhaps the newly-formed pack of Infected had scented new prey and begun to chase it. That behavior, too, was known. They could move quite purposefully when they scented a living human nearby.

Nearly a mile farther down, her head going progressively lighter with the heat, pain, and effort, she found a break in the trail. The caisson continued on, roughly headed east to the nearest pass from the Black Hills. The tracks of the Infected diverted off to the north.

The Infected, she would not follow; she would end her life with more dignity than merely being an hors d'oeuvre. And the caisson…She would need better transportation than her own two feet.

An odd, sharp shadow on a nearby outcropping of rock caught her eye. She approached, noting the grass flattened nearby. There was a small pile of horse manure, and then, perhaps not shockingly, footprints near the rocks. They were not clear—gravel like that at the base of the outcrop did not hold such shapes very well—but she could tell at least they were made by boots instead of bare feet or moccasins. She inspected the outcrop, noting darker areas where the rock had been chipped by tools. There, a chisel mark. There, chips knocked off, as if a hammer had slipped from its target.

But had this happened before or after the massacre at the camp? Rock weathered so slowly that it was impossible to tell. Though if this had not been done by tribesmen—and the evidence, what little there was, suggested not—would they have allowed such a thing in their territory?

Marta pushed up her goggles, frowning, and turned back toward the camp. With each new piece of evidence, the problem felt larger and more tangled, and her time subsequently felt shorter and less adequate to work through such a mess. She stumbled, tripping over a root. Her nerves, almost numbed by constant pain, roused themselves enough to go into a head-spinning shriek of complaint. She caught herself against a tree and simply leaned for a moment, fighting to keep her breath even.

Slowly, she straightened, glancing at her hand, which was pressed against the bark. Each of her fingernails was surrounded with a rim of bruised, unhealthy black. She snatched her hand back and scrubbed it against her trousers. Whatever dirt she scraped away didn't change that dark color, the sign of a body preparing to rot as it breathed.

"Hell," she whispered.

Back in the clearing, she pried a skinning knife from the ground, contemplating the chipped but still serviceable blade. She could stop herself from succumbing and have a comparatively natural death instead. But no, she still had time. There was a whole suite of grotesque and uncomfortable symptoms she had to look forward to before she lost her mind entirely. Why waste what precious time she had left, when such foul doings were afoot?

What better testament to leave behind? If anyone ever found out about it.

Marta tucked the knife into her belt next to the machete and then brought up her hand to rub her forehead. That there was some foul plot being executed by men of some duchy—though she would lay good odds it was the Grand Duchy of Denver. She remembered, almost remembered, soaring over the grasslands, looking for the green uniforms, and then…then…At any rate, the conclusion that these duchy men were attempting to unleash a new plague of Infection upon the Dead Plains was inescapable. It was a disgusting, horrifying, enraging thought, and every fiber of her being that believed such a cosmically unlikely thing as justice was possible cried out that this must be stopped. How, then, when her time was so limited?

She had tried to warn the band camped along this creek and had been too late. That did not mean it was too late for every band within the Black Hills. And if she did warn one, surely they would be able to warn their brethren.

That made the only question *how*.

Marta stared moodily at the ravaged camp, plucking at a ragged thread from her sling with her fingers.

The Infected only ate other humans. They would leave any other animals alone. Those animals would have fled or, in the case of the unfortunate dogs, tried to fight for the sake of their masters. The Lakota used horses extensively.

Where, then, had the horses gone? They were prey animals, first and foremost, no matter how well trained. At the approach of the Infected, they would have broken their picket lines and fled.

But perhaps not too far.

Marta cast over the ground again, moving a bit faster, until she picked up the location where the horses had been picketed. From there, it was an easy matter to follow the course the panicked animals had taken through the trees.

They had fled east and then across the stream, as if spooked again. Marta thoroughly soaked her boots in the process but kept on top of the trail. Not much farther into the trees on the other side, she heard the sound of hooves on the pine needles, the soft breathing of a large animal.

Ah, and even luckier, perhaps some of the horses had thought to come back, now that the danger had passed.

She slowed, moving toward the sound. A dappled gray horse stepped from between two trees and regarded Marta warily.

That was the problem with this plan, Marta realized: they were horses. She'd never been much of an animal person. Particularly not animals that could kill her by kicking her. She much preferred machines, where if she ended up mangled, it was at no fault but her own idiocy.

Animals liked Simms. It was just one more reason to keep him around. So what, she wondered, would he do in this situation? Stroke his damn muttonchops, most likely. He always did that when he was thinking. Then what?

She could envision Simms going gaga over a lamb or a duckling. She had, in fact, seen those things. She could not quite imagine him soothing a horse and then leaping athletically onto its back. If nothing else, she didn't really want to meet the horse large enough for him to do that. No, not helpful. What did he do around animals? He always insisted they were very like children, but she'd never had much use for children either, the way they insisted on being sticky and asking repetitive questions.

Think.

Feeling foolish indeed, she rubbed her hand on her cheek, as if stroking a phantom muttonchop. Calm, she thought. Cool. Soothing.

"There, there," she said, taking a step closer to the horse. "There, there."

The horse gave her a thoroughly unconvinced look.

All right, what else?

"You're a very pretty girl," she cooed in her best imitation of a Simms-exposed-to-kittens tones. "Such a pretty girl. You could just crush me underfoot, couldn't you, you terrifying manure machine?"

The horse sidestepped once as she approached, ears flicking, but didn't move farther than that. Perhaps horses were subject to the sensation of horrified fascination, just like humans. "Pretty, pretty girl. Oh goodness, what has happened to my vocabulary. Lovely. Heavenly. Luscious. Lively. Vivacious. If you let me catch you, I'll name you after Deliah—"

…on second thought.

"No, scratch that. I'd like you to be cooperative and not break any more of my bones. I'll name you after Dolly. She seems nice enough when she's not shrieking her head off just to hear the sound of it."

Another side step from the horse.

"Please don't. Please. I haven't the energy to chase after you, Dolly. I don't have the time for this. I really don't." The horse flicked an ear again as Marta's voice cracked. No, focus. "But being around a pretty thing like you will make me feel all better, I'm sure."

And so on, approaching the horse a little bit at a time. Her mouth was thick, tongue about to stick to the roof of her mouth when she finally reached the animal. Perhaps she'd succeeded in hypnotizing it with boredom.

The horse had no saddle or bridle. She tried to remember how she'd seen them deal with the horses before. Carefully, she patted the horse's shoulder. The horse shuddered its skin and snorted at her, pawing the ground. With even more care, as if the creature might explode without notice, she grabbed a section of her mane.

The horse seemed used to that, thankfully. "There's a good girl, Dolly," Marta rasped.

The next question was how to get on the creature's back. While Marta was quite tall for a woman, she was also exhausted, sick, and only had one arm. She cast around for a handy rock and found one not far away in the form of a nicely jointed outcrop.

Feeling dangerously close to hysterical laughter, she tugged on Dolly's mane. The horse followed, of all mad things. Marta led Dolly over to the rock, using that to aide an undignified scramble onto the shockingly patient beast's broad back. Perhaps the horse was just relieved to have someone with opposable thumbs in charge again.

Doing her best to remember a few riding lessons that had occurred decades ago and forced onto her by her parents, Marta nudged Dolly with her knee until the horse turned, nose toward the heart of the Black Hills.

"I hope you know where you're going," Marta said. "I certainly don't."

Dolly only flicked one ear in response, somehow even more unimpressed than she had been before. Yet, as foolish as Marta knew it to be, it was a strange relief to have something other than herself to speak to, even if no answer was possible.

Or, well, if she ever thought Dolly did answer, it would be time to use that skinning knife on herself in some creatively brain-destroying way.

She nudged Dolly into a walk, a gait that didn't jolt her too badly. Her only hope was to follow the stream back into the hills and look for another band camped along its banks. As the sun began to fall toward the western hills, she told the horse of all she had observed, all of her theories.

Dolly snorted and turned, ears pricking up, then began to walk a bit more quickly on a course moving away from the stream. A nudge, a tug at her mane did nothing. Marta swallowed hard, watching the ground move past them. She looked down at her hands, at the spreading black now creeping up her fingertips, outlining the delicate dendritic pattern of veins. Swallowing against her stomach cramping again, she leaned forward and buried her face in Dolly's mane. "I hope you know where you're going," she repeated.

The horse, of course, did not answer.

Geoff didn't actually look at the map he'd stuffed into his jacket until his horse had carried him a fair distance from the Black Bull camp. By necessity, he had to head toward the foreboding, dark shapes of the Black Hills. The streams flowed from there, and those were his best bet for cover in the night, hiding among the trees sturdy enough to survive on the prairie.

Still, he did not hazard a fire. There was no knowing how far Del Toro might send scouts in pursuit of him.

He only paused when the growling of his stomach—why hadn't he sneaked into the mess for dinner first, *then* raided the general's tent?—had reached dizzying levels. He hobbled his horse, then removed the bridle so the animal could graze a bit. Then with a sigh, he took his own dinner from his pocket—jerky and hardtack.

He was a bit jealous of the horse, all told. But he couldn't afford a fire right now, when it could call unwanted attention to him. As he woodenly chewed on a dry mouthful, Geoff unearthed a spy's lantern from his pack. The little contraption was collapsible and equipped with mirrors to bend the emerging light into a tight beam, ensuring no tell-tale glimmer would escape so long as he was mindful where he pointed it. He had to pause twice while putting it together and lighting it to get a drink from the stream and unstick the gummy mix of hardtack and meat from his aching teeth.

After a covert glance around—ridiculous habit, as he was alone out here but for the horse, and owls posed no hazard to his secrecy—Geoff unfolded the map he'd stolen. It was a little worse for wear from its earlier adventures, a few marks made with wax pencil rather than ink smeared and sharp creases thrown in black relief by the lantern's light. But it would do.

At first look, the map seemed fairly standard, the symbols on it marking the movements of troops. But Geoff quickly realized that was not the case; while the arrows indicating lines of movement were there, the unit symbols were odd indeed. And there, far to the side, someone had neatly delineated the presence of the Black Bull camp with the standard symbols.

There were other odd markings on the map, as well. Green boxes had been drawn near many of the creeks. A few of them had been crossed off with black Xs. And each of those green boxes decorated the center of the line of movement arrows, the ones for the non-standard units.

Geoff frowned, reaching up to stroke his missing mustache, the expression turning into a grimace as he found only prickly skin.

And what of Cheswick's part in this? The map had been on the top of the pile, and Geoff hadn't heard the sound of any paper shuffling before or after Cheswick had gone on his strange lecture about natural sciences. He rather doubted the man had anything to do with the troop movements, even without the impromptu geology lecture. Cheswick, he recalled from school, had always acted rather like a pacifist, if such a thing were possible in one so young. It wasn't so much that he couldn't have fought back; it was just that he never did, somehow seeming to prefer taking the blows and the insults quietly because he didn't want to make a fuss.

Well, he was certainly making a fuss now. Perhaps he had something to do with the green boxes and their checks, though what geological phenomena required the presence of troops, however irregular? While Geoff had made his fair share of despairing jokes about terrain being the greatest enemy when he'd been in the Expeditionary Forces, it wasn't something one sent troops against.

There was no key to the map, no helpful notes to answer any of those questions. Of course, it was never that easy. Well, perhaps the simplest way to deal with the question was to go to one of the sites that had its box marked and see what he might find. It seemed a safe enough assumption that whatever Del Toro intended for that place had already happened. One of the marked creeks was perhaps half a day away, so long as he rose early.

Not that there was anything here but his own unquiet thoughts to keep him awake.

Geoff folded the map back up and stowed it, then unpacked his little bedroll before turning down the lantern. He missed the trappings of civilization keenly at times like these, with rocks digging into his back. But at the same time, there was something intensely refreshing about being on the scent and not having to look over his shoulder to worry what his employer might think.

Or at least, not until the end of the chase. But he'd already committed to seeing this matter through, and at the end, the chips would fall where they might.

And if his chip was to fall, at least he'd have his honor intact. The damnably pragmatic side of his character couldn't help but point out that honor didn't make much of a cushion.

If it did, the rocks wouldn't be bothering his back as surely as questions worried at his mind.

Marta woke to the sound of voices, a babble her mind couldn't immediately sort out, men and women, young and old. She opened her eyes and found only the dark hint of a curving wall that angled overhead.

Her mouth tasted very odd indeed. Disjointed memories rolled through her mind—the crash, the poisoned stream, the destroyed camp—bringing a surge of panic in their wake as she wondered if human flesh had some kind of aftertaste and that was the fresh horror to which she awoke.

No, that really didn't make any sense at all. She was fairly certain the Infected didn't have thoughts like this, as incoherent and sleep-fuzzed as she felt. Though wouldn't that be a new sort of nightmare to contemplate, an eternity trapped in a half-rotting body, able to think but not control what then happened?

She groaned quietly. That did nothing to ease the fears about having become Infected. She sat up, trying to move her right arm as she did.

Oh, but that hurt. Not as much as it had before, perhaps, but still enough to make her ears ring.

That seemed answer enough. It was well-known science that the Infected felt no pain. Even such basic functions were impossible for them, considering the relentless way they continued on even after injury.

Light pierced the dim space. Instinctively, Marta shaded her eyes with her left hand. Someone spoke to her, an older woman by the sound of her voice. It took her a moment to sort the sounds into words—not a language she knew. But there was an interrogative tone at the end, indicating she'd just been asked a question.

For the moment, none of that seemed at all important. As her eyes adjusted to the bright daylight, Marta saw her own fingers first as a shadow cutting across the sunbeam. But then, slowly, she realized that they didn't look quite as she had last seen them. She lowered her hand back down, inspecting her own skin with wide eyes.

While her fingers were dirty and battered enough to cause despair at the idea of ever playing at the role of grand lady again, all of her skin had resumed its normal, rich brown color. The black sign of Infection had vanished.

"Impossible," Marta whispered. Only obviously, it was possible; her life had become incontrovertible proof. Thus, there had to be an explanation for it as well, and one she would find out.

The woman, something dangerously close to amusement in her tone, asked the same indecipherable question again.

Marta squinted at the woman. Her iron-gray hair was long and plaited into braids. She wore a leather dress decorated with fringe and delicate bead work, symbols and stylized animals. The woman gave her a stern look; her face was quite craggy and suitable for such quelling expressions.

"I don't suppose you speak English?" Marta asked. The woman's expression didn't change. "What about Spanish?" she continued, switching to that language. Nothing again. Marta cursed herself for never having learned the Lakota language, for she was surely in the midst of a camp. Though it wasn't as if learning any of the native languages was at all easy, since first it required someone from within the tribes who was willing to teach. They tended to keep to themselves, and for good reason.

But just because the Lakota didn't trade with the duchies didn't mean they weren't trading with other tribes. Marta unearthed once more the memories of her misspent youth to the west and switched languages yet again. "Perhaps Goshute? Do you speak that?"

This time, there was a flicker of recognition on the woman's lined face. She nodded and disappeared from the doorway, letting the flap fall back to reveal daylight outside.

Momentarily blinded, Marta covered her eyes with her left hand again while she waited for her vision to readjust. Now that she'd gotten over her initial shock at not only being alive, but apparently set to continue being alive until she next did something suitably harebrained, she focused on what her other senses could tell her. The voices outside, while muffled and not speaking in a language she could understand, indicated at least eight people in the immediate area, of various ages. The tent smelled of smoke, stew, hides, and someone's unwashed feet—she practically felt at home. But how had she gotten here?

Her memory was a nightmarish blur, fragmentary images made incoherent with what she now realized had been a fever, another sign of the progressing Infection. It was all twisted shapes of trees moving by, the unsteady motion of the horse beneath her, worse than a boat in rough seas. And then she could vaguely recall the babble of voices—perhaps the very same ones that she heard now—and the sensation of falling into waiting hands, followed by the swift prick of…of what? A needle? The tip of a knife? A porcupine's quill?

Marta opened her eyes and looked down at her left arm. Her already soundly abused shirt had been slit up the sleeve. Seven punctures, scabbed over, the skin around them still irritated and red, ran down the inside of her arm in a neat row, from her bicep to below her elbow.

As if they had been waiting just for this attention, the little wounds took that moment to assert that they were very, very itchy. Perhaps her right arm being in a sling was a small advantage, there, though her makeshift sling had been removed. In its place were bindings made of strips of wool blanket and leather. It also hurt far less than it had; while the broken bone ached, her arm had been set and splinted, and that supplied an almost immeasurable amount of relief. So she had been found by someone good at the medical arts.

But so good they could *cure* Infection? Impossible. Or perhaps more accurately, *improbable*. The evidence suggested that these Lakota had done just that. Unless she found another explanation, all of which seemed equally if not more improbable, she must accept it as truth.

A shadow passed before the tent's doorway, cast by a middle-aged man, his long black hair also plaited. His chest was bare and flecked with dust. Marta made note of a scar on his left side, what had been a bullet wound, and quite a nasty one. Rather than wary or hostile like she expected, his expression was borderline jovial. "Chumani said you speak Goshute?"

Chumani must be the older woman who had gone to fetch him. And whoever this man was, he certainly spoke that language with more comfort than she did. "I'm a little out of practice."

"Unusual, though. What's your name?"

"Marta Ramos." She managed a little sitting bow.

His eyebrows went up a little, and he tilted his head as if thinking. "Do the Goshute have a name for you?"

This, she realized, could either be very good, or very bad. Reputation tended to work only in those extremes. "I've heard the Newe call me the Red Coyote." She smiled crookedly. "When they thought I wasn't listening."

"Oh, so it *is* you." The man managed a long-suffering tone, even though they'd only just met. He pointed to the side; the destroyed remnants of her coat were rolled up near the tipi wall. "I've heard stories."

"You needn't sound so pleased."

"Pleased or not, I greet you from my heart." The man snorted, an expression of amused resignation coming to his face. "And what trouble has this coyote brought?"

"Trouble enough. Who am I about to lay my burden upon?"

"You need not sound so pleased, either." He gave her an ironic little inclination of his head. "Khangiska."

She gave him as respectful of a bow as she could manage while sitting and with her arm bound tightly to her side. "Well, Khangiska, I'm afraid I'm the bearer of bad news."

"I can't think of a time when one of you has come to us half-dead and it's been good news." He waved a hand. "Tell me."

"There are Infected loose in your lands," she stated bluntly. "And the Infection was spread on purpose. I don't know by whom, but I suspect."

Khangiska had stiffened as soon as she stated there was Infection in the area. But as she continued on, his expression went from one of denial to something far darker. "Tell me everything."

She did, without hesitation. While she had many of her own questions, starting with the terrifying hope of her fingers returning to their natural brown color, the true priority was preventing the Infection from spreading further. That should have been something that crossed all peoples, all nations. That it was plainly not still sickened her.

Khangiska only became more sober as she continued on. "Which creek was the camp at?"

She shook her head. "I don't know. I lost my maps in the crash, and while I did memorize a bit, I...didn't have the necessary frame of reference at the time. I don't think I could even lead you back there if I tried. The horse brought me here."

"We noticed." Even deadly serious, there was a dry note to his voice. "I'll send a scout to follow the horse's trail, then." He turned to leave the tent.

"I'll go along—" She would certainly like to see the site again, now that she felt immeasurably better and didn't have her own impending demise weighing on her mind. While she resisted the thought that it might have made her less effective as an observer and clouded her judgment, a second look wouldn't be amiss.

"No. You were very sick and need to recover." Khangiska grinned briefly. "I'm not going to have that argument with the medicine woman on your behalf." He turned toward the door flap again.

"Wait!" She leaned forward. "I *was* very sick. I should be dead. What did you do?"

The older man gave her a humorless smile. "The Lakota have strong medicine. We always have."

"Good God."

Geoff had gone in to the Black Hills determined to have no expectations, to approach the site with keen eyes and an utterly open mind.

But there had been an expectation, unwittingly, in his mind. He had expected to see anything but *this*.

He pressed his handkerchief over his nose. He'd never been the sort to lose his stomach over something so ordinary as smell. But this was no ordinary smell, and it was all too familiar: blood. Blood going to rot in the ground, the stinking slurry of death and muck that comprised a battlefield when one fought the Infected.

Perhaps he should have expected. He was in the Dead Plains, after all. But the Black Hills had seemed so serene, even pristine, so unlike any place he'd ever been. He'd looked at the pine trees and hadn't felt the gnawing fear that death might be about to emerge from behind one of them. He'd seen deer and thought about a pleasant bit of hunting, since perhaps the noise wouldn't act as a deadly attractant.

He knew better now. What a pretty facade on an ugly truth.

The idyllic scene of nature, rows of stately pines and pale, lithe aspen trees, surrounded a clearing that had been torn and destroyed. Patches of long green grasses still survived among the torn, muddy furrows, poking up around flattened conical tents and scattered debris. The creek glimmered faintly in the distance, flashes of bright water visible between the trees.

Geoff dismounted with care, tethering the nervous horse to a tree. He couldn't safely take the animal any closer, not the way he was rolling his eyes and shaking his head. But Geoff didn't want to be farther from the horse than a quick, limping run, either. Not when he didn't know where the Infected might be.

He walked carefully into the churned clearing, after retrieving his lorgnette from his pack and removing its protective layers of handkerchiefs. Viewed through the treated calcite lenses, the ground was alive with Infection; the site couldn't be more than a day old.

Obviously, the camp had belonged to the savage residents of the Dead Plains. What he did not understand was why they would camp in the open if the Infected scourge still roamed. Surely they had posted guards, had lit watch fires. The corpses of two dogs indicated they'd had those as defense at least, if an inadequate one.

He didn't understand this at all. And why were there no bodies? The Infected were always hungry enough to eat at least a few of their victims.

Something moaned nearby.

Geoff was too well-trained to freeze. His thumb found the trigger for the sword's sheath, and he slid the blade free in one smooth movement. With his other hand, he tucked the lorgnette away in his coat pocket as he turned, trying to locate the source of the sound.

Another moan, but…muffled, somehow.

It was close. Terrifyingly close. Why hadn't the creature attacked yet?

Again, that hair-raising sound.

Geoff frowned, gaze coming to rest on one of the fallen tents, at the bulge in its rumpled hide exterior. It was about the proper size…

Carefully, he moved toward the tent, steps small by necessity to compensate for his limp. He skirted half-burned shards of wood, a bead necklace ground into the muck, a shattered bow. Using the razor-sharp tip of his sword, he sliced open the bulging layer of hides, revealing what lay beneath as if by some unholy birth. It did not burst out, bloody and ready to feast as he suspected.

But it was one of the Infected.

It had been a young woman, barely more than a girl. One of the natives, hair torn from its braids and stiff with mud and blood. She'd had a round face, something he would have found innocent and pretty if he hadn't already ruthlessly cut off his feelings of empathy; it was dangerous to look at the Infected as anything but monsters. A few bead necklaces, like the one loose in the dirt, were still tangled around her neck. Clouded eyes fixed on him, and she slowly gnashed her teeth, showing off streaks of brown flesh caught between them.

Slowly. Every movement was slow, lacking the jerkiness that was the hallmark of the Infected and their tortured nervous systems.

Geoff frowned, prodding the torn hides aside with the tip of his sword. This Infected wasn't overly damaged. It still had all its limbs and didn't appear to have any major bones broken. But it did have several arrows broken off in its flesh, ragged ends quivering in pools of black blood in its thin chest and belly.

Those weren't the sort of wounds that should have kept it on the ground. Only the head was a viable target, or the legs to at least slow it to a literal crawl.

The Infected flailed sluggishly, trying to free one arm to reach for him. It moaned again, thin and strange.

But it could still call back the others. Geoff raised his sword; with one well-aimed stroke, he separated the head from the body. "Mercy," he said quietly. "God give you rest." He'd never believed such things off the battlefield; on that bloody soil, there was nothing else upon which to hold.

He waited until the Infected girl's odd, weak thrashing had ceased. The Infected never moved like that unless severely damaged; a few arrows wouldn't be able to accomplish that. He pried one of the arrows from her stomach. He was not familiar with the tribes in the area, but assuming it was their work seemed reasonable. No man of the duchies would be trying to defend himself with a bow in such a situation. With care, he raised up the arrow and inspected what remained with the lorgnette.

There was no Infection at all on the head of the arrow, where the thick black blood should have been alive with it. What could cause such a thing? The Infected were immune to poisons, to all diseases.

Or were they?

Geoff snapped the head off the arrow, where any poison might be, and carefully wrapped it in three of his spare handkerchiefs before stowing it in his pack. Having Infected blood even that close left him feeling entirely uneasy.

He only had more questions now, and no answers. Cheswick's talk of geology certainly didn't match with this scene of carnage. For that matter, Cheswick had been a borderline vegetarian in school, yet another topic for harassment; he'd once fainted at the sight of a particularly rare roast. Geoff found it inconceivable that he could then be even an accomplice to such carnage, but what was here that the man could find of interest? What was here that Del Toro would need a geologist *for*? That was worth the risks of the roving packs of Infected?

He took out the stolen map again and scanned over the markings on it. A line of attack arrow had been drawn directly through this location. Roving packs of Infected…

But perhaps not roving. Frowning, Geoff mounted the horse and began to ride a wider circle around the area, looking for the tracks of the Infected. They had come as a group, from the area indicated by the arrow on the map. And they had left as a group as well. On that side of the camp, perhaps a mile down the trail, he found the tracks of a caisson.

Odd how such a simple sight could make his blood run cold. The Gatling guns had been mounted on caissons, but there was no sign of shells, no indication one had been brought here and fired. The strange device belonging to Professor Nielson, too, had been mounted on a caisson.

No. The thought was too horrifying. To be able to control the Infected in some way, direct their movements, use them as a weapon of war? The notion was absurd on its face. But that damned device—what did it *do*? And to what end?

Geoff looked the map over, finding the next location he could where the green box had not been marked off: French Creek. There were two more marked sites roughly between him and it; on the way there, he could see if the carnage would be repeated. His mouth set into a grim line, he folded the map back up.

If this was what Del Toro left in his wake, what would he find where the man hadn't yet been?

Marta was bored. That was perhaps the price of no longer having her impending death occupying a large portion of her consciousness; it freed up her mind to think of other things. Things like how utterly, savagely bored she was with lying around, and she'd only been awake for a few hours. Things like how incomplete her picture of the puzzle was, and how Khangiska seemed determined to cut her from it entirely for a silly little reason like her almost having died and become a ravening corpse.

She had to wonder at his priorities.

In fact, the only reason she was still lying around on her little platform of rugs was that when she'd tried to scramble up and give chase, she'd ended up sprawled out on her side, her vision gone to a black tunnel.

After a minor eternity, the iron lady Chumani returned, with another, much younger woman in tow. There was enough of a family resemblance there that Marta could already guess they were mother and daughter. And the easy way the daughter kept smiling—quite unlike her mother—put Marta very much in mind of Khangiska. Simple math. Marta pried herself from the suddenly high gravity of the ground and sat.

"You speak Goshute too, don't you?" she asked the older woman.

"A bit," Chumani admitted. "Ehawee, my daughter, does as well."

The girl gave Marta a bright smile. "My father has taught me." She sat next to Marta and offered her a wooden bowl filled with a thick, purplish red liquid. "I have some wojapi for you. And fry bread. It should be easy on your stomach."

"Thank you." Marta eyed the wojapi doubtfully for a moment, but the mere presence of any sort of food set her stomach grumbling. She used the fry bread to scoop up the soup and found it pleasant indeed—sweet and tart, made from berries. "Oh, this is excellent. Thank you."

"I'm glad you like it. I made the fry bread myself," Ehawee said.

Marta glanced up at Chumani, who watched her impassively. "Were you listening in?"

Chumani nodded. "It's best that I know." She crossed her arms. "You didn't say who brought the sickness."

"I said it was men of the duchies." The boots and the caisson tracks were evidence enough for that.

"But not which duchy. I heard the question in your voice."

"I don't know for certain."

Chumani tilted her head. "But you suspect?"

"What I suspect is immaterial. I don't have evidence yet. And until there is evidence, it's nothing but speculation. Does it matter?"

Ehawee looked like she might say something, but Chumani spoke first. "It always matters."

Marta frowned slightly to herself, then focused for a moment on soaking up the last bits of berry soup with her fry bread. "Tell me, Chumani. Men of the duchies don't really come onto the plains now, do they? Let alone into these hills." Now that she'd had a bit more time to collect her thoughts, without the specter of death on her shoulder, she thought of the more subtle things she had seen at the site, like the broken outcrop face.

Chumani shook her head. "I have been told you still fear these lands." She cracked a slight smile. "And our men do their best to encourage that fear."

"But they came here before."

"They were everywhere before. Hunting the buffalo and leaving him to rot in the sun." Chumani looked like the words tasted bitter beyond imagining. Ehawee simply looked horrified.

"But the buffalo don't run in this area."

"Not in Paha Sapa," Chumani agreed. "But there were trappers, I think. I know a story or two."

Marta nibbled on the last shred of her fry bread, offering her empty bowl back to Ehawee. "Thank you, Ehawee. That was lovely. I don't suppose I could have more?"

"You should just have a little at a time until you feel better," Ehawee said. "Or you'll make yourself sick again."

"You sound like Simms," Marta muttered.

"Who?"

"A giant with a red beard." She waved her hand to dismiss the topic and looked back up at Chumani. "Were any of the duchymen interested in the rocks around here?"

"There are pretty stones in some places," Ehawee offered. She held up one of her necklaces, to show off a few colored types of quartz that had been polished, likely in a creek.

Chumani frowned, however. "Before the great plague, men from the duchies had begun to build a town in Paha Sapa, even though they had agreed this was our land. They were excited and secretive and would not let us near it."

"They'd found something." Marta turned the thought over in her mind. There was a very limited set of rocks that the men of the duchies found interesting. "It was gold, wasn't it?"

"So it goes in one of the stories. But the duchymen always want gold." Chumani shrugged. "Before they could call for more of their people, the great plague happened. They were swept away. And the duchies are afraid to come onto the plains again. The buffalo have returned to their great herds. Things are better, now."

Gold. If it was true, if gold had been discovered nearby and the fact of it temporarily forgotten, there were many in the duchies who would kill for that information. And even more who would kill to get to the gold and claim it for themselves.

And perhaps some mad fools who would be willing to commit genocide over it and release a fresh scourge of Infection.

Marta licked her lips. "Do the stories say where this town was?"

Darkness had fallen before he'd gotten even halfway to French Creek. Geoff strung a makeshift hammock high up between aspen trees, unwilling to lay his bedroll out on the ground, when he knew there were Infected in the immediate area. He might have risked it if he'd had a dog with him, but horses weren't quite as reliable.

Swaying gently between the trees in a way that was just short of sickness-inducing, he chewed on more tooth-breaking jerky and gluey hardtack mixed with water, watching the countless stars shimmer overhead. One began to forget, after a while, the way the choking smog endemic to the city erased the sky. He dozed lightly as he tried to recall the names of the constellations.

He snapped into sharp wakefulness in the small hours of the morning, a distressed whinny from the horse echoing in his ears. Thankfully, he'd secured the animal well so he couldn't bolt; after a few minutes, the horse lapsed into silence, pawing at the ground.

In the soft darkness, he heard a low, despairing murmur, a strange, burbling moan. One hand clutching the hammock for all its dubious security, he slowly sat, then took up his cane from where it lay along his side.

The sound, unsettling to the point of nauseating as it grew louder, came again to the south. Geoff cursed silently; the light night breeze blew in that direction. If it hadn't scented him yet, it would shortly. Or at least in the Expeditionary Forces, they had assumed the Infected hunted by smell. They'd certainly never come up with a more probable mechanism.

The burbling sound grew louder.

Geoff took the little spy lantern from the branch upon which he'd hung it and turned the flame back up. He directed the beam at the ground, searching for the Infected.

Better to take care of it—them?—now, before his horse was frightened half to death. Or before the sounds called more Infected to the area. The chance of drawing more Infected in—as well the potential for unwanted human attention—made the pistol he tucked into his belt a last resort, saved only for emergencies.

He swept the warm yellow beam of the lantern over the ground in a careful search pattern, wishing now that he'd picked an area with fewer trees. There, movement! The Infected creature limped awkwardly, one foot twisted outward. He caught a white slash of bone, slick and shining in the lantern light. Streaks of mud and perhaps blood painted it from head to toe. It barely wore the shreds of a leather loincloth.

Anyone who thought there could be dignity in death had never seen the reality of Infection, Geoff thought grimly.

It was alone. He considered waiting and letting it try to climb the tree, since that would hamper it nicely for an easy kill. But the longer he let it remain animate, the greater the chance more would join it. In fact, as the Infected shuffled toward the tree, it let out another moan, this one strong and not burbling at all, and Geoff winced.

He'd strung a rope up to help him get in and out of the hammock. Geoff hung the lantern up again, angled to provide light while he was on the ground. Cane tucked securely through his belt, he eased himself over to the rope and climbed quickly down, bracing his feet against one of the aspen trunks.

Before he was even halfway down, the Infected had jerked toward him, accelerating into some semblance of a stumbling run. This was one was fresh, then, very fresh. He hastily dropped the short distance to the ground, hissing out a breath at the spike of pain that sent up his bad leg.

The Infected was only a few paces from him. Still fighting for balance, Geoff raised the cane and pressed the release for the sheath. It struck the creature square in the face, sending it reeling to the ground. A temporary reprieve; already, the creature struggled to its feet, jerking violently back and forth and hissing. Geoff raised his sword—

Bony hands grabbed his arm. The sickening burbling sound filled his left ear as something blunt poked his shoulder.

Geoff jerked to the side, tearing away from the grip, which was far weaker than it should have been. Ragged fingernails scrabbled and caught at the rough cotton fabric of his shirt. It was another Infected, male as well, though this one was peppered with wounds. A broken stick protruded from its gaping mouth, another from its throat, the source of both the horrible sound and its inability to bite. Its movements were oddly sluggish, much like the Infected he had seen in the destroyed camp.

But that still meant he had two opponents, instead of one. This straightforward combat had just become immeasurably more difficult.

The first Infected regained its feet, almost overbalancing at its own violent movements. It stuttered into a run toward him. Geoff skipped clumsily back to escape the line of its charge, all the while trying to keep an eye on his second opponent. He hazarded a swing at the creature; his aim was slightly off, and the blade buried itself in the flesh of its neck, grating on bone rather than sliding between.

Geoff cursed as the Infected lunged at him again, almost jerking the blade from his hand. He wrestled for control of the sword, the sharkskin wrap of the hilt tearing at his palm, but allowing him to keep his grip. As long as the blade was in the creature's flesh, it couldn't reach him.

Of course, the other was still moving, however sluggishly. It snapped at him, bumping his arm with the splintered end of the stick again. It couldn't bite him, he reminded himself. Use it as a tactical piece. Geoff kicked the thing solidly in the midsection, sending it reeling back.

With a snarl of effort, he grabbed his sword's hilt with his other hand, and yanked the first Infected hard, driving it into the second. A muscle in his back popped under the strain of throwing that much fighting weight.

The two Infected collided and tangled limbs. Geoff took that chance to yank his sword free, sweeping the blade back and driving it at the quick one's neck again. This time, he struck true; the blade bit deep and snarled between two of the vertebrae. The Infected dropped, twitching, on top of the other, head hanging by a strip of skin and muscle. Black blood flowed out in a massive gout, momentarily obscuring the face of the other Infected.

While the remaining Infected tried to free itself, Geoff moved in, trying to make out where the thing's neck and face were in the bloody tangle. There was a large, flat rock nearby; he'd thought about using it earlier as a hearth, but then had let paranoia overrule his desire for a fire. He speared his sword into the ground and snatched up the rock, raising it over his head with a grunt of effort. He drove the rock down into the jerking, rolling head of the squirming Infected with all his strength.

Crack. The awful burbling stopped, as did the creature's weak movements.

Geoff stood for a moment, the sensation of grim satisfaction cut by the fading surge of adrenaline brought on by combat. The old war wound in his leg had not stopped him from performing nearly as well as he might have as a soldier. And two Infected were dead; while it might be a drop in the bucket, it was a start.

He took his sword back up and retrieved the sheath. After a moment of consideration, he dragged the first Infected off of the second. Using a handkerchief, he pried one of the odd sticks from the second Infected, thinking of the way it had moved.

The "stick" was actually a broken-off arrow. He frowned, then dropped it on top of the body. What sort of delightful devilry had the savages invented? And more importantly, how could he take it home to the Grand Duchy of Denver?

He considered throwing away the dirtied handkerchief, but rolled it up with the bloody side in and stowed it in a different pocket. He might have need to it again. Then, after pausing to listen for his horse, for more sounds made by the Infected, and hearing nothing, he climbed laboriously back up into the tree. His upper back twinged now as he climbed.

Perhaps in some ways, he wasn't quite the soldier he'd once been. But he could pretend.

And like the soldier he had once been, he stared up at the stars, waiting for the hammering of his heart to slow, hoping that sleep would come and knowing that it would not. There had been so many other nights like this, out on the Canadian Front, more than he could count, but not so many he could not remember, more was the pity.

In true death, the faces of the Infected looked all too human.

Marta had intended to slip away in the heat of the afternoon and go looking for the abandoned settlement Chumani had mentioned. If she took the horse she'd dubbed Dolly, she wouldn't even be stealing from the family that had taken her in.

This plan lasted just long enough for Ehawee to bring her another bowl, this one full of a thick buffalo stew. Somewhere between the last chunk of wild potato and mopping up the broth with more fry bread, her stomach had hatched a conspiracy in collusion with her broken arm and the warm afternoon. She didn't so much fall asleep as get hit in the back of the head with a blackjack by it.

Marta didn't wake until the evening, when Khangiska came into the tent, Ehawee trailing in his wake. She had another bowl in her hands. Marta eyed it with a certain amount of suspicion, even as her stomach growled eagerly at the sight.

She'd never been overly interested in food before; that was something Simms used as constant fuel for harassment when he was in a mothering mood. Perhaps almost being eaten alive by Infection had a way of making one hungry, though.

Not a thought she had any interest in testing.

Khangiska sat down across from her as she began to eat her third meal of an already truncated day. "The scout I sent to track your horse has returned."

She raised an eyebrow. "I trust he found things as I said they would be?"

"How I wish you were wrong." The older man crossed his arms, frowning. He looked tired. "The camp at Elk Creek has been slaughtered, as you said. I've sent out all the men and a few of the women to find the surrounding camps and call them. Word will spread from there."

Elk Creek. So that was the name of the stream she'd crashed near. Good to know for later.

It felt good to think that there might be a later. Better than she would have imagined. "You'll need to hunt down the pack of Infected quickly."

"It hasn't been so long since the great plague. We understand how to deal with the living ghosts." Khangiska fixed her with a stern gaze; it would have been intimidating if she weren't immune to that sort of thing. "But from what you said, and what Chaska saw, it is men from the duchies. They have done this, somehow. I want to know where they are."

"I don't know. If I did, I would tell you."

His eyes narrowed. "I'm certain you would."

"I am not lying, Khangiska. I don't feel bound by loyalty to anyone outside of my own crew. The duchies are no friend to us." She flashed him a sharp grin. "They're the rabbits we hunt, most of the time. But it isn't even about loyalty. If they're trying to start a fresh outbreak of the plague, everyone is in danger. They should have no friends."

His dark gaze sharpened, but then he nodded. "But you have seen nothing of them but their boot prints."

"I think they must be the reason I crashed. The memory isn't clear, but…" She thought of the wreckage that had surrounded her, the neat holes punched through the intact pieces of wood and metal. "I was shot down, and I find it doubtful that your people would waste bullets shooting at an aeroplane." Let alone have the sort of rifles necessary to stop even that delicate of a machine. "I was downed very near Elk Creek. That is ultimately what led me to finding the camp."

"It would be easier if you knew, but we will prepare for war all the same. They cannot hide from us in our home."

Marta nodded. There was no argument she could make, about this being an attack, an act of war. Using the Infected as a weapon only made it all the more despicable. "Prepare quickly."

He offered her a sober nod, then rose to his feet far more smoothly than anyone of his apparent age had a right to do.

"Wait."

"Hm?"

"I need more data. I need more information so I can ascertain what is truly happening. It's more than just the deliberate spread of the Infection, but I don't know what."

"The scouts will be back soon. I'll bring them here so you can listen to their reports as well."

Marta shook her head. "No. I need to go see for myself. I'm sure your scouts are very good, but they're not so good as me."

"Once they've returned, you can decide if there is still more you need to know." Khangiska's tone was final. "For now, continue to rest. We'll have need of you in the council."

"But—"

"Patience, coyote."

Frowning, Marta watched him leave the tipi.

Ehawee remained behind, waiting for her to finish eating. "You don't need to be nervous," Ehawee said. "You're our guest. They'll just want to ask you questions like Father did."

"I imagine so. I'm not worried about that." She gave the girl her best, conspiratorial, *we're all women here* smile. "I've faced large, inquisitive groups of men before."

Ehawee shot her an odd look in return. "The women will be there as well. We need to know what has happened."

"Oh?"

The girl grinned. "If the men want to go to war, someone has to feed them."

Marta laughed. "The true mark of civilization." She finished the stew and bread, then gave the bowl back to Ehawee. "If you feed them all like this, it's a wonder they're not too fat to fight."

Ehawee rose to her feet, bowl balanced in one hand. "You need to regain your strength. The great plague is difficult to fight. Mother says only good luck brought you to us in time."

Considering it had been blind chance and the homing instincts of a skittish horse, Marta found herself unable to quite argue with that. "Ehawee, what sort of medicine did you use to help me?"

"You should ask Mother."

"I will. Thank you." Something slotted into place in Marta's mind about the girl's mother, the decoration of her clothing, her obvious authority. "Is Dolly all right, by the way? The horse who saved me?"

"Yes!" Ehawee grinned. "What kind of name is Dolly?"

"A…ah…good friend of mine has a daughter named Dolly," Marta said, suddenly feeling a trifle awkward about the entire situation.

Ehawee wrinkled her nose. "Why would you give a stallion a girl's name?"

Marta stared at the girl. "I had other things on my mind at the time. And I've never owned a horse."

"You must come from a very poor family," Ehawee commented, then rose to her feet. "I'll ask Mother if you're well enough to see…Dolly." She stifled a giggle.

"Yes, please do," Marta said, a tad stiffly. She waited until Ehawee had gone, then waited a bit longer, fighting off the urge to doze. Eventually, she rolled from the bed and rose to her feet, padding over in her socks to poke her head out the door flap.

"Is there something you need?" the familiar voice of Chumani asked to the side.

Marta smiled. The woman had been there every other time she'd tried to leave the tent. "Just to relieve myself again, I'm afraid."

Chumani grunted and set aside the grass she was weaving. "I'll make sure you don't get lost."

Which was really the problem. They both knew by not getting lost that what Chumani really meant was that she'd make certain Marta didn't go anywhere she wasn't supposed to. Fair enough, she supposed. It wasn't as if the people of any tribe had a reason to trust someone nominally from the duchies. And this current mess was not helping issues.

"I'm sorry I didn't thank you before, for healing me," she said.

Chumani grunted, not looking in the least bit surprised. "That's my calling."

Marta gave her as charming a smile as she could muster. It felt very wilted when met with the power of Chumani's disdain. "I don't suppose you'd tell me how?"

Of all things, it made the older woman chuckle. "Our medicine is not like the buffalo, coyote."

Marta didn't mind being a joke to someone all that much, particularly not someone who had saved her life and was intent on feeding her into a stupor, but it would have been nice if Chumani had bothered to explain the punch line.

Then it was back to the enforced idleness, which ate at her. She was perhaps not at her most useful, down one arm and still admittedly feeling exhausted, but her mind still worked perfectly well. She needed more data. She needed to find more of the pieces to put this puzzle together, to understand the *why* of this mad plan, which would ultimately lead to the *how*, and then to the solution. And the question of her cure was another matter entirely, one that might mean the end to the Infection throughout the world.

Though she could not help but wonder if it could also lead to the death of an entire people, as every duchy converged in an attempt to sweep up the supply of the mineral or plant that had produced whatever cure she'd been given. And if one duchy gained control of it…

Would this new sort of warfare, using the Infected as a weapon, suddenly become the standard? She shuddered to think of that, even as her blood still filled with the pounding need to *know*.

None of that mattered, however, if she couldn't get out of the tent. Khangiska did not need her; she'd already told him everything she knew. Hearing it from her lips directly really wouldn't make a difference. And there had to be more to this, more that would change the course of this coming war, or perhaps prevent it.

Though she did not feel any compelling reason to save the men of whatever duchy had decided to commit such an atrocity.

Escape seemed her only option; every time she raised the idea of leaving to do a bit of scouting on her own, she was firmly reminded that she was both a guest and needed to rest. Not a prisoner, but they seemed to have little interest in letting her out of their sight, and logically, she could not blame them. The tipi's only door was also not a potential exit; when Chumani wasn't there, one of the other women was. And at night, the entire family returned to sleep.

Cutting a second door through the side of the tipi would take too long and be a bit too obvious, but…

She rolled off the bed again and crept carefully over to the side opposite the door, ducking under a shelf-like overhang that covered that portion of the tent. The construction of the large tent was clever, with a liner inside to catch the rain. Marta explored the edge of the liner with her fingers until she found the tie that secured it to the pole behind. If she cut that tie to provide herself a bit of give, she'd be able to push the liner up. Then even if the hide cover of the tipi itself was stretched as taut as she feared, she could put a small slit in it with the tiny blade she had concealed in the heel of her boot, and that would give her enough room to wiggle under. She'd made it through tighter spaces than that before, and with people who had much more dangerous things than simply feeding her on their minds.

The sound of activity stirring outside the tipi sent her scrambling back to her bed, where she arranged herself hastily into something like repose. The flap moved, enough that Chumani could glance in to check on her, then shut again.

Marta retrieved the knife from her boot heel and went back to the other side of the tipi. Carefully, sweat beading on her forehead from the effort of doing something slowly and in silence—and with the wrong hand—she cut through the rope tying the tipi liner to the pole and created a slit in the hide cover. Better to wait for her actual escape until the night, when everyone but the sentries was asleep.

The tipi liner sagged alarmingly inward when she moved away from it. She quickly cast around for something to prop against it and came up with a basket that seemed to be filled with dried meat, and she tucked it up against the liner.

That would do for now. Hopefully, no one would notice from the outside. She put the knife away and went back to bed, intending to spend the rest of the afternoon napping. It wasn't as if she had anything else to do, just sleep and turn over bits of data in her mind.

When night fell, and after yet another bowl of stew, which she demolished just as hungrily as the last, Marta waited until the tent was filled with the snores and heavy breathing of the occupants. Then she slithered off her own bed, picking her way through the maze of resting human bodies, and crawled back to the escape hatch she'd made earlier.

She had a bad moment when she realized she couldn't crawl through belly-down, not with her arm still strapped to her side— and that immobilization was still very much necessary. That meant she had to go with the much more awkward belly-up squirm, made even more awkward by the necessity of doing it quietly. It felt like the tent was giving birth to her in the most undignified way possible. And then halfway out from beneath the tent, her foot slipped. Her boot knocked solidly into the basket she'd used to prop up the liner.

Marta froze, holding her breath. She could no longer see the inside of the tipi, or hear at all well into it, but no one stirred as far as she could tell. Quickly, she dug her elbow into the grassy ground beneath her and finished scrambling out.

Low to the ground and feeling awkward and overbalanced with only one moving arm, she crept around the tipi, looking for the line where the horses were picketed. Thankfully, she'd gotten the layout of the little camp at least partially whenever Chumani allowed her outside to relieve her bladder. The sentries were busy looking outward, listening for the tell-tale sounds of the Infected. They weren't looking for someone moving within the camp.

Marta spotted the horse she'd found at the other camp, hobbled at the end of the line. The beast gave her an annoyed look as she approached, ears flicking back.

"Hello, you beautiful creature," Marta murmured.

Another annoyed ear flick. But thankfully, *he* wasn't in a position to escape this time. Marta freed the horse and scrambled onto his back, only slightly more graceful than the last time. A few of the horses whickered inquiringly, heads coming up to investigate.

Quickly, she turned Dolly and urged him out into the woods. She'd figure out where she was actually going once the light came up and she had the lay of the land. For now, *away* seemed the best idea, and quickly. If she had enough of a head start, hopefully Khangiska would decide she wasn't worth the time to pursue.

She needed to go prospect for gold. Somewhere, in the back of her mind, she heard Simms make a terrible pun about things panning out. She ignored that figment of her imagination as resolutely as she would have ignored the real thing.

French Creek was an eerie place, even in the warm light of mid-morning. Geoffrey didn't consider himself a superstitious man in the slightest, but the sight of abandoned buildings had always filled him with dismay all the same. He told himself it was a reasonable sort of dread, since those sorts of places were perfect for the concealment of the Infected.

And he knew that they were near. He'd run across another straggler on his way to the site. There was now a large, unsightly tear in the left sleeve of his jacket because of it.

He approached from the creek, where he found the shattered, overgrown remnants of what he could only guess was a sluice. There was a frame at the bottom of it, containing the sharp edges of what had once been a screen of some sort.

Farther along was the overgrown clearing that had once been some sort of settlement, now long-since abandoned. Geoff observed the wreckage from horseback, using the safety of the trees. There were several shacks, fallen into complete disrepair. One of them had collapsed entirely. There was also what appeared to be a stable, or perhaps a very small barn, its logs weathered to a silvery gray. Had there been any streets or even paths, they were thoroughly overgrown now with grasses and saplings. Rusted rounds of metal sat in a collapsed pile toward the creek; it took him a moment to piece together those had once been pieces of a cart, one that had apparently contained hand tools.

This was not the first time he had seen such ruins since leaving the Expeditionary Forces. They were common outside the fences; people often thought they could strike out on their own, that the threat of Infection had abated because the cities had been rendered so safe.

But none of those places had filled him with such unease.

Geoff tethered his horse to a tree where he would be out of sight and approached the abandoned buildings. His hand itched to draw his pistol, but he scrubbed his palm against the seam of his trousers and ignored the urge. It would have been foolish to draw attention the previous night by discharging his pistol, and equally foolish now.

As he moved into the clearing, soft steps loud in his own ears, he realized what he had heard—or rather, not heard: there was no bird song. No sound at all but for his own breathing and the creek and brush of the trees as they were touched by the errant breeze. His hand tightened on the head of his cane.

One by one, he went to each of the derelict buildings, peering inside through the shattered windows or yawning doors. The shreds of civilization that had once existed made poignant comment to the utter desolation. Here, a broken plate, there a shredded blanket that had been turned dirty gray-brown by time.

As he approached the stable, he noticed something else amiss, however; there were fresh tracks here, men and horses both—and the ruts left by the wheels of a caisson. The simple sight of those ruts made the hair on the back of his neck stand on end. Was Professor Nielson's device close?

The sound of approaching horses caused Geoff to duck back into the nearest shack, for the sake of convenience; it had no door. Trying to get to his horse right now could prove deadly; he'd left the beast far enough away that it was very likely he would be missed.

Four men on horses rode into the clearing; three of them wore the distinctive forest green uniforms of the Grand Duchy of Denver, the black patches on their arms making their regimental affiliation clear. Geoff recognized General Del Toro immediately by shape alone. The man was built like a bull, as if his name had somehow dictated his physical destiny, his expression always with a hint of anger to it no matter his mood. Two soldiers of his regiment were with him, and between them rode the lanky form of Cheswick, several leather pouches strung across his person.

Hastily, Geoff ducked as the riders approached his location.

"—bloody inconvenience," Del Toro growled. "I'm weary of these delays."

"I'm certain Professor Nielson did his best, General—" Cheswick began.

"You lot always stick together. Go. Get your replacement samples, and be quick about it. The packs are wandering too far afield already. I don't want to lose any more to the vagaries of chance."

"Yes, yes, I'm so very sorry, General," Cheswick said, the words tumbling over themselves.

There was the sound of one horse, heading for the creek.

Del Toro continued on. "Captain Dowd, prepare the device. It should have been delivered this morning while we were waiting on the damned geologist. Lieutenant Gelleski, perimeter watch."

One man, presumably the captain, dismounted. Geoff hazarded another peep through the window, watching one of the soldiers disappear off to the right, presumably to go to the stable, the only building in that direction. The device must be in there, of course, the only building he hadn't yet checked. But if Del Toro was *here*, that meant the device hadn't been turned on yet. The man was far too concerned with preserving his own skin.

The more pressing concern, however, was the man riding out toward the perimeter. If he did a thorough, if quick, patrol, Geoff knew that his horse would be found. He tensed, trying to see some way clear of this; he had little doubt Del Toro would shoot him if he was discovered.

As he watched, Del Toro wheeled his horse and headed toward the creek as well, perhaps to keep an eye on Cheswick. That left Captain Dowd's horse unattended. If the game was up, it seemed best to go for that horse and abandon his own, then make good his escape. He could double back later, once they were tired of giving him chase.

Geoff spared a moment of sadness for his own horse, a reliable beast it had been, but only that. He crept from the shack and hurried toward the unattended horse.

Twenty feet—ten—five—two—there. He reached for the reins—

"Oy, you! Freeze!" The shout was accompanied by the unmistakable sound of a rifle being cocked. "That's right. Hands up."

He couldn't mount a horse quickly, not when he'd need to put all his weight on his bad leg as he heaved himself up. Gritting his teeth, Geoff dropped his cane and raised his hands. Slowly, he turned to face the man Del Toro had named as Captain Dowd. Or rather, the rifle that Captain Dowd held, which was really of primary import in Geoff's world right now.

"Didn't think I'd run across a horse thief this far out in the wilds," Captain Dowd remarked, the barrel of his rifle as steady as a rock, trained at Geoff's chest. "You look a bit familiar."

"Colonel Geoffrey Douglas," Geoff said stiffly. "Chief of Security for your employer, the Grand Duke of Denver."

Captain Dowd's eyes widened slightly. "You don't say."

"Are you aware, Captain, that you are on an entirely unauthorized expedition? Any act you commit now will not only reflect poorly on your regiment and the armed forces of the Grand Duchy of Denver, but be entirely illegal."

The man hesitated. That was good. Geoff began to lower his arms, and the man let him. "The orders came from the general himself," Captain Dowd said.

"The general did not consult with the Grand Duke on those orders," Geoff said, keeping his tone calm and rational. "I'm the head of security. I would know."

Another hesitation. Geoff could read in the man's eyes that he'd felt like something might have been a little wrong all along. That gave him hope, but he had very little time to try to talk this man around.

"And why would the general do something like that?" Captain Dowd demanded.

"I'd very much like to know that myself," Geoff said. "But I don't even know what it is you're doing out here. It has something to do with the Infected, though, does it not?"

There was no mistaking the unhappy disquiet in the man's eyes. He'd been getting orders that he didn't necessarily disagree with, but that he did not in the least like. Rifle still up but no longer quite so steady, he approached. "You don't know the half of it. We—"

Geoff had thought the luck he'd relied upon in the Black Bull camp had died when Captain Dowd spotted him. But if that was the case, its corpse burst into spontaneous flame at what happened next. A horse—no, two—approached at a rapid clip.

Talking would no longer do any good. Geoff lunged for Captain Dowd, banking on the distraction of the rider to hopefully prevent him from being shot. The captain let out a shout of surprise as Geoff grabbed for the rifle. They clinched, struggling briefly for the weapon. The captain's hand tightened in response, and the rifle went off with a deafening *crack*, the barrel of it thankfully no longer pointed at Geoff.

After another brief moment of struggle, his leg buckled, and he dropped to one knee, still trying to gain possession of the rifle.

At which point the barrel of another rifle pressed itself solidly between his shoulder blades.

Cursing, Geoff let go and raised his hands again.

The sound of more horses. With nothing left to lose, Geoff looked over his shoulder to see Del Toro ride into the clearing, his saber naked in his hand. The dark man's eyes widened at the sight of Geoff, narrowed, and then Del Toro smiled.

That worried Geoff more than anything that had happened yet.

"Why, Colonel. I hadn't expected to see you here," the general drawled, halting his horse only a few steps away.

Had Geoff's gaze had the power to set things ablaze, surely the man would have been a crisp in an instant.

More hoofbeats sounded, and Cheswick rode up to stop by General Del Toro. "General—"

Del Toro cut him off with a chopping hand gesture. "What was he doing, Captain? Other than making a foolhardy attempt at combat."

Geoff met Cheswick's gaze, saw his eyes widen slightly, saw the man open his mouth and draw in a breath. He gave his head a little shake. Whatever Cheswick might say, he couldn't imagine it would help. Not with calculating madness glittering in General Del Toro's eyes.

And perhaps this allowed him to repay a little of the debt he owed the man for his own past inaction.

"He was asking after the mission, sir," Captain Dowd said. "About the Infected."

If anything, General Del Toro's smile became even less pleasant. "You had but to ask. In fact, I'll do better than merely answer. Fancy a small demonstration?"

If Khangiska had bothered to send someone after her, Marta had dodged them so thoroughly that she'd never even heard the sound of their horses. Something about that left her feeling oddly disquieted as she did her best to navigate the woods at night. City born and bred, she couldn't help but think bitterly how much more helpful it would all be if there were a few street lights here and there.

She rode through the dawn and into morning, so surrounded by the peaceful bliss of nature at its most annoyingly natural state, complete with twitting birds and chattering squirrels, that she was ready to tear her hair out by the roots.

Then she heard the distant *crack* of a rifle shot.

Even more fascinating, that sound had apparently come from roughly the direction she was headed. Better and better. Dolly flicked his ears, as if to question her wisdom in wanting to continue on that direction, but didn't argue further. The urge to try to kick the horse into a faster pace was strong, but Marta resisted it. She had the distinct feeling she was only on Dolly's back at his sufferance.

Nearly an hour later, she came across the creek that she was fairly certain would be the one she wanted, unless she'd completely lost her way. And still no sign of the mysterious rifleman, with no other shots fired to confirm her impression of the location.

Curious. A hunter, perhaps? But it wouldn't be one of the Lakota. Neither Khangiska nor Chumani had mentioned that duchymen came on their lands to hunt, but that didn't necessarily mean anything. What data she'd extracted from them had been hard won to say the least.

Moving east along the stream, she noted the overgrown wreck of a sluice, obviously disused for decades. All that remained of it was the metal frame, badly rusted out, and a few cracked boards overgrown with vines. That certainly did lend credence to Chumani's story that there might have been prospectors here once, before the Infection had burned across the world.

Much more cautiously, she headed south of the creek, to where she could pick out what looked like an overgrown clearing in the trees. There were small, derelict buildings throughout in various stages of collapse. More interesting to Marta, however, were the signs of recent activity: boot prints, the hoofprints of shod horses, and yes, the ruts left by a caisson.

The caisson trail led toward the largest building of the ruins, what appeared to be a stable. Marta slid from Dolly's back, but kept her hand firmly on the horse's mane, with the idea of making a quick escape if something untoward happened. Yes, by somehow swinging up onto the horse's back using her off hand and just her grip on his hair.

Perhaps not the most realistic plan. But she didn't want the beast just wandering off, all the same.

At the door of the stable, she was compelled to let go of Dolly, though she gave the horse an admonishing glance and said, "Don't wander."

The horse gave her an unimpressed look that would have been more at home on the long face of Simms, and she was forced to wonder if he'd be just as intractable as the man as well.

There was little she could do about it at this point.

Marta reached for the left hand of the stable's double doors and swung it open. The hinges squealed so loudly, the sound could have by all rights removed the color from her hair if she'd been of a nervous disposition at all.

Far more interesting, however, was what she found on the other side. Marta stood for a moment, feet braced, and simply took in the sight, savoring it as if it was some sort of fine wine. To begin with, at the center of the stable was a device of some sort, a box with an ungainly, flaring horn that looked a bit like an ugly gramophone, affixed to a caisson, the tongue of it propped up on crates. Her fingers itched to take it apart immediately and ascertain just what it was supposed to do.

More amusing and quite possibly less useful, however, was the person neatly trussed with rough twine in one of the rotting stalls to one side of the machine: Colonel Douglas, looking exceedingly dyspeptic. In what could only be cruel mockery of the sort she could almost appreciate from an artistic perspective, someone had laid out his cane three feet away from him and quite out of his reach.

"Of the many possibilities I considered upon reaching this place," she drawled, "I'm pleased to say this wasn't one of them. You do have a habit of surprising me, Colonel Douglas. I haven't yet decided if it's lovely or nasty. Maybe both by turns."

He glared at her. "*You.*"

"Yes, me. Considering your current state, I daresay I'm not the one with whom you should be cross." She walked over to where his cane lay on the ground, rolled it up on the toe of her boot, and kicked it up into her own hand. Heavy, as expected; she'd seen the sword in it before. "Whatever did you do to your *face*?" There was a pale strip of skin on his upper lip where she'd been accustomed to seeing a carefully groomed mustache. Colonel Douglas wasn't the sort of man she tended to find physically interesting to begin with. Without the mustache, he simply looked…underdressed, as if he'd stepped out of the house without putting on his waistcoat. Bizarre. "Or did the miscreants who left you trussed up here decide to steal the last shreds of your dignity while they were at it?"

"Untie me at once," he said, stiffness fading into a far more frantic tone. "We're both in terrible danger!"

That gave her pause. "Of what sort?" Then she glanced at the machine. "Does this belong to those wretched fellows who left you in such a bind?"

His tone begrudging, the colonel said, "Yes."

Marta nodded. "What does it do that's so dangerous?"

"I don't know precisely," Colonel Douglas answered, the urgency returning to his voice. "But I've reason to believe it's something to do with the movements of the Infected."

Marta turned abruptly on her heel, points of data turning furiously in her mind. There had been caisson tracks here, and then at the massacred camp, where the Infected had acted in a decidedly strange fashion. "How do you know this?"

"Del Toro implied as much when he abandoned me here." Colonel Douglas squirmed a bit, as if to get her attention. "Untie me at once. We need to escape."

And General Del Toro involved as well. That made her think of…of…

She had to stop, hand resting on the sturdy box of the device as finally, she recalled soaring over the Dead Plains in her little aeroplane, scouting precisely for what Colonel Douglas had mentioned—the sight of General Del Toro and his personal regiment. She'd found their sudden movement from the Grand

Duchy suspicious indeed, and apparently, she wasn't the only one—only what did it mean that Colonel Douglas, the security man of the Grand Duke, was just as in the dark? But she recalled seeing a camp out on the grassy plain outside the Black Hills, of turning back for another pass, and then Gatling gunfire tearing through her aeroplane. She remembered grappling with the controls, the machine spinning out, and then…

Well, perhaps best she didn't precisely remember what came next. But she now knew the biggest pieces of the puzzle. Del Toro, his entire regiment, and somehow in control of the Infected—and indeed in pursuit, it seemed, for something so banal as gold. The thought filled her with rage, only her anger had never burned hot; it was cold, like ice sharpened to a fine, brittle point.

Colonel Douglas had been speaking. Marta shook her head sharply and looked back at him. "I'm sorry, what was that?"

"I was reminding you that you should be untying me," Geoff said, the words clipped. "And I told you that I saw the tracks of a caisson near the site of a massacre, one marked on a map I stole from Del Toro. More evidence that we really ought to leave."

Just as she had seen the evidence for a caisson at the camp at Elk Creek. "Right. Yes, you're right. Flight would be advisable." Marta nodded, drawing out the blade hidden within the cane. Colonel Douglas had just long enough to shoot her a wary look before she used a flick of the sharp edge to cut the bonds at his wrists. She offered him the sword almost absently as soon as he had begun to chafe a bit of feeling into his wrists. "Do you still have the map?"

"What do you need it for?" Colonel Douglas snatched the sword up with a disbelieving look.

"To see the best way to run. There's only one horse between the two of us. And he's not the stalwart or patient sort."

"You make an excellent point." With his other hand, he dug into his jacket and came up with a neatly folded, but slightly stained, packet of paper.

Marta snatched the paper from his hand and left him to deal with the rest of his bonds.

She wondered if she ought to make the point that it might already be too late. Quickly, she searched for their location on the map, trying to find a course of escape that would be perpendicular to the line of movement bisecting the site. There was handwriting on the map that she recognized as Colonel Douglas's, additional notes. "This is the site you mentioned?"

Colonel Douglas got to his feet, a bit ungainly; no doubt both of his legs were asleep. Absently, Marta retrieved the sheath for his sword and handed it to him. A muttered thanks, and he united the two halves, then leaned heavily on the cane.

"Which one? Yes. The Infected had been through, but they hadn't eaten anyone. Just turned them all. Within the last day, though yesterday was when I saw it."

Marta nodded, quickly tapping the location of the massacre she'd seen with one finger before beginning to fold the map back up. "This, the camp at Elk Creek, was the first target, I think. Del Toro's men placed the bodies of two men into the stream that supplied the camp with water. And when everyone had begun to fall ill…" But before they had realized the disease and enacted their cure, or perhaps even when they recovered, she thought. "A small number of Infected entered the camp, I suspect a hunting party Del Toro had captured and made to turn." A sickening thought indeed. "Like the ones you saw, they only completed the Infection's spread and added the entire family to the pack, rather than feeding. And then they moved on to the camp you saw yourself." She glanced at the device. "Or were moved, if you are right."

Colonel Douglas looked like he might be sick. "He has two of the devices; I heard him say as much whilst I was reconnoitering. If these truly do in some way attract or direct the Infected, then that gives him the ability to leapfrog the entire group around at will. Then it becomes simple mathematics. One by one, he can fold hunting camps into this new army of his, swelling their ranks even as he depletes those of his enemies. And he need not even fear for his own men, since he will always know the approximate location of the Infected in the area. Then once they have fulfilled their purpose...Del Toro has brought a surprising number of Gatling guns with his regiment." His tone sounded caught between horror and respect. Marta understood that feeling quite well. Colonel Douglas gave his head a little shake. "And all the revelations in the world will be useless if we are torn to shreds by the Infected. We need to leave *now.*"

"Perhaps not. The question becomes, how do these devices work? If we dismantle or destroy it rather than fleeing, that will effectively remove Del Toro's ability to direct the Infected."

"You may have a point," he agreed, his tone grudging. "All it's been doing the entire while I've been sitting here is tick. Drove me half mad." Colonel Douglas began to cast around, presumably for something heavier than his cane. "There is, or was, at least, glass tubing in it. Perhaps if we smash that..."

"It ticks..." Marta examined the device again, and indeed, there was a discernible ticking from it. "If there's tubing, it's inside the box." She felt around the exterior until she found the catch for the rear panel. Inside was an array of clockwork, the escapement heavy and etched with the mark of a maker in the Grand Duchy of Denver.

There was a clunk, a whirr, and the ticking changed in timbre, some mechanism within the device switching over.

"What did you do?" Colonel Douglas asked, his voice dropping spontaneously to a horrified whisper.

"I didn't touch anything at all," Marta pointed out. "You were watching me. Some sort of timer, perhaps?"

Oh hell.

Outside the stable, Dolly let out a panicked whinny. Automatically, Marta stuffed the map into her coat as she rushed for the stable door, Colonel Douglas only inches behind her.

Infected, nearly all of them brown-skinned, with ragged black hair and the tattered remnants of leather garments clinging to them with mud and blood, boiled from the tree line.

As one, Marta and Colonel Douglas snatched for the open door and slammed it shut. They both cast around for something to secure the door. Colonel Douglas found the old bar, now half rotted away, and hauled it up and into place. Marta grabbed the twine that had been used to bind him and hastened to wrap as much of it as she could around the still-solid iron hardware for the bar.

The stable wasn't so bad, as potentially defensible positions went. It had plainly been built with that in mind, perhaps as a shelter from attack by the Lakota. That had been before, unfortunately, time had rotted out most of the wood.

The entire building shuddered as the Infected hit it in a wave. The sound of hands slapping and clawing against wood was almost deafening and coming from all sides. Hacking their way out of a wall would do no good; the Infected were converging on them.

On the machine.

The Infected beat at the sides of the building. The doors shuddered and buckled, the old, rotted bar crackling. Colonel Douglas half-raised his cane, as if to try to break the device into pieces, but paused when Marta grabbed his wrist. "Colonel Douglas," she said, "we have a better chance of survival if they're dividing their attention between us and the device." She carefully did not mention that the division of attention had apparently not helped either of the camps they'd found.

Colonel Douglas nodded jerkily. "Captain Ramos..." He cleared his throat and continued in a steadier tone. "I do hope you have one of those hideously twisty plans in mind. As much as I normally loathe them, this seems a most excellent time."

Marta cast around again, looking for another escape route. Her eyes fixed on the tiny hay loft, or rather, its broken skeleton. It would be madness to go up there, a fall almost guaranteed.

A broken neck, she decided, would be preferable. "I'd rather thought running away sounded like a good idea. If we leave this device in place, perhaps that will distract them from us."

One of the boards splintered, a hand with cracked, bloody fingernails clawing through.

The Colonel blanched slightly. "Will you think me terribly unmanly if I scream while doing so?"

She grabbed the disintegrating remains of a feed trough, dragging it one-handed toward the wrecked loft. "Not at all, Colonel. Point of fact, I'm considering just that course of action myself."

"Oh, good." The colonel gave the rotted structure a horrified look, but then rushed to help her.

Behind them, the door shattered in a spray of fine wooden splinters. Marta hazarded a glance back to see Infected tumbling in over each other in a strangely boneless heap. Then scrabbling jerkily up to stand. Then charging toward them.

There was, indeed, screaming.

Geoff had the presence of mind to shove his cane into his belt as Captain Ramos gave the trough one last heave. He, too, could not help but cast a horrified glance over his shoulder as the doors failed. Both of them should have known better, and he most of all as a veteran. But there was the undeniable human urge to stare at the oncoming wreck of death.

Someone screamed. It might have been him, or Captain Ramos. He didn't particularly care. Geoff scrambled onto the narrow side of the table and lunged for the beams of the loft. One sagged under his hand, cracking, and he hastily grabbed the next one over, then hauled himself up with the strength of pure terror. Sharp splinters tore into the skin of his palms, caught in his shirt and trousers as he dragged himself onto the rotting wood, into the dusty darkness and cobwebs.

He didn't hesitate; as soon as he was in a nominally stable position, he turned and extended his hands to Captain Ramos, catching her outstretched left arm. With a sound that was at least this time far more manly than a scream—more of a rough, protracted grunt—he rolled and dragged her up and into the loft. Her feet kicked away grasping hands as she came. The woman was a constant thorn in his side, an unnatural creature through and through, and a wanted criminal. There wasn't anyone so villainous yet born he'd be willing to abandon to Infection.

For a moment, she lay on top of him, breath sobbing out of her and face gone as pale as her natural skin color could, an unhealthy yellowish sort of color. This was, he reflected suddenly, highly inappropriate. Almost as inappropriate as the fact that she was wearing trousers and no corset. And why had that suddenly come to mind, when the air of the stable filled with the groans of the Infected? The specter of death had a tendency to do strange things to a man.

Captain Ramos crawled off of him, elbowing him in the side in the process. He was almost certain that it had been an accident. Almost. "That," she gasped, "hurt."

"Whatever happened to your arm, anyway?" he asked. That little detail had struck him before, but now it seemed strangely important. Just past his ear, muddy, bloody hands with cracked fingernails clawed at the beam he'd used to drag himself up. It creaked alarmingly.

Hastily, Geoff sat, banging his own knee with his cane as he rearranged himself. The need to get away from the edge suddenly became quite pressing.

Captain Ramos was already ahead of him, crawling carefully along a different beam then the one he'd picked. "Del Toro's men shot me down while I was doing a flyover in my aeroplane." Wood cracked behind them, and they both shot alarmed glances back. The face of one Infected showed over the edge of one beam, then the wood crumbled beneath its hands and it vanished.

"Ah. So that was you." Geoff blew out a breath to knock a bead of sweat from the end of his nose. "They thought you were a man."

She laughed. "They always do."

Well, so had he, once. That wasn't a lesson he'd soon forget. He continued to crawl, trying to concentrate on the fact that there was a horde of Infected below them, wanting to feast upon their flesh, and not the equally undeniable fact that Captain Ramos insisted on having a nice bottom and was wearing trousers.

Damn it.

He reached the wall of the stable on her heels. The loft shook alarmingly as another enterprising Infected clawed at the beams. "I don't believe this will hold long at all," Geoffrey said.

"I concur." Captain Ramos gulped in a few breaths, her face still decidedly pale. She patted the wall next to her head. "See if you can dig through this wood. It's mostly rotted anyway. There have got to be fewer of them out there than there are in here. And it isn't as if they'll have any conception of what we're doing."

Geoff snorted. The Infected didn't *do* strategy. It was what made them both easy and bloody difficult to fight by turns. He turned his attention to the logs that made up the wall, which were perhaps in a worse state than the beams of the loft. A disturbing agglomeration of spider webs and droppings of some sort had to be swept aside by hand, but touching that was still far preferable to death. The roof had obviously begun to leak here some time ago, putting an entire section of the wall into an advanced state of rot. The wood felt strange and spongy to his hands as he began to peel splinters and chunks away from the log.

The entire structure creaked warningly, shifting slightly. "Gently," Captain Ramos hissed, grabbing at his arm. "Gently."

Geoff froze until the little tremor had passed. He licked his suddenly dry lips. Without the option of brute strength, he drew his much-abused sword. Grimacing at the damage he was about to do to the blade, he set to using that to dig at the rotted wood instead.

Perhaps it was his imagination, but he thought Captain Ramos might have winced at the sight as well.

"Do you have any sort of weapon at all?" he asked as he dragged up another large chunk of wood.

"A very small knife," Captain Ramos said. "I'd have better luck using strong language against them."

Geoff frowned, considering the tactical possibilities as he widened the hole he'd made. Warm September light poured in, as did sound. It was no longer eerily silent outside; he heard the sound of moaning from that direction as well. "See if you can find a sturdy enough bit of wood while I work on this. If you do, you can…borrow my sword." Oh, but those words did not feel natural coming from his mouth. Still, the reasoning was clear; a sword could be wielded much more effectively one-handed than a club.

"Ever the gentleman, Colonel," Captain Ramos said, the mockery of her tone rather ruined by the underlying shaky note of fear.

Geoffrey was not so proud a man that he thought his own voice to be any steadier. "A gentleman who very much does not want to die today." And he laughed, since there was really no other option in such a desperate situation, about to launch into such a mad plan.

His fingers were raw and bleeding when he'd peeled away enough rotted wood to make the hole useful as an exit. Mercifully, it was loud enough with all the activities of the Infected both inside and out of the building that the little noise of wood being dropped hadn't attracted even a single one of the Infected. That, he knew, would change as soon as they were on the ground. "We run straight for the woods," he said.

"Straight for the woods," she agreed. "As long as we have the building's wall between us and the mass downstairs, they should remain in place at least." The Infected tended to take a straight-line course to whatever they wanted. It was the sort of thing plans were often made around when it came to destroying them. She came close again, holding out a pitchfork of all things. "Here. I found this."

Geoff gave the makeshift weapon an appreciative look. The tines of the pitchfork were quite rusted, and the wood had gone gray with age, but it felt nicely solid in his hands. "That will do. I'll go first."

"I think I don't mind for once," Captain Ramos said.

He huffed a laugh. "I wish I could say it was an honor, Captain, but I think such a concept is alien to you."

"I shall blush with all the compliments, Colonel Douglas."

Without another glance, he pulled himself through the hole he'd made in the wall, dropping the pitchfork ahead of him so it speared into the ground. Then he lowered himself down as far as he could, hands tight against the splintered wood, before dropping the rest of the way.

He snatched up the pitchfork from the ground just as the first Infected rounded the corner. Without hesitation, he drove the pitchfork into the side of its head with a satisfyingly meaty *thunk*.

Captain Ramos grunted behind him as she dropped to the ground. He didn't look back. A moment later, he felt a tug at his belt, heard the sharp hiss of the sword being drawn. Smoothly done as expected.

Another Infected ran toward them from the side. With far more finesse of technique than he would have expected from a common pirate, Captain Ramos whirled, striking the creature's head from its body with a precise blow. "Now, we run."

They ran. Geoffrey used the blunt end of the pitchfork as a makeshift cane, propelling him along over the ground. What a pair they made, he thought grimly, neither of them able-bodied enough for anything but the most unsteady flight. But it didn't have to be graceful; it just had to get them quickly away.

"Left side!" Captain Ramos hissed.

He turned his head to catch a snatch of movement, then brought the pitchfork up in a hard arc, catching the Infected in the chin. He reversed the movement, driving the metal head down into the creature's skull. Two of the tines came up bent, the third snapping off. He turned and started moving again. "Behind you!"

Captain Ramos dodged to the side, away from the grasping hands of another Infected, not even bothering to look. She pivoted and lunged, blade of the sword going in through the Infected's gaping mouth. With a grunt, she jerked the sword free. Her eyes widened as she glanced behind Geoff even as she started running again herself. "Faster! Faster!"

Geoff decided that he very much did not want to look back just then. "Look for a tree," he gasped. He caught more movement from the corner of his eye and struck backwards with the pitchfork. This time, he didn't even stop to see if he'd landed a mortal blow.

"I'm looking! I'm—" The word ended in a yelp as an Infected barreled into her from between the trees.

Geoff shouted and lunged forward, driving the pitchfork into the thing's neck, shoving it off of her. Captain Ramos scrambled to her feet, blood oozing from a fresh cut on her head, and began running away as he jerked his weapon free.

"Where the hell are they all coming from?"

"More homing in on the device," she gasped out. "Keep running!"

How many more were there? Always more, his instinct told him. There were always more Infected, like the heads of a hydra.

A thunderous crashing sounded in the woods in front them. They both stumbled to a halt, weapons coming up.

Captain Ramos looked wildly around, then pointed. "There, that tree!"

"Not enough time!"

"Do you have a better idea?" And of all things, she shoved him.

Geoff, shocked, began to stumble in that direction, trying to force his screaming legs into a run again.

Horses burst out of the woods around them. He stumbled to a halt, stopping just short of being run down by an enormous, raw-boned roan. The beast flashed past him. He looked up, eyes wide, catching just the impression of a painted savage, bow out and ready. His gaze met the cool, assessing brown eyes of a warrior, and then the man was gone, borne toward the great mass of Infected.

He leaned on the pitchfork, gasping for breath as more riders moved past. They were silent, he realized. Weren't they supposed to be whooping and shouting as they entered battle? But they were grim as ghosts, the only sound the pounding of their horse's hooves.

Arrows cut through the air with sharp zips and whistles; an Infected at their back hit the ground, limbs moving feebly despite its apparently whole body. More proof, then, of some kind of poison known only to them. It was a footnote in this mess, but if he made it out of here alive, it was valuable information. Rifle shots cracked around them. Captain Ramos stumbled over to it and lopped the creature's head off with a grunt. Then she shoved the body over with her foot, looking at the two arrows embedded in the Infected's flesh. She yanked one of the arrows free and inspected as if it held some great meaning "Interesting."

The Infected, in complete disarray with too many warm bodies around in disparate directions, fell swiftly. Most dropped to their knees or fell bonelessly to the ground with arrows standing out from their rotting flesh, immobilized as Indian warriors galloped by and severed their heads with practiced swings of their hand axes.

Geoff stared at it all, trying not to gape as yet more horses passed them, more stern-faced warriors. "Captain Ramos, what is the meaning of this?"

She offered him his sword back. "It seems they did follow me after all."

"Patience, coyote. I said *patience*. You *do* know what that word means, right?" Khangiska crossed his arms over his chest.

Marta shrugged her left shoulder. "It worked out all right, I think. If you'd taken any longer, the Infected might not have been in such a nice group, waiting for slaughter."

Behind her, she heard Colonel Douglas hiss, "What is he *saying*?"

She answered with an impatient little gesture of her hand. After they'd finished clearing out the Infected, the Lakota had trussed the colonel up quite neatly and hauled him away, draped over a horse's back like a sack of potatoes. They hadn't bothered to do the same with Marta. She wasn't certain if it was a sign of respect or, perhaps more likely, a sign of just how little of a threat they thought a one-armed woman with no weapons presented.

They'd both been brought to a nearby camp. Not Khangiska's, but all of the men there deferred to him; it seemed that had been the staging area for the war party. And unless she missed her mark, it seemed Khangiska was a bit more important than just the head of one family.

Khangiska glanced over her shoulder at Geoff. "Is he one of *them*?" he demanded.

"Not precisely. Our culprits are a rogue regiment from the Grand Duchy of Denver, and he's the security man. He's been hunting them down this whole while."

"Right. A friend of yours?"

"No. I would say not. He's trying to put me in prison, where I believe I'll be hanged, actually."

Khangiska's eyebrows went up. "You're not making much of an argument for keeping him alive."

She shook her head hastily. "No, no. He's useful. I run circles around him. It's rather fun."

He snorted. "You *are* a coyote. Useful to *you*. And to us? He's seen too many of our secrets."

"Better the devil you know than the devil you don't." From the look on Khangiska's face, that expression hadn't translated into Goshute properly. Marta was saved from having to launch immediately into another awkward explanation by the sound of more approaching horses.

Two scouts rode up, their cheeks decorated with slashes of white pigment. One had another man slung over his horse much as Colonel Douglas had been. The prisoner had dark skin and a tangled mop of hair; he was dressed as a duchyman, though he had no coat. The back of his black waistcoat was torn, his sleeves rolled up to the elbows to reveal slim brown forearms.

The scouts had a brief conversation with Khangiska, one that Marta could unfortunately not understand, and then dumped the man on the ground next to Colonel Douglas.

"Good lord!" he exclaimed. "Cheswick!"

Marta exchanged a look with Khangiska, trying to convey that no, she had no idea what this was about either.

"Geoffrey? It is you!" the man said, rolling over. "I thought you were done for."

"What are you doing here, Cheswick? Did the savages capture the general?"

Before Marta could track the conversation further, Khangiska cleared his throat. She turned her attention back to him.

"Someone else who wants to see you hanged?"

"No. I don't know that one at all." She frowned, tilting her head. "Though, if that is *Professor* Cheswick, the ah..." She couldn't think of the correct Goshute word for "geologist." "The... rock talker...I may have read a few of his papers."

"Ah. He must be the one they're using to look for their gold."

"I imagine so." Marta decided to pull the conversation back to the track she'd been headed toward before Cheswick's arrival.

His lip curled. "And for that, they try to unleash the great plague upon us again."

"They think you're helpless against it as well." She answered his sharp look with a raised eyebrow. Not only had they cured her, they seemed to have some poison that would immobilize the Infected almost instantly—or perhaps the two were the same, she didn't know. And she knew he wouldn't answer if she asked. "You have a regiment on your doorstep. I imagine you want to maintain the reputation of the Dead Plains, yes? And the more you know, the greater advantage you'll have in defeating them." She felt no allegiance to the nearby Grand Duchy of Denver on even a good day. That General Del Toro had decided to use his personal regiment to whip up a new outbreak of Infection meant she had a decided interest in seeing them stopped. The fact that they had found some way to control and divert the Infected meant that she had quite the interesting task ahead of her when she returned to the Roost; it was the sort of technology that cried out to be shared.

Just as the medicine of the Oglala Lakota did. Somehow, she doubted Khangiska would find that argument compelling.

"I hear you."

She jerked her head toward the two duchymen, talking amongst themselves. "The man you just captured may know a bit. But I know for a fact that Colonel Douglas has detailed information."

"Are you arguing that I should torture him?" To his credit, Khangiska didn't seem happy at the prospect.

"No, I don't think that's necessary. If he gives his word to keep the hints of your secrets he knows, he'll keep it. I know the man. He's..." She glanced at Khangiska and decided not to use the phrase *rather in love with his own honor.* "Very honorable. He'll keep his word. Let him bargain for his freedom."

"If he is so honorable, why would he betray his own people?"

"Justice," she said. "It is a matter of justice." Well, what she expected, knowing Colonel Douglas as she did, would be that he wanted to haul the entire regiment back to the Grand Duchy in shackles—*somehow*—and see them tried for their crimes. As if a fair trial would occur. As if the judges would care one whit about outrages done to people they lied themselves into believing were "savage."

Khangiska made an open-handed gesture, something almost like amusement sparking in his eyes. "Then bargain."

"WHAT ARE YOU DOING here, Cheswick? Did the savages capture the general?" Geoffrey asked. And if so, where was the man? He'd much rather see Del Toro taken back to the Grand Duchy and brought publicly to justice. He wanted to see the bastard confess before the Grand Duke at the very least. Being killed by the natives in the Dead Plains just seemed a bit too…ignominious for what the man had done.

"No, no, the general rode away." Cheswick hesitated, squirming a little against his bonds. "I hid. I…When the general said he'd leave you for the Infected to eat…I couldn't. I thought if I hid and waited, I'd be able to come back and free you. But it was harder to get away than I thought. They've been watching me so closely…"

Geoff stared at the man, mouth unabashedly hanging open. Was this the same man who had once been mercilessly harassed in their school days? He had never thought of such an act of bravery coming from Cheswick, however mad his plan had been.

But really, how well had he known the then-boy?

"Stupid, I know," Cheswick continued. "I should have…I don't know. Taken up a rifle. But I was never a military man, and I thought this wasn't really the time to start. I don't even know how to shoot the bloody thing."

"Cheswick," Geoff said after a moment more of stunned silence.

"He'll be so angry, Geoffrey. So dashed angry. If he ever finds me again. I let my horse go, and yours as well, so he'd have something to chase, but if he catches me…Oh God. But I had to do it. I couldn't stand it any longer. This is all my fault."

"Cheswick," Geoff said again.

"Gabriel. My name is Gabriel. Remember?"

Geoff blinked his eyes a few times, trying to rearrange the world within his head. "Right," he said weakly. "Gabriel. It will be all right."

Cheswick—no, Geoff reminded himself, *Gabriel*—laughed. "I'm beginning to feel as if nothing has ever been all right, Geoffrey."

"We have a plan." It was a lie, but the man looked so distressed that he couldn't help himself. He wondered if he should have tried this when they were in school. If he should have talked to the man, even just to lie to him.

Gabriel nodded. "All right. You have a plan. I remember, you always had plans, even when we were boys."

He smiled, but the expression felt awkward. It felt as if Gabriel recalled them being much closer than they had been. "Gabriel, what are you even doing *here*?"

"I found a few notes that led me to think there might be gold in the Black Hills. Ones from before the Infection. And the geology of this entire area is so fascinating…I applied to the Grand Duke for an expedition." He swallowed thickly. "I didn't think it would be like this. Not at all. All I wanted was to come up here for study. I didn't want any of this!"

Geoff felt as if his blood had gone to ice. "Did you actually speak with the Grand Duke?" And still, the question remained open—was the Grand Duke involved?

Gabriel shook his head. "No. I always just spoke with General Del Toro. He said the expedition was important enough for his personal attention."

"Why didn't you *tell* anyone, Ch—Gabriel?"

"Who would believe such a mad thing?" he answered bitterly. "No one ever believed the far more believable things that happened to me at school, at uni." He shook his head. "I know, you think me a coward. But in truth, Geoffrey, I had no inkling of what would happen until I'd arrived at the camp. And then it was too late. I've been trying, ever since, to think of a way…to just find a way…"

"I don't think you a coward at all, Gabriel." And it certainly felt like truth when he spoke it. "A coward wouldn't have tried to come back for me."

Gabriel laughed, the sound as bitter as his voice. "It's the thought that counts, is it?"

He didn't have a good answer for that. This was not the time to deal with another man's demons. And also, Geoffrey feared, not the time to tell Gabriel to buck up and have a stiff upper lip about the entire matter. The man looked positively stretched to the snapping point. He decided to change the topic back to facts, cool and calm. "The man with the device that's controlling the Infected…What can you tell me about him?"

"Professor Nielson? We talked a bit. He's…I don't really like him. All his ideas about experiments on the Infected." Gabriel looked distinctly uncomfortable. "I…may have stolen a few of his papers. I thought they would be evidence, but of what, I don't know. Another half-baked plan."

Geoff did his best to remain calm at *that* revelation. "Gabriel, you are a genius. Don't think otherwise. Where are the papers?"

"Rolled up in my satchel. The men who captured me have it."

Of course, profoundly out of his reach. Though perhaps it was foolish to get excited about this tidbit of information when, as far as he knew, they'd both be getting their heads cut off and their scalps removed shortly. Unless he was relying upon Captain Ramos, who was jabbering quite happily away at the chieftain, to save their lives.

Grim, terrifying thought, that. Geoff did not want to live in a world where even his subconscious thought it a good idea to trust that woman. "That's excellent, Gabriel, it really is. Look, I know there are two of the devices, but I only ever saw one. Where is the other?"

"I don't entirely know. They always moved them in tandem, you see. Move one while the other is in operation. For…safety. Hah. Safety. The general is probably on his way to move it, once he gives up on finding me. You've seen the map, right? It'll be two north of French Creek. Normally, I didn't go somewhere until… until after they had been." Gabriel looked like he might be about to vomit. "Today was a special case, you see, since I needed a second set of samples."

"Steady on, Gabriel. Deep breaths," Geoff said soothingly, filing that data away for later use. "Do you know where this Professor Nielson lives? Is he from the Grand Duchy of Denver?"

Cheswick nodded. "I've actually been to his workshop, not long before we left. The general wanted me to help him pack, since I'm accustomed to field work, you see." He began to recite the address as Captain Ramos approached, the leader of the savages on her heels.

Marta crossed the short distance to Colonel Douglas, Khangiska at her back. She squatted down in front of the two men, left elbow propped against her knee. In English, she said, "The Lakota are currently considering if they want to let you live or not." She glanced back at Khangiska, who looked appropriately stern. Well, at this moment, he really *was* appropriately stern. "Right now, they're leaning more toward not, I'm afraid."

"I'm sure you don't have anything to do with that," Colonel Douglas growled.

"Rude. And after I helped save your life, too." She glanced at the man next to Colonel Douglas, taking in his clothing, the callouses and scars of his hands, the broken fingernails. "Professor Cheswick, a pleasure to meet you. I found your monograph on the provenance silver seams of the Grand Duchy of Denver very interesting."

The man had been looking quite ready to faint but brightened considerably. "Oh, I'm so glad to hear that."

"My name is Captain Ramos, and I should very much like to see you survive right now." She smiled thinly. Now that she had his attention in a much more positive way, she looked back at Colonel Douglas. "They are willing to make a deal."

"What sort of deal?" the colonel asked.

"Your word of honor that you shan't tell anyone the Dead Plains are populated by people of the native tribes, rather than packs of Infected. Not one hint of their existence, nor their methods for keeping themselves safe." She'd seen Colonel Douglas's knowing look when she'd investigated one of the arrows earlier; he seemed at least somewhat familiar with it. And while this sort of secrecy left a bad taste in her mouth, she had no desire to see the Black Hills invaded by the surrounding duchies searching for wealth or knowledge. Better to try to study the chemical composition of this weapon first and then release the information without a whisper as to its provenance, if such a thing was possible. Otherwise, she feared the prospect of a cure or weapon alone would lead to the worst attempted invasion of these lands yet seen. When Colonel Douglas frowned, she added, "The choice is really that you can either remain silent on the topic and keep your head, or remain silent in death, I'm afraid. That's not a point Chief Khangiska is willing to budge upon. And you as well, Professor Cheswick."

"Of course I give my word. How odd," Cheswick said. "I find I'd really rather not die."

Colonel Douglas was silent for much longer than that. Then he growled, twisting against his bonds for emphasis. "Fine. You have my word."

"He'll be pleased to hear that." She looked over her shoulder and told Khangiska in Goshute, "They've both given their word to keep your secrets in exchange for their lives."

"That's a start," he answered in kind.

She turned her attention back to the two men and continued on in English. "We've been given the task of hunting General Del Toro down ourselves, if he hasn't yet returned to his regiment. That will be some small compensation for the harm he has caused."

"We're not going to kill him," Colonel Douglas said flatly. "He has crimes to answer for in the Grand Duchy of Denver."

"All the more reason for us to find him before the Lakota do, yes?"

"And what of the regiment?"

"The Lakota have every intention of wiping them from the surface of the Earth." She saw no reason to sugarcoat that. Colonel Douglas was far too intelligent to fool with an obvious lie unless it was one he desperately wanted to believe. "And I believe if you thought about it, you'd agree they have every right."

"Just whose side are you on?" Colonel Douglas demanded.

"Not yours." Marta stared at him levelly. "They marched onto the lands of a sovereign nation and attacked without warning, using the most despicable of tactics."

"Why must it always be violence?" Cheswick asked plaintively.

Marta and Colonel Douglas both ignored him.

"I can't stop them." Colonel Douglas visibly braced himself, gritting his teeth. "But I won't be party to this. If we capture Del Toro and any of the rest, I'll march them out of here myself."

"Going to put them all on trial, are you?"

"The soldiers were following orders," he said stiffly. "But those sorts of orders are criminal, and you know it. The very thought of starting a new Infection! Strictly against every law of warfare in the civilized war—and the uncivilized too, I'd say. They must have an example made of them."

Which would really violate the promise of secrecy he'd already given, but Marta felt no need to point that out. The chance that he would accomplish that feat was so low that it was simpler to round it down to zero. "There will be no mercy for you if you are there during battle."

"Understood," he growled, spine stiff. "And these savages will receive no mercy from me!"

"Savages. Hah." She turned her attention to Cheswick. "And what of you?"

"What of me?" he asked.

"You said that you wanted to live."

"I do."

"Do you wish to return to the Grand Duchy of Denver?"

Cheswick shot an odd look at Colonel Douglas, then said very carefully, "It hasn't been particularly kind to me. And this is…I feel responsible. It was my research. Can you please ask the chieftain if there's anything I can do? Anything at all?"

"Gabriel," Colonel Douglas murmured warningly.

A shame, Marta thought, that Professor Cheswick was obviously of too nervous a disposition to be a pirate. He was rather pretty. "There are some very lovely rocks in the Black Hills," she observed.

"I was hoping to do a bit of research, but it's all gone so wrong now. The hydrothermal deposits alone…"

Marta let him go on a bit, occasionally asking questions to prod him ahead about the geology of the area; she wanted volume of words more than anything. Finally, when he'd begun to run out of steam she nodded, her expression becoming incongruously final. "Of course. Worry not, gentlemen. I think your lives shall be safe." Marta straightened and turned to face Khangiska, switching back to Goshute. "They've given me the information. I shall describe it to you, if you like."

He nodded. "Walk with me while you do."

Behind them, Colonel Douglas hissed, "Gabriel, this is madness!"

Marta began describing what she'd observed from Colonel Douglas's map as they moved away. Once they were out of earshot of the two men, however, Khangiska stopped the flow of information by clapping a hand on her shoulder, then said in perfect, if accented, English: "I think next time, I will negotiate for myself."

Marta shut her mouth with a snap, nearly nipping the end of her own tongue. She took in the amused twinkle to his eye, and laughed. "Well played, sir."

"We will say your cunning has still saved the life of your enemy."

"Let's hope I won't have cause to regret that." She dug into her coat and pulled out the folded map she'd taken from Colonel Douglas earlier. He'd never gotten around to asking for it back. "Here, look this over. Better than me trying to tell it to you. Though I'd appreciate it back when you're done, just in case the good colonel asks for it."

"Games within games, coyote." He took the map and unfolded it, looking over the markings. His expression darkened as he saw the spots that had been marked, the sites of probable massacres. "So many," he murmured.

She knew it had nothing to do with troop numbers.

"Colonel Douglas did mention earlier that they have Gatling guns at the camp, though not currently positioned for defense. If you ask the other fellow, Cheswick, once he's no longer around the colonel, I would lay even money he'll tell you precisely where in the camp they are."

"Mmm. I don't think I like you volunteering my home to him."

"Give him a chance to prove himself. I think he was honest when he said he wishes to repay you for his part in this crime. I know the look of men like him." She remembered the glance he'd given Colonel Douglas, the way he'd seemed to curl in on himself without moving. "They want for a different sort of civilization." She smiled crookedly. "And he'll love every one of your sacred hills as much as you do, if in a somewhat different way."

"I'll think about it." Khangiska folded up the map and handed it back to her. "The general is ours to punish."

"I had assumed as much," she answered smoothly. She had thought they'd be after the man, but she hadn't known he would have ascertained her particular plan. She had a few questions she wished to ask General Del Toro. "It's more an excuse to lead Colonel Douglas on a merry chase so he doesn't try to do something stupidly noble and warn the regiment you're coming."

Khangiska shook his head. "I will pray that you never have a reason to return to Paha Sapa. Just talking to you makes my head hurt."

Marta grinned. "I tend to have that effect on people."

"Go get your horse." Despite the pained expression on his face, his lips twitched. "I hear you named him Dolly."

Borne away from the Indian camp on his borrowed horse, Geoff probably should have felt some small amount of relief. He'd at least escaped with his life; many a man would not have survived the adventure he'd just had.

He did not like owing his life in any way to Captain Ramos.

And there was no time for relief now. Not with General Del Toro on the loose. Not with an entire regiment of men from the Grand Duchy of Denver about to be slaughtered.

"Do you have any idea at all where we're going?" he asked Captain Ramos after a few minutes of silent riding.

In answer, she dug the map from her pocket and handed it back to him. "Do tell me you got something useful from Cheswick."

"His name is Gabriel," Geoff corrected her, almost absently. Something about knowing the man's first name gave him an uncomfortable spasm of guilt. "And I still can't believe you bargained to leave him with the savages."

"It was what he wanted. Particularly since it sounded as if we were about to go hunting for the creature of his nightmares."

"Still…" Geoff unfolded his map, continuing to ride easily. It hadn't escaped his amused attention that Captain Ramos, for all the death-defying stunts he'd seen her perform, sat a-horse like a sack of potatoes. "Gabriel told me that they might have been searching for him for quite some time, though it's been long enough by now that they might have given up, I should think."

"We could pick up the trail in that area, though."

"Or better." He found the mark on the map, which Gabriel had told him was the site they'd been going to next. "He said after, they'd be going to join the men picking up the second device. Here." He flashed the map at her.

Marta nodded. "We'd best hope that your Gabriel bought us enough time to make the distance." Awkwardly, she urged her horse into a canter.

Geoff followed suit much more smoothly, casting one last glance at the map before stuffing it back in his pocket. "Not mine, Captain Ramos."

She seemed disinclined to answer, concerned with just hanging onto her horse.

Geoff took the lead, focusing on navigating the both of them through the woods and finding a path that a mediocre horseman could follow. It was tempting to see if he could lose Captain Ramos. But he was painfully aware that General Del Toro would have between two and five more men at his back when they found him. Captain Ramos might have only one arm, but she'd shown she could use that quite effectively.

They rode for over an hour in grim silence, but for the sound of hoofbeats and the snorting of the horses. They quickly moved out of the area of grassier clearings, climbing up into the hills. For the sake of the horses, they had to slow their pace as the time grew long, though Geoff reassured himself that Del Toro would be in the same position. Completely inappropriate to the gravity of the situation, his stomach grumbled loudly. Geoff glanced up, squinting through the trees; it was well past noon now. Perhaps Captain Ramos had acquired a bit of food to go with the deadly-looking ax she'd managed to talk out of the Indians.

He caught sight of something, a tell-tale shape from the corner of his eye. "Hold."

Captain Ramos clumsily drew her horse to a halt beside him as he slid down to stand on the ground and moved around the tree they'd been about to pass.

"What is it?"

"Evidence." A better look at it confirmed his initial thought. "Horse manure. And so fresh, the flies have barely gotten to it."

They were close. With a renewed sense of urgency, Geoff hurried to mount again as Captain Ramos nudged her horse forward, toward the new trail.

"Well spotted," she said, tone not in the least grudging. "We have them."

He caught more signs quickly: there a hoofprint, there a thread caught by a twig. They had the advantage now. Their quarry was close and didn't know it was being pursued. Geoff kneed his horse back into a fast trot, trusting Captain Ramos would keep up. As he rode, he drew his sword, leaving the sheath secured in his waistband. Better safe than sorry.

The sight distance was limited, with trees growing thickly on the hillside. So focused on keeping up the pace, Geoffrey didn't hear the murmur of men's voices until it was far too late. He burst out into the bright afternoon sunlight, into a small clearing made by fallen trees. He had enough time to catch the impression of the green uniforms, a caisson bearing a canvas-covered bundle, a blanket spread out for lunch—lunch of all banal things!—and then they were scrambling around him.

Geoff wheeled his horse and kneed him forward, cutting down the man nearest to him with a slash of his sword. He turned his head, doing a quick count of five more men total, and then the first rifle shot split the air. He ducked, and the horse surged away into a gallop, dodging back into the trees.

No sign of Captain Ramos. Lovely. Well, at least he was proving a nice diversion now.

Marta had hung onto her horse with grim purpose but hadn't quite been able to keep up with Colonel Douglas. It wasn't so much that she lacked the will. It was more that Dolly the horse didn't seem at all interested in going over a slow canter, and the one time she'd tried to urge him to go faster, he'd attempted to bite her. The horse could move like a striking snake.

At the sound of rifle shots, however, he moved into a thundering gallop like an avalanche as she jerked upright in surprise. Marta grabbed a fistful of his mane and held on for dear life. This was definitely nothing like the rather fat ponies she'd learned on, so many years ago. And it reminded her why she'd decided she preferred her vehicles powered by steam, rather than grass.

More rifle shots cracked. She saw a flash of movement, Colonel Douglas weaving through the trees. She yanked Dolly's head to the right so that they moved away from him, circling. Likely, the soldiers thought he was alone.

She found the clearing through a gap in the trees, getting a rough estimate of the number of men and their position, and then wheeled, giving Dolly his head to free up her hand. She hoped she wouldn't live to regret it. Or have her last moment before death involve the regret-filled revelation that perhaps the horse hadn't liked being named for a girl after all.

Dolly charged into the clearing. Marta yanked the hand ax from her belt and raised it high, then drove it down into the head of the first man they passed. Her entire arm nearly went numb with shock. Dolly squealed and lashed out his hind feet in a kick as another of the soldiers swung toward them, taking the man in the chest.

Then they blazed out of the clearing.

Only three men left, if she counted correctly, and trying to split their attention between two targets.

Splinters of wood erupted from a tree next to her, taking the brunt of the rifle shot. Dolly bolted, and she fought to regain control of the horse, which unfortunately required her to drop the hand ax. Behind, she heard another shot, and then a strangled scream, which she thought far too high to be Colonel Douglas.

Down to two men, then.

As she finally got the stallion back under control, trying to turn him, she heard more pounding hoofbeats. Two horses charged toward her, a lighter flash behind them indicating a third—was that Colonel Douglas? Marta prodded Dolly with her knee—miraculously, it worked. The horse moved toward the others, paralleling their course.

The second man, large and dark and angry and most definitely General Del Toro, raised a pistol. She hastily pushed Dolly back out among the trees as a bullet tore through her sleeve, grazing her arm in a hot line.

The lead rider drew a pistol of his own, taking aim at her.

She ducked.

And the movement ended in a meaty thud rather than a sharp crack as he ran his head into a low hanging tree branch. Marta caught the sight of him flung backward from his horse in a heap, just out of the corner of her eye.

Then there was just Del Toro, presumably far too canny to be taken out by an inanimate object.

Colonel Douglas thundered past her, hunkered low against the neck of his horse and looking unfairly like a natural rider.

Marta gritted her teeth and hung on grimly. This couldn't be any worse than navigating the rails at night with no lights. She made Simms do that all the time.

Perhaps this was her karmic punishment. She nearly dropped from the horse's back, only a yank on Dolly's mane saving her as she jerked away from another low-hanging tree branch. "Slow down, slow down. There's a pretty girl. A good fellow. Whatever you like. Perhaps you're a fellow who likes feeling pretty. That's all right. Just slow down." It was difficult to sound soothing when she was being shaken all over the place.

Dolly slowed of his own accord as they moved out of the trees again, onto bare rock sown with patches of grass and scrub. Two horses were there as well, riderless. And perhaps fifty feet ahead, Marta saw Colonel Douglas and General Del Toro squared off. At the edge of a cliff, of all melodramatic things.

Marta slid from Dolly's back, hoping she didn't look nearly as wobbly as she felt, and walked toward the two men. Del Toro's coat was torn, she noted, and he had a lovely bloom of color on his cheek, just the size of a fist. Colonel Douglas's nose had sprung quite an impressive leak, which he was ignoring. He had his sword up and pointed toward the general's throat, tip resting gently against his skin.

General Del Toro, on the other hand, had his pistol up.

"I don't particularly care what state you're in," Colonel Douglas said. "I'll take you back in pieces gladly. We can patch you back together for court."

"Pathetic, Colonel," Del Toro spat. "The Duke's been going soft ever since he hired you."

Both of them ignored Marta. This was an odd feeling for her; she was markedly taller than either of the men and not used to being ignored unless she wished to be. Slowly, she bent to fiddle with her boot as the men continued to snarl at each other.

"Meaningless insults from an honorless cur," Colonel Douglas growled.

"You're less of a man than she is! And is that your backup? A doxy? The only thing foolish enough to follow you. I'll shoot you both and have done with it!"

Marta straightened back up. She waited for Del Toro to look at her, then away, and then she lunged, slashing across his forearm with the small, razor-sharp knife from her boot.

Del Toro screamed, the pistol dropping from his suddenly floppy fingers. He clutched at his arm, cursing her soundly, his pained shuffling putting him even closer to the edge of the cliff as he tried to move away from her.

"Doxies have ears, you know," Marta said. She wiped the little knife on her pants leg.

Colonel Douglas lowered his sword, then carefully put it back in its sheath. The cane once again whole, he leaned on it. "I would have had him in a minute," he said conversationally.

"I have no doubt, Colonel," Marta said dryly. "I just couldn't stand the suspense." She looked at Del Toro. "This was entirely about gold, was it not?"

He glared at her. "Gold for the glory of our duchy. No price is too high for that. And more land as well."

"All you had to do was clear away its rightful occupants by turning them on each other with Infection." She tilted her head. "And at the end, you were going to gather all of the Infected in a canyon and cut them down, do I have that right?"

"A neat plan," he ground out.

"Indeed. I wanted to make certain I had it all to rights. And where did you find these fascinating devices, by the way?"

The general bared his teeth. "People with ideas find *me*."

"So that was the genesis of this mad scheme."

"Oh, I couldn't have done it without Professor Cheswick finding the gold for us. But Professor Nielson had such a clear vision. And to think, his colleagues thought him mad and drummed him out into the street."

Knowing what the man had wrought, Marta could not find any sympathy in her heart even for such a misunderstood inventor. Though she had to admit, quietly, that she would very much like a look at his engineering notes. Perhaps she'd take the time to look over the other machine well before dumping it into the canyon and seeing it smashed. Unfortunately, it was far too bulky to make the trek back to the rail lines.

Colonel Douglas turned his attention back to Del Toro, who had stopped cursing and limited himself to heavy breathing. "General Del Toro, you have sought to use Infection as a weapon of war, a criminal act counter to all conventions of warfare. You've invaded lands not your own without the express permission of your lord. For those crimes, I now place you under arrest." He smiled grimly. "And I'm certain I'll think of many more charges while we're on our way to the nearest rail station."

"Ha." Del Toro stuck his hands out before him, as if to receive a pair of handcuffs, though the effect was rather ruined by the way he still had to clutch his right wrist with his left hand. Even with his broad face tight with pain, he smirked. "Do what you wish, Colonel. No judge would dare to convict me, not over dead savages. And then I will have my revenge on you!"

Marta stared at the man. While in tone he sounded nearly ready to twirl his black mustache for effect, she had little doubt he spoke the truth. Del Toro had established himself in the Grand Duchy long before Colonel Douglas had ever arrived. He had a reputation and was no doubt owed countless favors. And she'd seen herself how the courts of the Grand Duke worked; no one of note was convicted unless the Grand Duke wished it. Even ignoring the fact that the Grand Duke was quite likely involved in this plot, he would still not want these events to see the light of day. It would reflect scandalously on him, for the commander of his military to have become something so monstrous. Even if Colonel Douglas hadn't sworn on his honor to keep the existence of the Lakota secret and thus hopelessly hampered any chance at prosecution, the verdict had long since been written.

It was ugly, twisted, and inescapable. How Colonel Douglas still managed to be an idealist in his own odd way, she could never guess.

She thought of the bloody ground at Elk Creek, of the Infected tumbling over each other. All of those lives destroyed in pursuit of wealth, murdered as surely by this man's hand as if he'd shot them each himself.

The course to justice seemed very clear.

"I'll very much look forward to the day you are hanged," Colonel Douglas said.

"It will never happen." Del Toro smirked.

"Colonel." Marta looked at the colonel. "I regret to inform you that I agree with General Del Toro."

Del Toro laughed, a triumphant note in his voice. Colonel Douglas's eyes widened, then narrowed. Marta's shoulder moved in a small shrug. Then she lunged at Del Toro, driving her left shoulder into his chest. The force of the collision drove her back onto the balls of her feet. Del Toro overbalanced, arms windmilling as Marta shifted her weight and followed the heavy blow with a kick to the stomach.

With a strangled scream, Del Toro disappeared over the edge of the cliff.

Colonel Douglas stared at her, open-mouthed, for only a second. Then his hand tightened on his cane. Marta read his intention in the way his muscles tensed. She snapped her foot out in another kick, sending the cane spinning from his hand and clattering down the rocks toward the woods on their other side. Hastily, she danced back.

"*You*," he said, naked horror in his voice. Whatever strange camaraderie they'd begun to find had vanished into dust in his eyes. "What have you done?"

"What I had to do." Her own voice sounded strange and hoarse to her own ears. She felt oddly dizzy. "You have the map, Colonel Douglas. You ought to be able to find your way out of the Black Hills on your own." She could feel it, a line she had crossed without even being aware of its existence.

And yet. She would do it over again.

Marta turned and began to walk quickly away toward where Dolly waited. She half expected Colonel Douglas to tackle her. But when she had squirmed her way onto Dolly's back and hazarded a glance behind her, the colonel remained still as a statue at the edge of the cliff.

"You're being awful quiet," Simms remarked.

Marta didn't have to look up at him to know he was stroking his red muttonchops. That seemed to be his automatic reaction to any emotion outside of simple calm. Stress? Stroke the muttonchops. Puzzlement? Stroke the muttonchops. Boredom? Better than doing nothing, she supposed.

"Still are right now, point of fact," he continued.

"I find I haven't anything to say," Marta muttered.

She poked at the glass jar nearest to her on the work bench. In it sat a broken-off arrow, coated with dried, black blood. It was the only sample she'd been able to acquire. She really ought to start working on it, but she didn't want to undertake anything overly delicate until her right arm had healed and she had her steadiest hand back.

"Want to talk? I hear it's supposed to help."

"Not in the mood." She poked at the jar with her finger again, then abruptly said, "I almost died. Of Infection."

There was a long, awkward pause. She could almost hear the muttonchops being stroked. "But you got better."

"I did."

"Well, that's all right, then." There was the scrape of wood on stone as he pulled a stool up to her workbench. "That's what I like about you, Captain. You don't do anything by halves."

She grunted.

"Also what scares the hell out of me too, every other day."

Marta sighed. "Would you think it odd if it occasionally scares me as well?" There were other things she could tell him, things that were far too raw. The image of Del Toro spinning down into the void haunted her, somehow, and she didn't wish to speak of it until she'd sorted out her own feelings about both almost dying… and killing.

"I'd like that, actually. It'd mean you're less mad than I thought."

That pried a small laugh from her.

"Better. I've got something that ought to put a smile on your face." A broad hand reached around her arm to set a grubby piece of paper in front of her: the list she had left Simms. Every item was crossed off.

"Good work, Simms," she commented.

"Turn it over," Simms said.

She flipped the list. The handwriting on the other side she recognized immediately as that of Deliah Nimowitz. And that did make her smile, the fond expression a bit crooked with a helping of *oh goodness, what sort of interesting mess has she gone and caused now.* She read over the note. "You were gadding about with Deliah while I was in the Black Hills?"

"Wasn't my idea, trust me."

"You don't even *like* Deliah."

"I like her a fair bit less now," Simms grumped.

Marta couldn't help it; she grinned, finally turning to face Simms. For all that had gone terrifying and wrong in those brief days in the Black Hills, for all the grinding unpleasantness of the journey home, it was perhaps a reminder that she was *home.* That some things did not change, like Deliah and her schemes, or Simms and his delightful, long-suffering grumpiness that she'd long ago realized was his way of admitting to a grudging affection. "Do tell."

And she saw it, with her smile, a glint of answering humor in Simms's eyes, even as his long face maintained its put-upon expression. "Well, Captain, therein lies a story."

"Very sorry to hear about your aunt, sir."

Geoff grunted, waving his secretary away. The lie grated on him, like fingernails dragged across slate. Whatever else could he say, though? It was bad enough that he'd come dragging in almost a week late, thoroughly sunburned and far thinner than when he'd left.

The sunburn faded quickly, however. And the vanishing weight, everyone seemed more than willing to put down to a stoic sort of grief. At least the passage of time had allowed his mustache to return to a reasonable shadow of its former glory, though something in him said it would never be quite the same again. It felt as if the events of the Black Hills would be as sharp a dividing line in his life as the day he'd shattered his leg and ended his military career.

Geoff dropped into his chair, eyeing the mountain of paperwork piled on his desk with something close to appreciation. Catching up on events during his absence would be a welcome distraction, something else for his mind to chew over instead of that wooded cliff, the flurry of movement, the sight of Del Toro dropping away, and then later, the wreckage of what had once been the Black Bull camp.

Blood, so much blood, but no bodies, much as it had been in the Indian camps. Somehow, it plagued his nightmares more than the solid proof of a massacre would have.

"Sir?"

"What is it?" He dragged his gaze up from the piles of papers.

"The Grand Duke wants to meet with you after lunch. One of the regiments has gone missing. They were supposed to be on training exercises, but no one's heard from them in weeks."

He stared at the young man until he stopped talking.

"Sir?" the secretary ventured again after a moment.

"Tea," he said. "And of course, tell the Grand Duke that I am his servant." The gross humor of the situation made his stomach cramp. "Always."

He began to sort through the reports, placing them in order of urgency. One minor occurrence, a fire, he almost just dropped into the wastepaper basket, until he noticed the address of the residence. It was the one Gabriel had given him as belonging to the inventor of those horrifying devices, Professor Nielson.

Geoff crumpled the report in his hands. Well, it seemed that Captain Ramos had, unsurprisingly, returned to the duchy ahead of him. She didn't have everything, however. He still had the papers Gabriel had given to him, locked away in a safe deposit box. What he would do with those, he hadn't yet decided.

And really, it might depend on if he even still had a job, after this next meeting with the Grand Duke.

The secretary returned with a little silver tea tray, which he set on Geoff's desk. After a moment of hesitation, he added a silver flask. "You look like you need it, sir," the man said.

"Very thoughtful of you." He waited until the secretary had left him in peace again before doctoring his tea with a healthy dollop.

He'd had a great deal of time to think, on the way back to the Grand Duchy of Denver. For days, it had just been him and his borrowed horse—and the memories of that last moment, the cliff top. He'd thought the ruined camps and the mass of Infected at French Creek would be what haunted him, but no. It was Del Toro's scream as he dropped from sight, and Captain Ramos's wide brown eyes as she said those clipped, precise words: "What I had to do."

And the worst of it was, the more he thought of it, the longer he considered the implications, the crimes, the politics involved, he found he could not disagree. As if he had unwittingly allowed that woman to become judge and sin-eater in one shocked moment.

For that, for the most profound thing she had ever stolen from him, he could quite easily hate her.

Geoff contemplated his half-full teacup and carefully filled it back to the brim with whiskey. He tugged a few more papers from the pile. A rather stained envelope fell in the minor avalanche to slide across his desk. He frowned, looking at the unfamiliar handwriting that scrawled his name across it.

And it was surprisingly heavy.

He tore the envelope open, and several rocks fell out. Most were round and polished, as if taken from a stream, pretty and colorful things. One was a rough lump, its edges dusted with... with...gold. His eyes widened.

Geoff shook the envelope again, and a folded scrap of paper tumbled onto the desk. The paper had plainly been torn from a book of some sort, the text on the front and back the tattered portions of an index. A brief note on it simply read: *It's come out all right in the end, Geoffrey. There is no plan. Yours, —GC*

He picked up one of the smooth stones, rubbing it between his fingers, and a faint smile came to his lips.

Do Shut Up, Mister Simms

I T WAS A BEAUTIFUL day at the abandoned silver mine affectionately known to its occupants as the Devil's Roost. The sun shone down from a nearly cloudless blue sky. A panorama of forests and fields spread out below, with the city that acted as the heart of the Grand Duchy of Denver occupying an evil yellow haze in the distance. Birds sang. A hawk circled lazily as if drawing a target around the sun. A soft breeze ruffled the leaves of the aspen trees and the needles of the stately pines, occasionally sending a bit of foliage to land on the electrified perimeter fence with a loud crackle. Just beyond the fence, a few deer grazed idly.

Meriwether Octavian Simms, known by his own preference to everyone he'd ever met simply as "Mister Simms," or "Simms" if they were feeling a bit froggy, didn't trust any of the wholesome, natural goodness one bit. He held a mismatched cup and saucer—blue and white Zhonghua china and lumpy green *oh look daddy, I made you a present isn't it lovely* respectively—and sipped his tea with the air of a man who knew the other shoe was about to drop any second now, and if he was truly lucky, it would land square on his head and kill him before he had a chance to suffer.

He was never, ever that lucky. Which was probably for the best, because in his more honest moments of introspection, which he perforce tried to keep few and far between, he had to admit that he actually *liked* a little bit of adventure. He would likely go just as mad as his best friend and partner in crime if forced into a life of boredom, though very likely in a much more quiet and unimpressive way.

Simms was the right-hand man of Captain Marta Ramos, infamous rail and air pirate, scourge of the Grand Duchies, and general smug pain-in-the-arse. How he had attained that position was a mystery still even to him, and something he really only bothered to wonder about at times when angry people he did not know were attempting to insert knives, bullets, or cannonballs into his more delicate anatomy. These were the sorts of things that happened far too often to a person caught in Captain Ramos's orbit.

That Captain Ramos was not currently in residence at the Roost didn't change the fact that Simms could all but feel an invisible noose tightening about his right ankle. No one had tried to kill him for months. The half-hearted efforts of the Grand Duke's security forces hardly counted; they couldn't hit the broadside of a barn, let alone a large man sprinting away in terror. He was due.

Simms took another sip of his tea and tugged a scrap of paper from the pocket of his buckskin jacket. The paper was only slightly stained as of yet, and covered with Captain Ramos's almost unreadable, slapdash handwriting. Before her departure on her adventure up into the Dead Plains—Simms was simultaneously relieved she hadn't asked him along on *that* nonsense and terribly hurt that she'd decided she didn't need him—was a list of things she expected him to accomplish while she was gone. Mostly things, he noted, that were really supposed to be her responsibility and she had slagged off as too boring, such as testing the entire crew to make certain they were all still reasonably accurate with their machetes.

Fine. He didn't mind being boring old Simms, the giant redhead with the muttonchops, *don't mind him, he's really a kitten underneath it all*. He didn't mind, truly.

Only he did, very much.

All of the items on the list were crossed off but for the last three, two of which required a foray down into the city: *Check if Count Blatherthwait*—"Balthertate," Simms muttered to himself—*has moved his safe yet* and *Weekly drop box round*. Neither were terribly exciting tasks, which explained why he hadn't gotten up the motivation to take the little railcar down out of the mountains and wander around, pretending to be a civilized member of society.

And then of course, the last item was there only to annoy him, he was certain: *Don't do anything silly*.

The very idea. Simms didn't do silly things, ever. The whole point of his existence, it often felt like, was to stand by in horrified fascination as Captain Ramos did every silly thing her more cracked mental faculties could invent, as if natural law demanded the presence of a witness at all times.

He stuffed the list back in his pocket and took another sip of his tea. Behind him, the metal door that covered the defunct mineshaft opened with a clunk, though any proclivity toward metallic squealing had been removed by the liberal use of oil. Footsteps crunched in the gravel behind him, rapid and purposeful. "Mister Simms!"

Simms recognized the light, melodious tones of Amelia Cavendesh. She'd been well on her way to becoming a professional opera singer before she'd dropped in on the crew during a raid and declared her intention to join—while still wearing a full costume ball gown. He'd never asked why. It wasn't really any of his business.

Far more importantly, Amelia wasn't even supposed to be here. That morning, she had departed for town, wearing a red jacket and a jaunty pair of striped trousers guaranteed to scandalize anyone who realized she was female. In her wake had been Gregory Kinzer with a thoroughly disreputable bowler pulled low over his eyes and Lucius Lamburt, the nattiest of the bunch in a tweed three-piece suit, a little four-leaf clover pin at his lapel throwing off sparks of morning sunlight. Yet here Amelia was, returned far too early, and with a tone of breathless urgency in her voice.

Simms sighed and set his teacup back down. "Hello, other shoe," he muttered.

"Simms?" Amelia stopped behind him.

He turned to face her. "What is it, Amelia?" It had to be bad news. Of course it was; no one ever came rushing over to tell him it was a lovely day or there were fresh biscuits in the kitchen, just waiting to be taken.

Not that he was still a bit bitter about *that*. Really, he didn't mind that everyone in the Roost, including his daughter Dolly, had gotten at least one biscuit and he'd only arrived in time to see crumbs.

"It's Lucius, Simms."

Of course it was. "Of course it is." Outside of Captain Ramos herself, Lucius was the biggest source of headaches in the crew. He didn't so much make trouble as locate it and gleefully roll in it like a dog who had discovered a dead squirrel.

Amelia stared at him with wide blue eyes. The close-cropped blond curls that framed her face made her look ridiculously young. "…sorry?"

"No, go on." Just the name "Lucius" alone meant that this was going to be something particularly horrible. Lucius was a bit unhinged in a way that Simms only liked when he could point the man at people who deserved to be knocked over. And it was still an open question on if he was actually a *man* as such; he resembled nothing so much as an extraordinarily pallid gorilla that had been creatively, if only partially, shaved. "What did he do?"

"He didn't really *do* anything…"

"Pull the other one," Simms said dryly.

"Truly. We'd just gone to Black Hawk, since you gave us the week free. Just for a bit of shopping." The free week wasn't lack of initiative so much as the captain's request, delivered in the form of a merry, "Now don't have too much fun without me!" right before she shut the canopy of her aeroplane.

"Shopping. Really. Did Lucius find anything pretty?" Simms used a sardonic tone borrowed directly from Captain Ramos; it wasn't as if she was using it at the moment. Lucius was a man of simple tastes and crazy eyes that made store clerks nervous.

No, the shopping had likely been for Amelia and Gregory Kinzer, the normal crew lookout. Both of them were of that peculiar mindset that Simms had never been able to really understand, which held that spending money was fun, and looking at things without spending money was nearly as much so.

Amelia's shoulders hunched slightly. "He found a lovely floral bonnet."

"Really?"

"Of course not." Her tone turned nothing short of miserable, the words pouring from her quickly enough to stumble over each other. "We only left him alone for a minute, Simms, I swear." She glanced up at him. "Well, perhaps more than a minute. Gregory and I found this lovely tea shop…called the Amber Moon, I think, and he needed a new teapot you see, and it turned out to take longer than we thought because then I wanted to try out one of their varieties of oolong and it just…"

Simms felt he ought to think of something clever to say to stop the tidal wave of needless patter. Unfortunately, clever on demand was not really one of his skills, and he couldn't help but feel a little bit bad for Amelia, even as he dreaded how this story would end. "And what was Lucius doing at the time?"

She blew out a breath. "He might not have been with us."

"Might not?"

"Might not," she agreed miserably.

Simms sighed. "Amelia, you realize I'm not Captain Ramos, right? She's nowhere around. Watching you do gymnastics while standing still entertains her far more than can be healthy, I suspect, but it's giving me a headache. Out with it, please. It can't be that bad."

"Well, he was there for a moment, right when we'd started tea. But then a waiter came up to him and gave him one of *those* winks, you know? And Lucius excused himself. Said if he was going to drink, he wanted to do a proper job of it. But when Gregory and I caught up with him, you see, they were dragging him out in irons."

"That's normal, isn't it?" Sadly.

"But they were carrying someone else out behind him on a stretcher."

"Also normal."

Amelia's shoulders hunched up like she was going to try to crawl back into the collar of her shirt. "It was the garrison captain for Black Hawk."

"Oh."

"They'd been playing dice. That's what the men in the bar told us. And Lucius accused the captain of cheating."

Simms huffed out a breath. "All right. So he's in the gaol in Black Hawk. That isn't so bad." He'd been to Black Hawk before; the gaol was small and really more of a drunk tank for unruly miners. If he scraped together a bit of cash to flash at the gaoler, he should be able to recover Lucius. And then, if he was feeling very uncharitable, tell the captain all about that when she returned.

Amelia cleared her throat, shoulders moving toward her ears again.

Simms stared at her, a strange mixture of dread and fatalism trickling down his spine. "Or not?"

"Not," she agreed.

"Not what?" He wasn't going to play guessing games; she'd better bloody well just say it so he could have his stroke and get it over with.

"He's…not in the gaol at Black Hawk."

"Then where is he? On the moon? In a jam jar? In an inner tube, floating down Left Hand Creek on a river of lemonade?"

She had the good grace to cringe rather dramatically at those last words. "Not quite that bad."

"Then tell me. I'm old, Amelia. Ancient. My heart can't handle this much suspense. Out with it."

"He's down in the city."

There was no world in which that could possibly be good. "…what?"

"He's in the central gaol. Down in the city."

"*How?*" He hadn't thought it possible to fit that much disbelief and dismay into a single word. Already, this morning had been quite the journey of self-discovery.

Amelia muttered something.

"*How?*" he thundered.

"He mentioned the captain's name! They know he's part of the crew."

"Oh." He couldn't think of anything else to say. There wasn't an adequate word in his vocabulary for this kind of situation. Maybe if he went back to drinking, his pickled brains could come up with something right before he passed out in the gutter. Better not to experiment, as tempting as it was in this moment.

"It's all my fault, Simms." Amelia hunched over in a posture of abject misery. "I *know* we're not supposed to leave Lucius on his own, but we didn't want to take him into the tea shop, and we weren't going to be in there that long. I thought, how much trouble could he really get in, we'd be just down the street?"

He couldn't help but wonder if there was something more she wasn't saying. Lucius was a champion drinker, to be sure, but for that very reason he couldn't really get himself completely sodden that quickly. Had Captain Ramos been standing here, he was sure, she'd have been able to take a sniff and pick a bit of lint off Amelia's cuff and divine exactly what had gone wrong. He probably could have had much the same effect by bellowing at her. He found he didn't really have the heart. The damage was done. Shouting at Amelia wouldn't change anything, and it wouldn't even make him feel better. Simms had never been fond of shouting.

He heaved a sigh. "All right. Well, we can't leave him down in the gaol. If they know he's one of Captain Ramos's lads…bloody hell, they haven't hanged him already, have they?"

There was a moment of utter panic in Amelia's face, perhaps as she realized that option was very much on the table, but then she quickly shook her head. "The Chief of Security is out right now, remember? Captain Ramos is following him, isn't she? They wouldn't hang Lucius while he's away. At least I don't think they would."

"I don't think we should depend on that." But it was a valid point. Captain Ramos had been a thorn in the side of Colonel Douglas, the Chief of Security for the Grand Duchy of Denver, since before he'd actually arrived in the duchy itself. The man would be very put out if he returned home from wherever he'd gone, only to find a potential source of the whereabouts of his nemesis had been dropped off the gallows in his absence.

On the other hand, Lucius could be *very* annoying when he put his mind to it. Or when he didn't. Or when he was asleep.

"All right," Simms said. "All right."

"All right?"

"All right," he repeated, as if that would compel the situation to comply. Really, he felt as if he was winding himself up to plunge into a lake, one which might or might not contain some sort of horrifying flesh-eating eel. "We'll just have to get him out."

"We...*How?*"

He hadn't gotten nearly that far yet. "I'll think of something."

The amount of confidence shining in Amelia's eyes, as if she expected Captain Ramos's labyrinthine thought processes to have somehow rubbed off on him, was something close to terrifying. "Yes, Mister Simms!"

"Gather up the crew, Mister Cavendesh. Prepare—" No, taking Diabola, the raiding engine, would be an incredibly bad idea, even if having access to a roof-mounted Gatling gun and a ramming guard would make him feel better. Neither of those things would do much good against the thick stone walls of the city gaol, which was not located on a set of tracks anyway. Subtle. He needed subtle. He was utterly abysmal at subtle. What would the captain do? "—the large railcar."

"Will do, sir!" Amelia turned to hurry back into the Roost.

And just like that, he was "sir" again and everything was most assuredly his problem. Simms watched Amelia's retreating back. *Don't do anything silly*, indeed. Why hadn't Captain Ramos put that on a list for everyone else? *They* were the silly ones.

The door slammed shut behind Amelia, and Simms heaved out a sigh, looking down at his now cold, half-finished cup of tea.

He hooked one finger in the cup's handle, and tossed the liquid out in a shining arc. It splashed against the electrified fence with a satisfying sizzle.

Boring old Simms to the rescue.

"That's…the seventh guard," Amelia said. She reached up to adjust the magnification loupes on the goggles that obscured her face, an old pair that had once belonged to Captain Ramos and been stored in the railcar. "No, wait. That's only the sixth man again. He's turn around and come back."

Simms blew out his breath in something a bit too morose to actually be a laugh. "*Only?*"

"That's…yes. Only six on the roof," Amelia confirmed. She squirmed back from the cornice she'd hidden behind and pushed the goggles up to rest in her hair.

"Only six. Well, that's all right then," Simms muttered. He'd just brought along the normal crew, which meant Amelia and Gregory. They still hadn't found a regular replacement for the late, lamented Elijah, and Simms didn't trust their newest navigator; the man had a nervous disposition and a tendency to scream. And Lucius was, of course, the reason they had come to this rather run-down but nicely tall hotel, and were currently staring down at the large, ugly building that housed the Grand Duchy of Denver's central gaol.

Two nested walls of concrete blocks surrounded the building, which had originally been a fortress before the Grand Duke had gotten around to buying his beloved army something prettier and less drafty. The gaol itself was made of unadorned, coal-smoke-blackened stone in an unimaginative, square shape. A smaller wing, not quite so dark in color because its stone was newer, seemed to bud from its side. From experience, Simms knew that to be the women's wing, a regular place of residence for Captain Ramos until Colonel Douglas had taken over as Chief of Security and started off their relationship by putting her in the much more secure men's wing. That old knowledge wouldn't be helpful in this case anyway, as Lucius *would* insist on being a man and thus tucked into some dank corner of the much larger, more labyrinthine original gaol.

Of course, just locating the man within the gaol was the least of Simms's worries. The six guards patrolling along the roof of the building itself were joined by eight more, two on each of the walls, and who knew how many more down on the ground and inside the building. That many guards against just three of them weren't odds he liked at all.

Worse, he couldn't really trust Lucius to play much of a role in his own rescue. On the many occasions—more than he liked to count, just thinking about it forced him to wonder what he was doing with his life, *honestly*—he'd helped Captain Ramos remove herself from these walls, it was normally a matter of finding a clever way of getting a tool or two into her hands within the walls and standing quietly back. She could easily let herself out of nearly any bonds, pick her way through any locked door.

Subtle was even less Lucius's style than it was Simms's. Unless the rescue plan involved Lucius punching something vaguely human-shaped repeatedly, he really couldn't be trusted to lend a hand.

"We're not going in there, are we?" Amelia asked.

"We'll just use the army I've got in my pocket instead," Simms said dryly. "I just wanted to know how bloody hopeless it looked. Maybe Gregory will bring some better news."

Gregory had been sent to check on the sewers. That stinking undercity was the stuff of Simms's more hallucinatory and claustrophobic nightmares, thanks to more than one Captain Ramos-led adventure. But if it was the only way to save Lucius from the hangman's noose, Simms would have to just force himself into the hated, hellish depths. He could burn his clothes on the other side.

And have Lucius sew him a new set for penance. When the man was actually sober, those blunt, scarred fingers of his could turn a shockingly lovely seam.

Amelia looked dismayed at the prospect as well, but nodded all the same. "I hope so. Not looking to get shot today, that's for sure. I've heard sometimes you find interesting things down in the sewers, at any rate."

"You and Captain Ramos and your damned *interesting*," Simms grumbled. "Just how desperately have you wanted to see a bloated rat that choked on a severed finger literally explode?" He wasn't all that interested in making her feel better. It was half her fault they were even thinking about crawling through that much muck to begin with.

There was the sound of boots scuffing on stone accompanied by a repulsive squishing sound. Simms glanced over his shoulder to see Gregory climb over the cornice. The light breeze saw that the eye-watering stench he now produced reached them before his voice even could. To Simms's weather eye, his trousers were also decidedly dark and clinging from the knee down, which was also a good sign.

The expression on Gregory's face, however, was not. The man looked nauseated, for a special class of nausea that involved regretting things he had yet to even eat. But rather than satisfied or triumphant underneath the unhealthy yellowish tinge of stench-induced revulsion, his already pinched face seemed about to fold in on itself with upset.

Maybe it was just the smell, Simms told himself. Just the smell. "What's the news, Gregory?"

"Not good, sir," Gregory said. There it was again, that "sir." No one ever called him sir when there was good news. And was Gregory…yes, he had come to a halt and seemed to be standing in something like parade rest.

Bloody hell.

Simms coughed and pointed to the side, prompting Gregory to move so he was no longer upwind. Simms's voice still came out a bit choked, but he told himself that was residual stench and not nervousness. "Not good or bad?"

"Bad, sir."

"Then why not just say that?"

"I was trying to soften the blow, sir."

Simms shut his eyes for a moment, counted to ten like he'd sometimes had to do when Dolly had been three years old, precocious, and very opinionated about things like naps and trousers and what a lovely age *that* hadn't been. "Just. Out with it. I'm not going to explode."

"Says you," Amelia muttered.

Simms gave her a sharp look.

"Made it into the sewers. Quite a ways in. But…there was a grate in place over the main branch to the prison. Looks new." Gregory reached up to run his hand through his hair, but then seemed to think better of it. "And it's got some kind of mechanism to it. Not sure what it'll do, but whenever I see that many wires and cogs, I reckon it can't be good."

Simms took another deep breath. "Did you try the second branch?"

"I did. Same thing."

Simms cursed, loud and long and creatively. It was actually a bit nice, in a weird way. He never got to utilize his extensive vocabulary like this when he was at the Roost, since you never knew if Dolly was going to pop up out of nowhere and ask him again just what *ballocks* meant.

"Well," Amelia interjected after a moment when his voice had reached a more normal volume, "that means we won't be crawling through the sewers, yeah? So look on the bright side. It could be so much worse."

Simms rounded on her. "Don't *say* that!" he shouted. He'd been *thinking* that, to be certain; it wasn't as if he *wanted* to go into the sewers and have nightmares for the next month.

Amelia took a step back. "What? Why?"

"Because—"

"Oh, I'm sorry, am I interrupting something?" The low, amused tones of a woman wafted over from the other side of the roof. Far too familiar low, amused tones.

"Because of *that*." Simms turned, gesturing toward the newcomer with open hands. How had she known? How? Had she been dangling from a chimney by her heels, just waiting for someone to say those unfortunate words?

The woman smiled. The expression looked very nice on her, the graceful lines of her dark face and her tawny eyes showing cool amusement. Of course *everything* looked nice on her, including the simple black clothing she wore, coat and trousers and boots, just the sort of thing for sneaking about on rooftops and spying on innocent people who desperately wanted to not have their lives complicated. "Hello to you too, Simms. Are you going to introduce me to your friends?"

Gregory gawked openly. Amelia opened her mouth, shut it, and said, "Yes, Simms, why don't you introduce us?"

Because he didn't believe in introducing people to poisonous spiders as something other than a danger to be avoided and possibly squashed. He bit back that reply carefully. Because the hell of it was, as highly suspicious as her arrival seemed and he'd be damned if he'd trust her, with the Captain away they did need her help.

So much for *Don't do anything silly.*

Simms sighed. "Gregory Kinzer, Amelia Cavendesh, this is Deliah Nimowitz."

"Oh dear, that does sound terribly unfortunate," Deliah practically purred once Amelia had explained the Lucius situation to her.

"And I just took a look down in the sewers," Gregory offered.

"I never would have guessed," Deliah said, smiling. And somehow when she did it, it didn't come across as overtly snide, even though Simms knew that was exactly how she meant it. The few times he'd had to cross paths with Deliah, one of which was without Captain Ramos as a safety net, had convinced Simms that an icy wash of smug ran through her veins in place of blood.

But Gregory smiled, even a bit fatuously, and Simms resisted the urge to grind his teeth. It would do no good at this point. "It wasn't such a big job, really. I didn't get too far in because all of the main lines into the prison have been blocked off with welded grates." He glanced at Simms. "I suppose we could get through those, but I don't fancy trying to haul a welding torch down there."

"An interesting idea…" Deliah drawled, turning to look at Simms with overly wide eyes, as if she was pretending to be innocently curious. "Nothing to say, Mister Simms?"

Simms had assumed his *I think this is very stupid and want no part of it* position, which meant standing in stony silence with his arms crossed over his chest. He did not like Deliah Nimowitz, not in the slightest. She made him severely uncomfortable, itchy almost, and the sensation had everything to do with their introduction: Deliah had helped her elderly, senile grand aunt Clementine end her own life and then left the corpse to be partially consumed by an adorable little dog named Chippy.

Simms grimaced at the direct question. Well, best to make it clear that *he* wasn't a total, head-floating idiot. "I wouldn't fancy any kind of open flame down there. Flammable gases and all. But I suppose you could try, if you like."

It was telling that Simms still thought of Chippy with immense affection, despite the fact that the first time he'd laid eyes on the dog, his muzzle had been coated with dried blood.

That Deliah and Captain Ramos seemed to have some sort of… of…*canoodling* going on was really none of his business, except for the fact that he was fairly certain friends didn't let friends go to bed with poisonous reptiles as a matter of principle.

"I think not. I just had these boots polished. Ah, but that all does sound like a bit of a puzzler," Deliah said. And then she glanced at Simms again before he could fully lapse back into sullen silence.

He didn't like that. "Well, you don't need to worry. We've got it all well in hand."

"But Simms—" Amelia began.

"Shut it," he hissed, and did his best impression of a sweet smile back at Deliah. The expression felt entirely alien on his face, skin and muscles objecting to being pulled into such unfamiliar lines. He had a bad feeling it came out looking more like a grimace than anything else. "We have it well in hand, Miss Nimowitz. But thanks all the same."

Deliah smiled with perfect, practiced sweetness right back at him. It looked a lot better on her, of that he had little doubt. "Of course, Mister Simms. I wouldn't doubt you for one moment. I imagine Captain Ramos is off getting everything sorted right now, isn't she?"

"No, she isn't," Gregory said. "She's gone off on a scouting trip."

Simms glared at him. He'd tried to introduce Deliah as a distant acquaintance of the captain, and Deliah had objected and called them close friends, tilting her head back and laughing in a very particular way that had made Gregory scrub the palms of his hands against his trouser seams. Something about that laugh made her eminently more believable than Simms, it seemed, and the hell of it was he couldn't even bring himself to object to her reclassification of that relationship.

"Oh, has she?" Deliah's eyes widened in the least surprised expression of surprise Simms had witnessed since the time he'd asked Captain Ramos if she'd noticed that the new Chief of Security was a too-clever-by-half tosser.

"Didn't she tell you?" Gregory asked, shooting a worried look at Simms. "Well, she has. Which means we've got to figure out this mess ourselves, haven't we?"

"And we will—" Simms began.

"—but as luck would have it, I've a need to briefly get into the prison myself," Deliah said smoothly. "There's a gentleman inside with whom I simply *must* have a conversation. And at that, a conversation that doesn't invite some silly guard to eavesdrop."

Simms stared at her. That seemed all too convenient, that Deliah would be here just at the right time, hovering about in the right place for no apparent reason. But he had nothing else upon which to build a complaint. "That sounds a bit tricky," he finally said, tone grudging.

"Perhaps a bit. The fellows at this gaol aren't at all wise to my tricks yet." Deliah smiled sweetly. "It wouldn't hurt anything to see about breaking free your man Lucius whilst I'm considering the disposition of my own prisoner."

"Right." The other shoe had already dropped. This didn't comfort him at all. Rather, it seemed that he was dealing with some sort of bizarre, alien creature that had at least three feet, and thus yet another shoe waited out in the aether. And, considering the sudden presence of Deliah, he imagined shoe after shoe would be striking him in every rude bit of his anatomy until he extricated them all from this situation. Unfortunately, he didn't have a good way to do so. That Lucius needed to be sprung from prison was an inarguable fact, and that Simms had no plan and no ideas was equally inarguable.

That didn't mean he had to like it in the slightest, however.

"Why would they be taking you through to have a look?" Amelia asked curiously. While this wasn't an unknown idea for their crew, she wasn't often around when Captain Ramos pulled outrageous stunts that didn't involve large firearms.

Deliah smiled, the way a schoolmarm might, pleased that her star pupil had asked just the right question to prompt a lecture. "I've a few options, really. But I think I'm in the mood to be a nun today, ministering to dregs of society." She looked around a bit expectantly.

If she was hoping for some sort of appalled reaction, she'd come looking in the wrong place, and Simms found that grimly satisfactory. Simms himself had been a Methodist at some point in his past, now murky with alcohol, and simply hadn't ever gotten around to going back to the church after he'd extricated himself from the bottom of the bottle without the need for divine intervention.

Amelia had been some other brand of Protestant—Lutheran, perhaps—but Simms had heard more than one blistering rant cross her lips about the way women were treated by religion, and he didn't see her going back any time soon. Not that church was such an option when one lived in the depths of the mountains in an isolated mineshaft governed by the most determined heathen in the known world.

And Gregory...well, Gregory was really *himself.* And he seemed to take a strange sort of comfort in the fact that death was a permanent fixture from which nothing ethereal escaped to flit to Heaven or Hell. Simms had learned to not engage in any philosophical conversations with the man because it always left him feeling vaguely unsettled about the disposition of the metaphysical universe.

And thus was Deliah stymied, though she smiled gamely on, bereft of any censorious looks.

"You're dressing as a nun?" Amelia asked, her tone indicating she was incredulous not of the ruse in general, but of Deliah's ability to pull it off.

Deliah laughed, though she gave the other woman a sharp look. "No more unusual than your own Captain Ramos doing such a thing."

"Perhaps not," Amelia admitted, frowning. "I suppose it's the sort of disguise that would get you the run of the place. Within reason. Hasn't the Captain pulled that one before? It seems so obvious."

"It sounds familiar," Gregory agreed, and glanced at Simms.

He smiled. "Not in the last two years." Which had been in the Duchy of Missoula. Simms stopped himself before voicing that bit of information out loud, however. Deliah didn't need to know where Captain Ramos had worked in the past. What she might be able to do with such information he didn't know, and didn't want to guess because it would make his head hurt.

"So long as she didn't botch it horribly, it won't be of any matter to me," Deliah said, her tone filled with studied laziness.

Simms eyed her with a new sort of suspicion. He'd heard a tone eerily similar to that from Captain Ramos on more than one occasion before. Normally when she was trying to coax him into doing something daft by pretending that no, really, she didn't care about a silly old thing like that anyway. "Say you do help us spring Lucius," he said, stringing the words together slowly. "What's in it for you, then?"

"The goodness of my heart and affection for your dear captain," Deliah said.

Simms simply stared at her. "Pull the other one, it's got bells on." He'd only been desperate enough to ask Deliah for help once, when Captain Ramos had allowed herself to be captured during the horrid mess with the tin orrery some time ago. Deliah had lent her aide only in order to get back a piece of jewelry—one of four—they'd quite rightfully stolen from her. Simms wasn't all that impressed by the strength of Deliah's supposed love.

"How unkind, Mister Simms. Suspicion is so unbecoming."

"Sure keeps me unbecoming dead," he muttered, stare slowly heating to a glare. "Now how about you tell me what it is you want, or you can shove off. I've got a man to rescue." It was an empty non-threat, really. He had no idea how to get Lucius out of the prison, and it was a sad reflection on the choices he'd made throughout his life that Deliah Nimowitz really was his best hope. But he didn't have to tell her that.

Or at least, he could pretend that he was too thick to know that obvious fact.

"Well, if you do insist on making it some kind of exchange rather than just a matter of neighbors helping one another..." she purred. Maybe she really did think he was that stupid, or that stubborn.

Simms wasn't certain if he was pleased or insulted. "I insist."

"There is the small matter of my jewelry..."

Of course, it always came down to the jewelry. Well, he supposed he could bargain for an earring, since Deliah already had the other back thanks to the other prison break. However, he didn't like to think what the captain would say to him if he gave it away easily. "I don't know if I can bargain for that without Captain Ramos's say so," he said, making a show of stroking his muttonchops with great reluctance.

Deliah rolled her eyes. "Oh, but you are *tiresome*, Mister Simms. I've never known a man happier to let a woman make all his decisions. It's a quality I could *almost* like if it weren't so annoying." She heaved a sigh. "Fine. There's a rather grand ball in two days' time, and I find myself in need of a dance partner. I'd thought to invite the dear captain, since she does fill out a pair of trousers nicely when she's a mind to, but I doubt she'll be back in time."

"Likely not," Simms admitted. "She only just left." Something about the entire exchange left him feeling unsettled. He'd expected an argument, not just a few insults—uncreative insults at that, the sort he'd expect from a drunken mining town tough—and had been prepared to bargain. This seemed a little bit *too* easy.

Deliah began to approach. There was something about the way she moved that put Simms in mind of a cat. But not in the nice, fluffy cat who wanted a bit of cream way. More the moggy about to pounce on a bird and educate any young bystanders on the brutal nature of the great chain of life way. "And how do *you* feel about dancing, Mister Simms?"

He had seen more frightening things than Deliah Nimowitz. Most of them had involved Captain Ramos and peyote. He stroked his muttonchops with one hand, hoping the movement looked thoughtful rather than nervous. "I'm crap at it, actually. Two left feet."

"Well, that's all right. You don't actually have to dance. Just stand there while I look pretty and try not to dribble pâté on yourself."

"I've known how to eat for years, no need to worry. I'm an expert."

"So will that do? A small favor for an equally small favor?"

Simms glanced over his shoulder at Amelia. She shrugged. Well, of course she would. She hadn't ever had to handle Deliah in person. He glanced at Gregory, and the man grinned. "I dance quite well, you know," Gregory offered.

"That won't be necessary, Mister Kinzer." Simms could only imagine that Deliah would eat the man alive and not even leave any bones behind as evidence.

"Much appreciated, yes, Mister Kinzer, but Mister Simms here is the man I need, I'm afraid. He's so nicely…tall."

Deliah was many things, but tall wasn't one of them. This stirred up a new drip of dread into his stomach. He didn't like this one bit.

"Oy—" Gregory started.

"That will be all, *Mister Kinzer.*" Simms used a tone of voice that he'd spontaneously developed upon first finding himself in possession of a precocious three-year-old. It froze grown men in their tracks. Sadly, even after years of refinement it barely made Dolly blink. He turned his attention back to Deliah, whose face was suddenly just inches away from his. When had she gotten that close? And really, was that *necessary?*

"Just a bit of dancing."

"Just a little dancing," she agreed. "You have my word."

"All right," he said.

"All right?" Perhaps she'd been expecting more of a fight.

"An evening in a tight coat surrounded by snooty nobles won't kill me. Being left to hang definitely will kill Lucius." Very carefully, he stepped around her and headed toward the parapet again. That was the most important thing, after all. Though now, a morbid sort of curiosity had begun to fill him. What did Deliah want with *him* specifically? And for a ball? This couldn't be good. But it was the same sort of horrified fascination that caused him to follow Captain Ramos time and again.

Only in this case, he wouldn't feel at all obligated to haul Deliah out of any fires she decided to start. God help him, beyond owing her his life, he genuinely *liked* Captain Ramos. She was the closest thing he had to a family outside of Dolly. He had no such feeling of affection toward Deliah.

"All right," he repeated, looking down on the brooding shape of the gaol once again. "What's our part in this?"

Deliah sat down on the parapet to his right, swinging her legs over the edge. She idly kicked her feet, smiling to herself. "It's simple, really…"

Frowning all the while, Simms listened to her plan.

"Anything yet?" Gregory asked.

"If you ask me one more time, I'm going to thump you," Amelia seethed.

"Well, this isn't very comfortable," Gregory said, his tone perilously close to a whine.

"Do you think *this* is?"

This of course being Amelia's overhead position as lookout, hanging from the spire of the grand duchy's only cathedral, the Basilica of the Immaculate Conception. They'd put her in a makeshift rope harness, which apparently was creeping up in places rope had no right to be.

"Both of you, shut it," Simms said, his tone too tired to be properly called a growl. They'd had to make an overnight foray back up to the Devil's Roost to get supplies for this little adventure, and he hadn't slept a wink between Dolly being in a temper and his ever heightening levels of paranoia as the morning approached.

Simms was squashed next to Gregory on the narrow, walled walk shadowed by the spire, regretting with every breath the rather garlicky lunch the man had apparently eaten before they'd returned to the city. He and Gregory were braced against the sharply sloped roof, the largest grappling gun from Diabola, its brass fittings still blacked out from their most recent night run, sitting across their laps and slowly cutting off their circulation. Of course, the tiles of the roof, having baked in the sun all morning, were far more likely to kill them first by broiling them alive.

The cathedral was, incidentally, the tallest building in this section of town once the spires were taken into account. And it had a very, very nice angle on the prison, as the two buildings were neighbors separated only by a small and overly full graveyard. For which neither warden nor bishop was apparently well pleased, according to Deliah, but that was the sort of thing that happened when you converted a former citadel into a gaol without bothering to worry about property values.

"What about—" Gregory shut his mouth when Simms elbowed him sharply in the ribs.

"Wait, wait…all right, the prisoners are out in the yard for exercise. So it shouldn't be too much longer now," Amelia said. "For which my backside thanks whatever god might be listening."

"Any sign of Deliah?" Simms asked.

"Not since she went in ages ago…no, wait. There she is. She's walking out right now. And…just looked right at me, you cheeky little thing! She's dropped her rosary on the ground, right there in the street…oh. Oh my. Oh my!"

"What?" Simms demanded.

Before Amelia could answer, there was a large, horrifying crunch, loud even from their elevated position. Amelia whooped, and then hastily lowered her voice. "Whatever those beads where, they played merry hell with that steamer. One of the wheels just…fell apart! I think it might be melting, that wheel. Oh, the steamer was full of pigs. That's a right mess. Went right into the gates of the prison like she aimed it herself and…now! The guards are on the move!"

Simms hastily scrambled to his feet, ricocheting along the half height wall and around to the front of the spire. He raised the enormous, heavy gun to rest on his shoulder. The weighted dart that had replaced the gun's normal grapple did its level best with the aid of gravity to pull the barrel straight toward the ground. Gregory grabbed hold of his shoulders to brace for firing as he leaned out, aiming down at the exercise yard. "Firing now!"

The gun had been designed to be mounted on the heaviest of their engines. When Simms fired the blunt, heavy dart that would carry the rope to its destination, the kick threw him back into Gregory, who made a soft enough cushion against the roof. Simms squirmed back off the man, with no time to care where elbows and feet went, and dropped the gun onto the narrow walk next to him. He snatched up the rope from where they'd loosely tied it to a cross-eyed gargoyle, and began hauling up the slack. With that much slack, it was no easy task; his forearms burned as he fought the sheer weight of the heavy rope. "Mister Cavendesh, report!" Behind him, he felt Gregory take up the end of the rope.

"Guards are still moving toward the gate. Uh oh...there's a couple of men going for the grapple. But—oh, good show, Lucius! Oh! That has to hurt! And in the ear too, you horrid sod!" She sounded quite cheerful in a bloodthirsty way. "Yes! Yes! He's got it!"

Simms glanced over his shoulder. Without Diabola to supply steam, the gun couldn't winch the rope back in as it normally did; all its compressed charge had been spent simply firing the line. Its best use now was as a counterweight for the heavy length of rope—and Lucius. Gregory, panting and swearing, shoved the gun with the rope tied securely to it off the opposite side of the parapet. The rope suddenly went taut in his hands. "All right, Mister Kinzer—hold!" Simms shouted.

Sweat poured down over Simms's forehead as they fought to hold the rope still as Lucius began to climb, more than balancing out the weight of the big gun as it dangled over the roof and trying to pull the rope back toward the ground. Behind him, Gregory swore again. "Going to tell Lucius...no more...bacon!"

"Almost to the top, boys. Almost to the top! Keep going!"

"How close is almost?" Gregory shouted.

Tension suddenly left the rope, and they both stumbled back, the weight of the big gun once more taking over. "A little more warning, Amelia!" Simms gritted his teeth.

"Sorry! Give him back some slack now, boys."

Growling and cursing again, they both turned and began hauling the gun back up toward the edge. Slack would let the rope drape over the outer side of the gaol's wall so Lucius could climb down enough to avoid breaking his leg or his neck. "Only ten, maybe fifteen feet of rope," Simms said. "He can jump the rest of the way."

"Oh, hurry. I think the guards are about to get sent back—"

"Is that enough?" Simms shouted over his shoulder.

"Just a bit more…yes! Stop there and brace!"

Simms braced himself as best he could, getting ready to be pulled from the other side for just a moment as Lucius climbed back down the wall. The rope jumped and sang with unsteady pressure. "What is he doing, bloody jumping?"

"Rappelling, Simms. It's called rappelling. And—he's on the ground. Haul up the rope, hurry!"

"Loose the rope, Gregory!" Simms let go, allowing the rope to slide over his leather gloves, but only briefly. "Now slow!" They only needed to get the weighted dart back up over the prison wall to get the pale rope out of immediate sight. If no one was looking for it, it'd be hard to spot against the stone walls of the cathedral. Hopefully the dart wouldn't knock over any headstones as it dragged through the graveyard, before they hauled it up the wall.

And they very much did not want to simply drop the big gun on the cathedral's roof. That would certainly grab unwelcome attention and quite likely add an unwanted skylight to the building.

"Report, Mister Cavendesh!" Hand over hand, they lowered the big gun to the roof below them.

"Hold on, just trying to find him again…"

The rope went slack again as Simms and Gregory lowered the big gun gently onto the cathedral's roof. They'd be able to retrieve it shortly, on their way back down out of the building. All that was left to do was haul up whatever free rope remained on the other side with the dart at the end of it, and with luck, no one had even noticed it. Which meant they might be able to use this particular method again if necessary.

Oh, how he hoped not.

"Lucius is…away from the prison walls now. He's moved into the alleys. None of the guards seem to be the wiser. I think…I think we've done it, Mister Simms!"

"Not until we've got him safely home and scrubbing pans." His hands ached, and if he ever saw another rope again, it would be too soon. But Deliah's plan had worked, and quite prettily.

Deliah.

Simms's mouth set in a grim line. He'd almost forgotten that the prison break was going to be the easy part of his day. "Or more like, *you've* got him safely home."

"What—" Gregory started.

Simms smiled sourly. "I have to find where the captain hid my good trousers. I have a dance to attend."

"Ah, Mister Simms. You *do* clean up well. Perhaps that's why Captain Ramos keeps you around." Deliah gave him a smile that might as well have been the blade of a knife. She sat across from him in a hired steam carriage, which swayed slightly as its wheels rolled over the cobblestones toward whatever destination she'd given the driver.

They hadn't been moving long, and as far as Simms could tell, they were headed solidly north, along the Platte River where it cut through the city. There were some very unsavory locations along that river, but toward the city center the riverbank housed some of the most expensive mansions in the whole of the grand duchy. Those estates created vast swathes of nearly empty space within the great electrified fence that surrounded Denver proper and kept the population safe. In Simms's opinion, houses would have been a far better use of the land, to bring more people into the relative safety of the city instead of giving useless rich people somewhere to ride their ponies. No one ever bothered to ask his opinion.

After a moment of stoic silence from him, Deliah added, "Don't you think, Mister Simms?"

He wasn't certain if she was fishing for simple agreement, or meant that in a far more insulting and abstract sense. Simms grunted; he might as well answer before she decided to get more pointed. "Must be. I make a lovely beard." That was certainly his use, more often than he liked. Captain Ramos playing the grand lady, and him there to get his foot trod on every time he said something insufficiently posh.

Though he had gotten to do a bit of work on his own in the past. He wasn't *entirely* useless. Just apparently too useless for expeditions up into the Black Hills. Fine. He didn't want to be eaten by the Infected anyway.

Deliah laughed, a musical, almost practiced sound. "Ladies do like to joke that a man is the most necessary and least useful of all accessories. Though speaking of beards, you could have stood a little more grooming in that department. Not really the mode with the fashionable set these days." She pointed delicately toward his muttonchops with her fan, a green silk sail with ivory sticks, and flicked it open with a practiced motion. The fan went well with her outfit, a rich dress of yellow and gold, her jewelry composed of chains of pearls.

Simms had gone with a gray suit. You could never go wrong with gray. It went with most of the dresses the captain had, even the most ridiculous, and normally allowed him to fade away into the woodwork. In a fit of annoyance, he'd picked a gold waistcoat to go with it, thinking something that bright would surely clash with whatever mourning dress Deliah would be wearing. He was even more annoyed that plan had backfired.

He should have guessed she wouldn't be going to a party of this sort as herself. Not if she was planning to work.

"Leave my muttonchops out of this. And do ladies say that about other *ladies* they use as accessories?" He wasn't in the mood to sit quietly and let himself be poked with verbal barbs. He only tolerated the captain doing that because she'd bloody well earned it. And because he was fairly certain, after many years of closer observation, that she was just completely incapable of having a normal conversation.

Deliah laughed. "Such a taboo subject. Not in the salons and tea parlors I frequent, more's the pity."

So much for that volley. Saying clever things had never really been his forte anyway. "What's my name to be for tonight?"

"Lord Reginald Granby."

"Do I really look like a Reginald?" He felt almost insulted.

"Not with those muttonchops, you don't."

Simms hastily covered one with a protective hand and laughed. Then glared. No. That had been a bit too familiar and easy. He had to keep in mind that he really did not like this woman. "And you are?"

"Your loving wife, Cassandra. We're visiting from the Duchy of Missoula. Too minor for anyone to have really heard of us."

Those simple facts, he could remember. Captain Ramos had drilled this sort of basic spy nonsense into him. He still claimed he didn't find it at all fun. "Right."

"I trust that Captain Ramos has impressed upon you how to act in these situations. You're really just along to look pretty like you do for her." She smirked. "Or perhaps act as a clothes rack for that lovely waistcoat."

"Suits me." He did not care if she thought he was an idiot, he tried to reassure himself. He had no interest in impressing her. If something did go horribly wrong, it'd serve her right, even.

Except for the bit where he'd get sucked under too.

Simms crossed his arms over his chest. "How is Chippy?"

"He's doing quite well. Marta never calls or visits, though. I think it makes him a bit sad." Deliah gave him an odd look, her eyes narrowing, as if she was calculating something. Or perhaps annoyed.

He frowned. "The captain wanted to shoot him, you know. I don't think he'd like to see her." Assuming a dog would even know he was in mortal danger because they wanted the necklace he'd eaten. Or that he had that long of a memory. Likely, all Chippy recalled of that weekend, if anything, was that those lovely people kept giving him dried venison to get him to shut up.

And as for the captain not calling or visiting…he'd gotten the distinct impression that she had, and it made his brain *ache* just considering it in that oblique fashion. He did not want to know, and he refused to ask.

"Yes, but she got over that and made friends with him."

"Not the sort of thing I'd forget, if I was a dog."

"Good thing you're not."

"Not likely to forget it as a man, either. Cold-blooded murder has a way of leaving an impression." Simms felt immense relief as the carriage slowed and halted; Deliah was giving him another of those narrow-eyed looks.

Simms saved himself from further conversation by half-rising and opening the carriage door himself before the driver could get to it. Pretending to be a proper gentleman now, he even helped Deliah alight from the carriage and offered her his arm.

She didn't have to dig her fingers into his sleeve quite so tightly, though. "It wasn't murder," she murmured, and gave the driver a sweet smile.

"As you say, my dear," he returned, doing his best to sound posh and hideously jolly.

The driver had delivered them in front of a stately manor, midway up its long and elaborate drive. Carriages were everywhere, and well-dressed couples walked toward the brightly lit, three-story brick house. The strains of music were barely audible above all the chattering voices and laughter. The drive itself was lined with statues of chubby, smiling cherubs, which Simms had always thought were rather creepy instead of charming. Each cherub held a lantern aloft, brass fittings obscured by strands of creeper.

This was Lord Balthertate's house.

Simms actually paused for a moment to stare at the distinctive copper drain pipes. Well, it looked like he'd get to cross off one more item on that to-do list after all. Deliah tugged at his arm. "You're going to attract attention," she whispered angrily.

"No, I won't. I'm gawking like a back-country noble at a fancy house," Simms said back. "And you're not here to mess about with the safe, are you?"

"What? Of course not. I've something far more interesting in mind."

He wasn't certain if he ought to feel pleased or filled with dread. Considering the number of times he'd heard something similar from the captain, dread was definitely winning. Simms started walking again, following the stream of couples.

"Something the dear captain wants from the safe in particular?" Deliah practically purred out the words.

"I wouldn't know," Simms said, cursing himself. "Above my pay grade."

"Surely she tells you everything."

He considered, once more, the bitter pill of being left behind. "Not everything."

A footman in dress livery, which included a burnt orange waistcoat, waited at the front door. Deliah dug around in her little purse for a moment and produced two invitations, which she handed over. Simms smiled and nodded, even though no one had actually said anything.

The music was much louder inside, another footman waiting to direct them to the dining room for a buffet—as there would be no formal dinner service—the ball room for dancing, or the salon—at the back of the house—if anyone fancied a friendly game of cards. And of course, for the lady, the dressing room was right that way, advice that Deliah only pretended to take by prodding Simms in that general direction. He would have liked to head immediately for the dining room, since food was really the only thing he found at all enjoyable at these affairs, but instead Deliah dragged him toward the ballroom as soon as they were out of sight of the footman.

There were fewer people on the floor than he'd expected; the room was populated mostly by ladies in shades of dress ranging from pastel to jewel tones, gauze and tulle and a thousand sorts of lace. Most of the men partnering ladies were significantly older than Simms. With so few men to be seen, a group of ladies had organized themselves into their own lines of dancers, laughing and giggling as half of them tried to recall the men's parts.

Well, who knew how these lordly types worked, Simms thought. Or their fancy parties.

He was passingly familiar with the dance, a Cakewalk, but he'd never been much of one for dancing. He tended to lumber when he walked, and had no sense of rhythm. And he stepped on Deliah's foot almost immediately; he wished it had been on purpose.

Deliah smiled as if she was having a grand time. "You're not terribly good at this, are you?"

"You're the one who wanted to dance," he said stiffly.

"Does Marta make you dance often?"

He snorted. What a bizarre question. And when had Captain Ramos become "Marta" in the conversation? "She says she values her feet far too much."

"Well then. You must be good at something else..."

Simms fought the urge to frown. What was this all about? "I don't see how that's any of your business. Aren't you here to do work?"

"Yes, but we need to make certain everyone sees us first. So do keep smiling, Mister Simms. Or rather I should say, my darling Reginald." Then Deliah stepped on his foot; from the look on her face, he could tell it was quite deliberate.

Deliah made him dance the next three, all the while deliberately treading on his feet every time he accidentally stepped on hers. His toes were quite grateful when she finally let him escape, proclaiming that she just *had* to go visit with the other ladies, but don't worry dear, she'd be back for another dance soon.

Toes aching, Simms made his escape to the dining room. He carefully avoided the footmen and their silver trays of wineglasses. Being teetotal still seemed to be an oddity among the upper classes, and he didn't want to attract attention by explaining that no, really, he'd just like some water and please he didn't drink at all no matter how nice the vintage.

The food tables, laden with roasted fowl, a terrifying array of breads, miniature cucumber sandwiches, candied fruits, and vegetables cut into an assortment of fanciful shapes, proved a welcome refuge. After a minute of searching, Simms spotted his favorite of all foods: tiny sausages. He carefully emptied half the pan onto his plate after a covert glance around.

Plate held in front of him like a shield, he slowly wandered through the rooms as he ate his sausages. The delightfully spicy little mouthfuls, juicy and flavored with garlic and cumin, almost made this ordeal worth it. Almost.

Some months ago, Simms and Captain Ramos had snuck in with a tour of Lord Balthertate's tenants, the sort of thing that was considered to be good practice by the lords, a single day of mingling with the common folk whose rent kept them in sausages and velvet. That day, the enormous safe had been in the library, brand new and only hidden with a silken drape.

He made his way slowly back to the library, bouncing from conversational clump to clump like he'd seen Captain Ramos do so often, with his plate of sausages as an excuse as to why he didn't do more than smile, nod, and chew.

The library doors were wide open, perhaps as an invitation for everyone to be impressed by the Count's extensive collection of books. As Simms and his sausages entered, however, there were only two people there, a young man in a maroon jacket and a woman in something girlishly pink. They were standing far closer together than polite society would consider proper, heads bowed.

Well, Simms wasn't polite society, and he didn't care in the slightest. He walked right past them, unnoticed, and headed toward where he'd seen the safe before.

For a moment his heart sank; the silk drape had been replaced with a set of bookshelves now. He stopped in front of it to scan over the titles, frowning to himself. They were all books of poetry, short, shallow little volumes. Curious, he stepped around to the side of the shelf. It was shockingly deep—far deeper than it had any right to be.

Transferring his plate to one hand, he knocked on the wood. The couple on the other side of the room sprang quickly apart. Simms spared them a glance and said, "You'd be better off in the gardens. It's a warm night."

The young woman laughed nervously, but then reached out and took the young man's hand. Simms pointedly turned his attention back to the shelves. He knocked on the wood again, farther back.

Yes, it certainly did sound different. No longer quite so hollow, as if that wood were pressed against something solid.

Like a safe, perhaps, though it was the wrong shape for the one he'd seen before. This alone let him cross that item from the list. Where the other, larger safe might have gone wasn't a question he was compelled to consider, and he had no desire to go snooping around the rest of the house and risk being caught in an awkward situation. Captain Ramos enjoyed that sort of impromptu play acting, but it gave him heartburn.

And on the topic of heartburn, his buffet plate was nearly empty.

Simms popped the next to last little sausage in his mouth and headed back toward the dining room. Luck had only been with him in the library, it seemed; he caught a flash of green and yellow from the corner of his eye, and there was Deliah turning around the bannister from the grand staircase and bearing down on him like a messenger of doom.

A very smug messenger of doom; the curve of her lips, when visible between flutterings of her fans, bore a definite resemblance to a cat who had just torn its way through a shop filled with exotic birds. Well, he supposed that was a good sign; it meant they'd be out of here soon and his debt would be discharged. He liked the idea of going back to owing Deliah absolutely nothing. And he absolutely did not want to know what she'd been doing. The idea of plausible deniability was an old friend to him.

"Oh Reginald," she trilled out in a spot on, almost eerie imitation of a high-society lady, better than any he'd heard even from Captain Ramos. "There you are, you dear man. I've been looking all over for you."

Simms brandished his sausage plate, now sadly empty, in answer. "Just a spot of food. Something amiss…dear?" Oh, but he did not like the way that word felt in his mouth.

"Oh, nothing amiss at all. It has been a lovely evening." Deliah plucked the plate from his hand and smoothly transferred it to the waiting tray of a footman. "I thought another dance was in order, and then I'll be quite fatigued."

"I'd no idea you were so delicate." He didn't mind getting out of here at all, even if he did give the buffet table a longing look as Deliah prodded him back toward the ballroom. He'd liked the idea of having an entire meal on the tab of Lord Balthertate, but he liked the idea of being free from the entire situation even more.

He only had to hope that she wouldn't feel the need to crush his feet under her heels again.

That was apparently one dream too far. Laughing all the while, Deliah carefully stepped on his left foot as they joined the reel that had just begun. Deliah, like Captain Ramos, was more than happy to poke him in the direction she wished to go while he pretended to lead. And he wasn't about to object, because the sooner they reached the doors that lead back into the foyer and made a graceful exit, the sooner he'd be free of this farce of an evening.

There was just a row of dancers between them and the ostentatious doors from the ballroom, which were, Simms noticed, carved in a cross-eyed cherub motif and covered in gold leaf. He'd never really liked cherubs.

As the musicians began to play the closing bars of the set, he could all but taste freedom in his mouth, around the greasy delight of the sausages, and they were almost to the door—

"Good lord, Miss Stenwick, is that you?" Oh look, Simms thought, another shoe. He kept his eyes fixed forward; Captain Ramos had trained him a little too well for that, in her long lectures on How To Not Look Suspicious Because We Don't Want To Be Fingered Like Jammy Bastards. Deliah turned her face away, but it was to no avail.

"Oh, it is you!' A man stepped up to Deliah's left elbow. He wore the all-too-familiar forest green jacket of the Grand Duchy of Denver's security forces, the bars of a captain decorating his epaulettes, and two gold stripes on his cuffs. A dress uniform, Simms recognized. The man was tall, which was to say he was still significantly shorter than Simms, and had his black hair in short, neatly oiled curls, his officer's mustache in proper trim on his olive-toned upper lip. The guard captain was also, interestingly enough, sporting a rather rakish cut on his cheek, and had his left arm in a sling.

Simms let Deliah go in as graceful a manner as he could, which wasn't at all graceful but at least he refrained from flinging her away as if he'd just been handed a boiling-hot potato, and wondered just what she had to do with the Grand Duke's dogs.

"Ah, Captain Paulos. So nice to see you!" The expression on Deliah's face changed subtly, becoming a bit more girlish. "I didn't expect to meet you in such a place!" She flipped her fan out, fluttering it wildly.

"And who is your friend?" Captain Paulos asked, eyeing Simms.

"Just about to leave," Simms said, affecting a jolly tone. "Old war injury is playing me up. Glad to be leaving this lady in good hands, however. Your timing is excellent, Captain." He edged a careful step back. His duty was discharged; he could smell another of Deliah's schemes just about rolling off the man and wanted no part in it.

"Well, pleased to meet you, sir," Captain Paulos said. He had eyes only for Deliah anyway.

Simms wasn't about to tell him how small the odds of anything along that vein were. He edged another step away.

"I'm a bit tired myself, Captain," Deliah trilled. "Though it is lovely to see you."

"Quite all right, Miss Stenwick. I'm not really in any condition to dance right now, myself," Captain Paulos said, lifting his injured arm slightly in indication. "But I did want to thank you for your advice about the Amber Moon Tea House in Black Hawk. Their facilities are…quite superb."

"Oh, say no more, Captain Paulos. It's our little secret," Deliah fluttered. Was that… nervousness? A hint of some tightness around the corner of her eyes stood out like a crack in her facade.

Simms, who had been edging back another step, froze. The Amber Moon Tea House in Black Hawk? No, that was too much of a coincidence. Captain Ramos's paranoia had to be rubbing off on him. But, as the captain was fond of saying, it wasn't paranoia when someone actually was out to get you. And Captain Paulos's wounds were obviously very, very fresh. "Dashed shame about your arm," Simms said, doing his best to sound jolly rather than suspicious. "Since she is a lovely dancer." *If you like having your feet flattened.* "Whatever happened to you?"

"Oh, I shudder to tell a story so indelicate in front of a lady…" Captain Paulos said. But his eyes sparkled with eagerness, the look of a young man who desperately wanted to tell a story, in the hopes of impressing the aforementioned lady.

"Oh goodness, Captain, please. I feel a bit faint from the excitement already." Deliah's fluttering fan presumably hid the nasty look she shot Simms from the dashing soldier.

Simms kept his face fixed in such a bland expression that he felt as if his cheeks might go numb. "Well, perhaps the lady's constitution is too delicate. We can always repair for a bit of brandy. I do like a good story, particularly if there are fisticuffs involved."

"Brandy does sound rather nice. It's been a frightfully long day..." Captain Paulos said, crossing over to stand next to Simms.

"Oh no! Don't desert me, gentlemen. I'd be utterly bereft." Deliah laughed girlishly.

If she fluttered that fan any harder, Simms thought with near evil amusement, she might begin to fly. On the other hand, what looked suspiciously like nervousness at the idea of Simms and the man having a private word just fed his paranoia. Simms leaned in close to give the captain a conspiratorial whisper. "Surely it can't be anything *that* risqué if it was on the lady's recommendation. She's just playing coy, I wager. You can't have gotten up to too much trouble in a tea house."

"Well, my dear chap, it wasn't the tea house that was the trouble," Captain Paulos murmured, grinning.

At which point Deliah snatched at his sleeve. "Captain!"

"Not the tea house?" Simms asked. "Whatever else were you doing?"

Captain Paulos gave Deliah a somewhat concerned look. Then he smiled fatuously. "Oh, my dear lady! Fear not. What happened later is no fault of yours at all. You needn't be concerned." He gave Simms a covert smile even as he seemed at a loss how to pat Deliah's arm soothingly with only one hand available. "You see, after I'd had the lovely tea Miss Stenwick recommended—thank you for giving me that lapel pin to wear, by the way—one of the waiters was kind enough to let me know where I could find a private dice game at their sister establishment. Not a suitable place for a lady, that, Miss Stenwick, so I won't speak its name. But the game went very well until a rough sort of fellow impugned my honor and that of my regiment, and I had to go rounds with him."

"Oh, you poor thing," Deliah cooed. "I do hope you won."

"Of course I did," Captain Paulos said. "The other fellow was in a frightful state when I'd done with him."

Simms knew he was lying. Not because he shared Captain Ramos's odd, almost preternatural sense about it, which she still claimed was directed entirely by observation. No, he knew Captain Paulos was lying because he'd heard this story from the other side, and knew for a fact that Lucius had been walked out of the saloon, while Paulos had been hauled out on a stretcher.

And he knew this because a tickle had started in his spine the moment Captain Paulos had mentioned the Amber Moon Tea House. He recalled the morning two days ago, when Amelia, Gregory, and Lucius had left for their fateful trip to Black Hawk: Lucius had been wearing a four-leaf clover pin in his lapel as well. Lucius was a shockingly natty dresser for a man with a face like misshapen dough, but he wasn't normally one for that kind of sparkling embellishment. Captain Ramos always cautioned Simms that correlation and cause weren't the same thing, but he'd also learned well by observation that coincidences in their lives rarely *were*.

"A lapel pin, you say?" Simms's voice sounded hollow to his own ears. "What a lovely gift. What did it look like, if you don't mind me asking?"

"Oh, I don't have it on me…Miss Stenwick, please, don't tug on my sleeve so. I'm sorry, but my arm is still quite tender." Captain Paulos shook his head. "A neat little four-leaf clover pin. And it did make me quite lucky, up until that common rogue decided to put on airs."

"How lucky," Simms echoed. His gaze fixed on Deliah now. She was holding on to her smile with the sort of game determination normally seen from a cat when it was about to be removed from a piece of furniture and given a bath. "Now I recall where I've heard your name before, Captain Paulos. You're in command of the Black Hawk garrison, are you not?"

"Goodness, you are good at this! Indeed I am, sir," the man answered. He rose up a bit on his toes, perhaps swelled with pride, but didn't quite click his heels. "Third month on the assignment! Though I'm on medical leave for a bit now, I'm afraid."

Perhaps Captain Paulos kept talking; Simms couldn't hear much of anything over the sound of blood rushing in his ears as he stared at Deliah. He might not have Captain Ramos's deductive faculties, but she'd taught him, using a combination of gentle prodding and un-gentle mockery over the years, to string logical conclusions together from evidence. And this was ample evidence. The conclusion was clear: Deliah had carefully put Captain Paulos in a position where he'd run across Lucius. She hadn't expected Paulos to be here now; Simms wasn't supposed to know about any of this.

Deliah had helped them rescue Lucius from gaol after she'd very carefully orchestrated him being put there. And why? The only reason Simms could see was that she wanted him to be *here* for some reason. She'd wanted him to owe her a favor. Or perhaps she'd wanted Captain Ramos to owe her a favor.

"*You.*" Simms glared at Deliah, his hands curling into fists. He normally had an even temper—someone who associated with Captain Ramos had to if they wanted to survive. But this was beyond the pale, and he no longer had the self-possession necessary to recall where he was and what role he was supposed to be. "It was your doing!" He grabbed Deliah's arm.

"Mister Simms, please!" Deliah said, eyes wide.

Captain Paulos, hand still occupied by a wine glass, tried to snatch at Simms's arm and only succeeded in slopping something white and nicely fruity on his sleeve. "I say, Mister…wait, did you say his name is *Simms*?" Then his eyes widened and he snatched his hand back. "Simms?"

Simms came back to himself to realize that the ballroom had gone utterly silent, and Captain Paulos was staring at him with something like horror, repeating his name like he was a monster from legend.

Oh, right. Lucius had drunkenly named Captain Ramos. Had the man really been brain-blasted enough to spout Simms's name as well? Of course. That was just his luck. And when had he gotten to be so infamous, anyway? It hardly seemed fair. No one ever offered him free cups of tea like they fell over themselves to buy Captain Ramos beers.

Still holding fast to Deliah's arm, Simms took a quick glance around. Contrary to his expectation, they weren't the center of attention. Rather, the natty men and brightly dressed ladies were all turned toward the double doors. A few women fluttered their fans nervously here and there.

What had he missed?

Through the doors of the ballroom, the grand staircase was visible, leading to the less public rooms of the upstairs. Simms hadn't bothered with even thinking about those, since he'd been after the safe in the library.

An older man dressed in a navy blue uniform of some sort hurried down the stairs. "Someone's broken into my safe! Call the guard!"

Simms had only seen the man once, and as a very passing glance when he and Captain Ramos had been in the house. And he certainly hadn't been wearing a uniform at the time. But a corner of Simms's mind, the one normally reserved for alerting him that he was about to die shortly after Captain Ramos had done something daft with the control panel of one of the railcars, informed him that was their host, Lord Balthertate.

So that safe had been moved upstairs after all.

"Something far more interesting, eh?" Simms shot a narrow-eyed look at Deliah. "What did you steal?"

Captain Paulos looked between them and slowly backed away. "In here!" he shouted. "Pirates! Pirates in here!"

"Let go, Simms," Deliah hissed. He felt her weight shift, and had the presence of mind to step back, yanking forward slightly and interrupting whatever trick she'd been about to pull.

"Oh no," he said grimly. "We're hanging together for this one." He shot a glance around the ballroom; still mostly ladies, who were drawing back from both of them in response to the Captain's shouts.

Simms spotted a set of doors on the far side of the room and started toward it, his hand still clamped on Deliah's arm. Hopefully the doors would lead outside, and they could make a break for it. But he wasn't letting the woman out of his sight, not when she'd so obviously intended to finger him for this crime. Perhaps just happy to be making a move toward the exit now that he'd destroyed her cover identity, Deliah trotted along readily enough.

Behind them, he heard Lord Balthertate shout again, "Thievery! Thievery!" And then, apparently taking up Captain Paulos's cry, "Piracy!"

Before Simms and Deliah had even made it halfway across the ballroom, the doors that had hinted at the possibility of freedom flew open. Men in navy blue uniforms that mirrored Lord Balthertate's boiled from the room beyond. Many still had glasses of brandy in hand. A few less than that number, but still far more than Simms cared to consider, carried decorative sabers, which they drew.

Simms stopped in his tracks and let go of Deliah, raising his hands as several swords pointed his way. They might be relatively dull and intended for decoration only, but he still didn't fancy finding out what one would do to any of his softer bits of flesh.

"Piracy!" Captain Paulos shouted behind them, at this point completely unnecessarily.

"Yes, I pirated your bloody sausage platter within an inch of its life," Simms growled, since at this point it seemed the only appropriate response. To the side, he heard a disapproving gasp, perhaps at his slightly coarse language.

Well, he thought with grim amusement, give them what they wanted. Deliah had gone all large-eyed and quivery next to him, obviously winding up for a round of weeping about what a brute he was. He pointed a finger at her as accusingly as he could with his hands still in the air. "She's the one wot done it," he said, doing his best to sound like a pirate in a penny dreadful. "She stole the lot of it. Sly she-devil, she is."

And to his satisfaction, two of the saber blades moved, wobbling perhaps a bit drunkenly, to point squarely at Deliah.

The look she shot him then could have curdled cream.

"You are an idiot," Deliah informed him for the third time.

Simms's response was the same as before; he simply continued to stare at the dark wooden wall over her head, trying to ignore the way it rocked and bounced in plain invitation to become motion sick.

They were in the back of the Black Maria, the enclosed and secure steam carriage belonging to the duchy's central gaol, careening along eastward the cobblestone streets on the long journey to those solid stone walls. The machine appeared to have no shocks to speak of; Simms was fairly certain that by the time they reached their destination, he'd be a few inches shorter, every impact jolting up his spine and unpleasantly jiggling the wad of sausages still sitting in his belly.

"A blithering idiot," Deliah continued.

There was a lot he could have said in answer to that, beginning with asking her just how she thought Captain Ramos would take it, that Deliah had tried to make him her patsy for a crime that was likely the same one the captain had been planning to carry out upon her return. And most definitely taking a detour through the little fact that Deliah had somehow thought it was an excellent idea to do all this on the night Lord Balthertate was having his regimental reunion. But he kept his teeth firmly closed on that question, because they weren't alone in the back of the Maria, and he didn't want to give her the satisfaction of knowing that she'd started rubbing his nerves raw like a thorn.

The policeman next to Simms, a stout fellow with a neat brown beard, shifted and grimaced, perhaps because they'd just hit a rather spectacular pothole. Simms thought it more likely that he had run out of amusement at the one-sided contest of insults. The other rozzer sitting next to Deliah squirmed a little on his seat and crossed his arms over his rather beefy chest. Both of them wore gray uniforms of the regular police forces. Simms had heard they were gray because the Grand Duke was too cheap to spring for the sort of dye that would make them a proper black. In the dim light from the street lamps that filtered into the Maria from the narrow, high, barred windows, they looked more than dark enough.

"Piracy! As if I could commit piracy in this dress."

And why not? Simms wanted to ask. *Captain Ramos does it all the time.*

Really, Simms had been hoping that arrest would separate them; he was very surprised when Deliah hadn't managed to talk herself away from the sabers. It probably had something to do with the extremely nice pocket watch and rather ostentatious diamond necklace that had been shaken from her hand clutch. Since her name definitely wasn't *Edgar*, it had seemed plain she had at the very least stolen the watch. Then Lady Balthertate had identified the diamond necklace as hers, just for good measure.

Deliah likely had other items from the safe on her person. But Lord Balthertate had quailed at the idea of searching a woman personally, or turning her over to any of the tipsy men at his party for that purpose. Curiously, no female guest had stepped forward as a volunteer. Thus Balthertate had decided it was a better idea to send her off to gaol with Simms and let the warden of the women's gaol deal with the nasty details. They'd been tucked away in the Maria once it had shown up, chuffing and shuddering up the drive and hiding the cherubs in clouds of oily steam.

"I can't believe you turned on me. Just like that. *She's the one wot done it,* my eye. Idiot." She took in a deep breath, perhaps in preparation for launching into another round of complaints. It had the secondary effect of drawing attention to her bosom, which was as well-displayed as it could be in what had been polite company.

Ultimately, he was more than happy to have the rozzers' attention fixed on Deliah. Simms wasn't much use for picking locks, but not long into their association, Captain Ramos had insisted on teaching him how to foul the locks of the most common models of handcuffs. And forced him to practice until he could do it with his hands behind his back and his eyes closed and her prodding him repeatedly in random spots with a wrench. Then she'd gone through all of his work clothes and sewn bits of wire into the cuff hems.

It was almost as if she'd been planning for this very moment. And for that, he could nearly forgive her the bit when she'd poked him very hard right in the armpit.

Simms let the words wash over him, his focus on his hands. He'd succeeded in extracting the wire from his shirt cuff, had managed to get it folded the right way round, and found the lock of the manacle. Thankfully any metallic scrapes or clicks were masked by the constant juddering of the Maria. The most difficult part of the exercise was actually keeping his face from screwing up with concentration. He worked the wire back and forth through the simple lock in motions he'd learned by rote until he felt it catch. Then he gave it a hard twist and felt the pressure on his left wrist release.

He was free.

"Don't you have anything at all to say for yourself, you worthless man?" Deliah demanded.

Simms stayed still, tensing a little as he waited. The next big bump the Maria hit, he lurched to the side as if falling over, giving himself a little room to maneuver. Movement caught at the corner of his eye, but he had to hope he could incapacitate one rozzer before the other was on him.

As the rozzer by his side turned to reach for him, Simms grabbed the man's wrist and dragged him forward as he swung his other hand up to strike. "How's this for worthless?" he snarled. The combined force made his fist hit the man's jaw with a sickening *crack*. The man in gray choked and went limp.

Simms shoved the limp man away with a thrust of his leg, hands coming up defensively as he turned his head to see…Deliah, also out of her cuffs, the much larger and presumably stronger man in a choke hold that he couldn't seem to escape. Simms decided to cut that fight and the disturbing burbling noises the policeman was making short by punching him in the temple.

Deliah dropped the man down onto the bench. She glared at Simms. "I still think you're an idiot."

"What, for not trusting you'd come fish me out of the clink after you got me put there? I wonder why." Simms cast around for something he could use to pry at the rear doors of the Maria. Nothing came to hand. He picked up one of the truncheons instead.

"I…would have."

"Then you should have told me that was the plan to begin with."

"Captain Ramos doesn't tell you her plans."

"That's because she just makes them up on the spot!" Simms glared at her. How did she know that? All right, to be fair, anyone who had ever spent more than ten minutes around Captain Ramos would know that she never bothered to tell Simms or anyone else the entirety of her plans. If she even bothered to have them. Frustrating beast.

"And besides," Simms continued before Deliah had a chance to speak, "she's never gotten me stuck in gaol. At least not on purpose. Yes, she's done a lot of things to me, but never that." Which was why, among other reasons and entirely contrary to every survival instinct he had, he trusted her. "And what were you after in Lord Balthertate's safe anyway?" he demanded. "I thought you put on airs about not being a common thief like the likes of us."

"Not everything in that safe was gold or jewelry," Deliah informed him primly. "There were some papers that I found to be of great interest. And quite a few other, very well-paying people would as well."

"Ah. Right. But…" That almost made sense. Though if the man had only lost a few papers, and ones he wanted to keep secret, why start an uproar at his own party over it? Unless he was hoping to catch the thief before he or she escaped…ah. And if Simms turned out to be the thief because Deliah planted jewelry on him, say, when they were dancing, no one would bother searching anyone else for papers. Balthertate wouldn't want to specifically ask about those once what appeared to be his stolen property had been found. Simms grimaced. "Twistier than a—"

basket of yarn the kitten's been at, he wanted to say, but his love of all things small and furry was none of Deliah's bloody business, "—a very twisty thing, the both of you," he finished lamely.

Deliah raised an eyebrow in a most sardonic fashion. "Thank you, Mister Simms."

Another massive jolt shook the carriage, and one of the rozzers groaned. Deliah braced one hand against the Maria's wall and kicked him with efficient precision. It served as a reminder to Simms that he needed to focus on the matter at hand, which was the fact that he really, really didn't want to end up in the grand duchy's gaol. Not when there was no knowing when Captain Ramos would be back in town to fish him out.

Just like she hadn't been around to fish Lucius out either. Lucius, who had been pulled because of Deliah's arcane machinations just to bring this farce about. Right. "Get stuffed," he ground out.

He turned and beat the truncheon against the ceiling of the Maria. It was hopefully the sort of signal one of the rozzers might use if he wanted the carriage stopped urgently because he needed assistance.

The reaction was sudden and immediate. The Maria jolted, a metallic shriek penetrating the wooden interior as the brakes engaged on full. Simms and Deliah stumbled toward the front of the carriage, the unconscious men sliding across the floor toward them. Simms barely avoided having the larger of the two men trap his legs against the wall.

The rear doors of the Maria rattled. Simms shoved himself forward, stepping none-too-gently on the stouter of the two rozzers, who had made the mistake of beginning to stir. "Best be ready," he whispered back at Deliah.

"Your plan is obvious," she returned dryly. He saw her pick up the other truncheon, the weapon sitting easily in her hand. One lock clunked on the doors, followed by a scrape and the grind of a second, very dirty mechanism.

The rear doors opened. Simms lunged out, diving onto the unfortunate man in gray who had opened the doors. He hit the ground with a meaty thud and a muffled shout, the much taller Simms on top of him.

Something whistled past his head.

Cursing, Simms ducked, and then reared back up as the rozzer landed him a solid punch in the mouth. Blood welling between his teeth, he gave the man a couple of solid blows with the truncheon to stun him and glanced aside.

The other policeman, companion to Simms's victim, lay sprawled on the ground with the truncheon rolling across the cobbles not far from his head. Deliah had apparently thrown it.

He might not like the woman at all, but he could at least respect that level of accuracy.

The rozzer struck Simms a glancing blow on the cheek. "Enough of that." Feeling strangely cheerful now that he was no longer stuck in an enclosed space, Simms rose to his feet, dragging the man up by the front of his jacket. "In you go, lad," he sang out, and threw him into the back of the Maria to join his fellows.

As he did so, Deliah jumped from the back of the black carriage, letting out an undignified squeak as she barely missed being hit by the disoriented rozzer.

Simms quickly turned and dragged the other, far more limp policeman up, to be shoved into the back of the Maria as well. Then he slammed the solid rear doors shut and engaged the only lock that didn't require a key. "That ought to keep them out of our hair…" he said to…no one.

Where had Deliah gone, and in just a few seconds? Simms glanced around, and caught a shimmer of gold and green reflected in a puddle. He heard the hasty click of heels on the cobbles.

Growling to himself, he gave chase, stooping to snatch up one of the truncheons as he ran past. One thing was obvious; he couldn't trust Deliah not to set the dogs on him if it came to that. Therefore, as best he could figure, the safest place to be was right on her tail. If she tried to set the rozzers on him right in front of his face again, he knew how to make a big enough stink that she'd get nibbed as well, and they'd be back in the same position as before. He doubted she wanted that any more than he did.

Deliah could run quite well, particularly considering the delicate shoes she'd chosen for the night, far more suited to dancing than fleeing down an uneven street from either police or an angry ginger. Simms, however, had the advantage of much longer legs and far more sensible shoes. He caught up to her in short order as she slowed to inspect a set of street signs and then turned right.

She whipped around to face him, something flashing in her hand. He brought up the truncheon out of sheer surprise, and was rewarded with the solid *thunk* of metal meeting wood.

"What are you *doing*?" She had to jerk her hand back twice to dislodge the knife from the truncheon.

"Were you going to kill me?"

"I thought you were someone else."

Well, that was a comfort, he supposed.

Deliah sniffed. "Point of fact, I was aiming for your shoulder. I think your delicate constitution could have withstood that. And I think I still might. Don't follow me!"

"You think I'm going to let you just run off so you can set the rozzers on me again? Not bloody likely."

"If you don't get away from me, I'll set the police on you for certain!"

Simms glared at her. He could see in her eyes that was an empty threat. She knew just as well that he'd take her down with him.

The shrill echo of a police whistle bounced down the alleyway, coming from behind them. There must have been a patrolling officer not far from where they'd stopped the Maria. Simms cursed, casting around for somewhere they could go. This area of the city wasn't immediately familiar to him; he didn't have Captain Ramos's memory for these things, and it was still far too middle class for what he might have known before keeping her company.

Deliah grabbed his sleeve. "Don't run," she whispered. "There's nothing more suspicious than someone running." She arranged her hands on his arm into a more companionable grip and nudged him forward. "Walk."

"This isn't going to work," Simms muttered.

"It will work perfectly if you just play it calm."

He bit his tongue; arguing or struggling against her iron-like grip would certainly attract attention. The spot between his shoulder blades itched fiercely under his suit jacket as they moved out from the alley and into a broader street. This late at night, there was hardly anyone else to be seen, most of the shops shuttered. Light still showed in the windows of a saloon here and there, however.

"This isn't going to work," he muttered again, still keeping at the stately pace she set.

"Quiet, Mister Simms. Do you argue this much with Captain Ramos?"

"Yes."

"It's a wonder she puts up with it." Deliah smiled and laughed lightly, as if he'd just made an excellent joke.

"She trusts me."

"Trusts you to be useless, perhaps."

Simms, past his endurance with these snippy comments no matter how desperate the situation, stopped in his tracks and refused to be moved. "Trusts me to have her back," he snarled. He pointed at her savagely, not quite poking her in the chest with his finger. "You've been sniping at me all evening, *and* you tried to have me put in prison. You have no room to be talking about *trust*."

Deliah yanked at his arm, trying to get him started walking again, but his last comment seemed to strike some sort of nerve. She leaned in close, her beautiful face twisting with ire, and hissed, "Of course I don't trust you. You've been standing in my way since the first time we met. And why?"

"Wait, what?" Simms stared at her. What was she talking about?

Deliah continued on as if he hadn't spoken. "It's clear enough. You want her for yourself, isn't that it? *Admit it*."

Simms continued to stare at her, trying to comprehend the words she'd just spoken, and any way they could be put together that didn't draw an utterly mad conclusion. Had she really just accused him of…of…*wanting* Captain Ramos? In the same way Deliah did? Perhaps being in love with her?

This, he thought, had to be what softening of the brain felt like.

Deliah *hmmphed* with a distinct note of triumph in her voice and yanked on his arm. Still trying to understand the view from Deliah World, Simms stumbled forward and followed.

They passed under a street light; the sodium yellow flame within hissed and sputtered. Simms felt a bit like hissing and sputtering himself. *You want her for yourself.*

It was too ridiculous, and he suddenly burst out laughing. "That's it? *That* is what you think?" Deliah gave him an uncertain, slightly panicked look. Perhaps he was laughing too loudly. He didn't particularly care. "For god's sake, Deliah, you've *met* Captain Ramos. Do I look *insane* to you? No. No. No, no, no. Goodness no. Oh, that's funny. You had me going for a moment."

It would be like wanting his sister in any kind of romantic fashion. If his sister had broken his arm, saved his soul, and made him question just how many times he'd been dropped on his head as a child. If his sister was someone he trusted with not only his life, but his daughter's life. If his sister was someone to whom he'd be wholly unafraid to say, *That is the most hare-brained idea I've ever heard in my entire life and you really ought to stop drinking topical medications, they're turning your teeth green.* If he even had a sister to begin with, since he was fairly certain if a daughter like that had crawled out of his mam's womb, she would have been put into the Platte River in a burlap sack filled with bricks.

No. Never in a million years. What had cracked in Deliah's skull to cause her to even think such a mad thing?

The shrilling of the policeman's whistle sounded again, very close.

Deliah shoved him into the doorway of a closed shop. The smell of grease, singed metal, and tobacco smoke breathed out from under the door: a tinker's, perhaps. She clapped a hand over his mouth. "Shut up, Simms. You'll have the lot of them on us!"

Simms bit the inside of his cheek, trying to think sober thoughts. It managed to calm his near-hysterical laughter down to little snorting giggles. "Sorry, you just…almost had me going there for a moment. What an idea."

"I was *serious*."

Mercifully, she clapped her hand over his mouth again before another guffaw could escape. There was an odd sort of doubt shining in her eyes, overtaking all the anger that she'd stopped disguising. The sound of several pairs of feet trotting up the street interrupted anything else either of them might have said.

Deliah yanked Simms down toward her by the tie. Their faces were almost touching. "Just pretend we're kissing," she whispered.

"It won't work," he whispered back.

"It will if you stop arguing."

Feeling very strange about the whole deal—the nice thing about pretending to be Captain Ramos's husband in public had always been the fact that he never had to touch her like that because it was always in societal circles where this sort of thing would be *very impolite*—Simms put his arms around Deliah. And kept their faces level, but there was no bleeding way he was going to pretend to kiss her.

Particularly not when he considered that her lips had in recent history been on Captain Ramos's lips and the thought was just too strange for a relatively straight-laced man like him to bear.

"No," he whispered, wishing he could see the street around Deliah's head. Her rather elaborate hairstyle, which involved black ringlets and feathers, made that impossible. "The answer is no. I most certainly do not…*want* my captain. Ugh, I feel ill just saying that."

Before Deliah could answer, light shone directly at his face. Simms jerked up straight, which he thought was a natural enough reaction. Around the glare of the lantern, he could make out the dark shapes of three men, presumably policemen from the shape of their clothes. "Sorry, officers. Didn't mean to be—"

"Move along—" one of the shapes began.

Another, with a much rougher voice, interrupted, "Oy! He said a giant with ginger muttonchops, didn't he?"

Simms didn't wait for the other two officers to confirm or deny that description. He shoved Deliah aside and launched himself into the center of the group, planting his shoulder into the chest of the middle man. The rozzer tumbled over, his breath—and no small amount of spit—exploding from him.

"Oy! Oy!" A truncheon whacked Simms solidly in the arm. That was followed by a meaty *crack*, a loud cry from someone other than Simms, and the sound of the truncheon hitting the paving stones.

"Run!" Deliah shouted.

Still half-blinded, Simms did just that. He felt fingers, far too delicate to belong to any of the rozzers, grasp at his. He snatched up Deliah's hand and dragged her along with him. "I told you it wouldn't work!" he shouted over his shoulder.

"Your damned muttonchops, Simms!"

"Leave them out of it!"

Behind them, the whistles sounded, calling every officer in earshot.

"Hell," Simms growled. He spotted another alley, not far off, between a shuttered haberdasher's and a pawnshop. Without a word, he turned for it, Deliah almost fluttering along in his wake like a kite. The cobbles in the alley were wet with things best left unmentioned, and terribly uneven. Simms felt Deliah stumble, and she cried out quietly, tugging at his hand.

At which point he realized that he had, in fact, taken her hand to begin with. He slowed, glancing back.

"Keep going," Deliah said, her voice strained. Her hand tightened on his.

They burst from the alley still at a dead run, though Simms could hear Deliah's steps had gone uneven. The rapid click of her heels was barely audible over the thud of his heartbeat in his ears. Down the street, he spotted a saloon, one large and still brightly lit. The sound of a fiddle spilled through its doors. If it was lively enough, they could lose themselves in there and perhaps even cause a ruckus to give the police something else to think about.

"There!" Simms tugged Deliah in that direction.

"No, not that one—"

Simms lost whatever she had been about to say as a chorus of cheers echoed down the street, coming from the saloon. He didn't bother to glance at the sign, to do more than note the large, smoky windows—not the sort regularly broken, then—before he shoved the doors open.

Silence.

He halted, Deliah stumbling behind him and catching onto his back.

The saloon was positively *filled* with rozzers, still in their uniforms. They had all gone utterly silent and turned to stare at him.

Simms glanced slowly back to look at the sign hanging out into the street: *The Blue Bottle*. "Oh, *come on*," he said, unable to contain his exasperation.

One of the gray-clad men nearest the door rose from his seat. "Something the matter—?"

The shrill, metallic whistling sounded in the street behind them, followed by shouts.

Simms turned tail and thundered back out into the street, nearly picking Deliah up by her arm. "How," she gasped, somehow still audible over the shouting in the street, the shouts now coming from the saloon, the sound of the door banging open over and over again as rozzers poured out after them, "did you not know that was the policeman's bar?"

"I don't go to bars! That's the captain's responsibility!" He dodged down one alley and into another, rushing through the narrow spaces between shops. He hoped that this would at least act as a temporary choke point and slow their pursuers. The rough edges of bricks tore at the shoulders of his jacket as he caromed off the walls, refusing to slow.

The real problem was, he wasn't at all familiar with this part of town. He'd never had a head for maps like Captain Ramos; he tended to learn streets organically. Once he knew them, had walked them with his own legs, he could remember nearly everything. But…

But it was all useless excuses at this point.

"Left, Simms! Left!"

He didn't have any better ideas, so Simms did as Deliah said and dodged left, down a narrow lane lined with shops and hissing street lamps.

Behind them, dogs began to bay. "What sort of rozzer brings his bloody hound to a saloon?" Simms asked despairingly.

Deliah was making curious noises behind him, her breath sobbing—no, she actually was sobbing. Simms hazarded a glance back, seeing the shapes of running men, of lanterns.

"Bugger this." He spied another alley and pulled Deliah into it, wracking his brain. Wait. He did recall something, almost, what was it? Right, Captain Ramos had made a joke once, about avoiding Congress Park above ground because it was such a *crush*. Crushers. The term the captain favored for policemen when she was feeling whimsical.

Were they in Congress Park? That would certainly fit with the fact that every bloody graybelly in the city was on their heels. So then…

Avoid it *above ground*. He had been here with Captain Ramos before, several times, but never above the surface. *This* neighborhood was the source of so many of his more stinking nightmares. *Bugger.* He'd thought he would escape the sewers when they'd proved a dead end at the central gaol. There were worse things than a bit of eye-gouging stench and exploding rats. Subteranian Simms to the rescue.

"Bloody destiny." He started running again, now practically carrying Deliah. "Just a bit further!" As they left the alley, he let go of Deliah and ran to the center of the deserted street, where a manhole cover waited. It should have had an electrical marquee over it that read *Welcome home, Mister Simms, this is your inescapable fate.*

"It's useless, Mister Simms. I can't go any further. It's no good."

He glanced back to see Deliah collapsed against the wall, sweat—and were those tears?—streaking her face and shining in the lamplight. Simms shook his head, latching his fingers around the manhole cover. His back twinged dangerously as he lifted the massive piece of solid iron. "There's always one thing I'm good for," he said, the words trailing off in a snarl of pure effort.

Gravity and Simms fought. This time, Simms won. The manhole cover moved, and he shoved it aside, enough that the both of them could squeeze through. Trying to shake feeling back into his hands, he hurried over to Deliah and dragged her back up to her feet. "Maybe that's why the captain keeps me around."

She shook her head. "I can't walk any more. My ankle—"

He gave up any pretense and simply carried her over to the open manhole. With care he'd never admit to, he lowered her in. The shouts of the police, the barking of the dogs were dangerously close. "You can climb with only one foot. Hurry."

It didn't even matter all that much if he couldn't get the cover back on the manhole; the dogs wouldn't be able to track them down there, even if their handlers were brave enough to try. And he could hope that Deliah had the foresight to bring some sort of lantern. But if not, there was one thing he did know, and that was how to find his way around in the stinking darkness under the city.

Captain Ramos had seen to that.

"Keep climbing down," he called quietly down. "Feel your way. Lean on the wall at the bottom until I get there, and…just try not to think about it when something crawls over your hand."

"When," Deliah muttered, her voice strained with pain. "Not if."

Jittering with barely restrained nerves, he waited until she was just far enough down the ladder for him to squeeze in his full height and followed her. He had to strain until he saw black spots before his eyes—or maybe that was the smell—but with a horrible scrape of metal on stone, the manhole cover fell back into place.

Darkness.

"Now what?" Deliah asked. Her tone was flat; it was impossible to see her expression in the absolute darkness.

"Now we walk to the Platte." Simms fought the urge to gag. It would pass quickly enough as the endless stench simply burned out his brain's ability to comprehend smell.

"I don't think I can walk any longer," Deliah said softly.

Almost, he offered to carry her on his back. But it was all too easy to remember that she'd attempted to metaphorically stab him there already tonight. And had already done Lucius one, just to further her own schemes. "We give it a while, I can move the cover back and get you out onto the street again."

An uncomfortable silence fell, but for the drip of something that Simms pretended with all his heart was water, and the skittering of both insect and rodent. Well, there was really no reason to worry about being quiet, not after the first few minutes had passed and no one on the street had thought to lift up the manhole cover. He decided to ask the question from this ridiculous scenario that still bothered him the most. "Why the blazes did you think I was…did you think I *want* Captain Ramos for myself?"

"Well, it's obvious, isn't it? She hasn't been answering my letters, so *someone* has been interfering. And you have been getting in my way since the beginning."

Simms snorted. "If Captain Ramos hasn't been answering your letters, it's because you've either put them in the wrong drop boxes, or she's been at the peyote again. She's not the most reliable letter writer on even the best of days."

There was a long pause, perhaps as Deliah mulled this over. It was difficult to tell in the dark. "Well, you obviously don't like me."

"I don't like you because I think you'll get her killed," Simms said, feeling his voice go strangely gruff in a way that had nothing to do with the surrounding smell. "I could throw you farther than I trust you. You don't weigh that much."

"You need to work on your compliments."

"I just lifted a manhole cover without straining anything, Deliah. That was not meant to be at all complimentary."

Another long pause.

"You've never trusted me," she said, almost accusingly. "You never gave me a chance."

"You murdered your grand aunt."

There was an odd, uneven splash, and something grabbed Simms—no, *someone* did, Deliah did. Her hand patted at his face, and then she slapped him, hard.

He was momentarily too stunned by such a deliberate act to do more than stare into the darkness where she had to be.

"Don't you *ever* say that again, you beastly man." Deliah jerked her hand back away from him. "You have no idea what it was like, to watch her drift further and further away every day. To watch her become less and less herself. And in those rare moments when she remembered, when she even knew who I was, she *begged me* to help her. She didn't want to go on like that. Could you stand that, Mister Simms? Could you watch someone you love dearly just fade away? She knew something was wrong, and it terrified her. How hard-hearted are you?"

Pretty bloody hard-hearted, he wanted to retort, but that wasn't true at all. She'd said something like that before, when she'd admitted her crime to Captain Ramos so many months ago. And Captain Ramos had accepted it, that Clementine Nimowitz had been going senile and wanted a way out. But it hadn't struck Simms then the way it had now. Maybe because he couldn't see Deliah now to be distracted by her habitually secretive expression. He could only hear her voice, and how it shook with emotion.

"You didn't sound so upset before." He felt like an utter cad. Was she playing him, though? He knew that Deliah was a spy, of some sort. She manipulated people for a living. Maybe this was more of the same, but in the stinking dark it was difficult to hold on to that idea.

"I didn't have a broken ankle before. It's done wonderful things for my composure, hasn't it?" She sniffled. "I despise crying in earnest. I'm not here for your entertainment."

"I don't think it's entertaining when women cry." It was bloody uncomfortable. Like it was right now. Stinking and uncomfortable. "What about the jewelry, then?" he asked weakly.

Deliah laughed unsteadily. "It was Grand Aunt Clementine's best jewelry. It was supposed to be mine, and it meant a lot to her. But in the end, it's a game. It's just a game, Simms. For us."

And by *us* he knew she meant herself and Captain Ramos, a game the two of them played against—*with?*—each other. That was the most ridiculous thing he'd heard in a day filled with ridiculous things. "My god, can't the two of you pursue a—a *relationship* like normal people? Flowers and chocolates and awkward dinners where no one knows quite what to say and then a quick snog in the doorway at midnight? Is that really too much to ask?"

"Do we strike you as particularly normal people?" Deliah asked with asperity.

She had a point. A painfully landed, nasty point. Which he might have deserved. But there really was no such thing as normal for people like…well, any of them really. And that included himself. They'd all taken a look at what regular society had to offer and returned a solid *thanks, but no, I'd rather spend my life at risk of being hanged than go to another party where I have to act as if there's nothing more scandalous than a naked ankle whilst people get put in jail for being poor every day.* Which, when he thought about it that way, put Deliah dangerously close to being in the same boat as the pirates, people with no home but what they'd gone out of their way to make for themselves.

And if she was serious, if he could trust her claim that she cared for Captain Ramos in whatever strange way those two shared, that gave them something else in common as well.

"All right," he finally said.

"All right?"

"All right," Simms repeated. He still didn't trust Deliah, not the way he trusted Captain Ramos. But in all honesty, he didn't trust *anyone* the way he trusted Captain Ramos…and that included Captain Ramos half the time. But there wasn't a point to being at war with Deliah, not like this. It was stupid, and it had gotten him into the grotty sewers *again* and ruined his best pair of shoes. "Let's head toward the Platte. It's going to be a long walk."

There was a long pause. Simms could only assume Deliah was staring at the bit of sticky blackness she thought housed him. "I already said I can't walk any farther."

"You don't have to. I'll carry you on my back."

Another pause. Deliah slowly said, "I didn't think this evening was going to get any more awkward."

He laughed. "Welcome to my life, Miss Nimowitz. I don't suppose you have a lantern stashed somewhere in your skirts?"

Hours later, like two maggoty cow pies had developed sentience and decided to try for a career change, they squidged out from one of the large, brick mains that dumped sewage and storm water into the river. Simms blinked dumbly at the sky, pink and gold with the promise of sunrise.

His back *ached*.

Huffing in the air that seemed almost noxiously clean, he took the last few steps over to the river bank and let Deliah slide from his back with an unpleasant squelch. This motion dislodged a large blob of something unspeakable from her skirts, which lay in an oozing puddle next to what had, in a happier life long forgotten, been his right shoe.

Only it didn't look quite right. Simms bent with a grunt to prod the mass with one finger. He found something solid beneath. Hoping he hadn't just made a terrible mistake, he picked it up. Beneath the layer of unmentionable filth, he found a water-tight oilskin pouch.

"You are still an idiot." There was no malice left in her hoarse voice that Simms could hear. Deliah flopped back on the bank, her eyes closed. "But I think I understand why Captain Ramos keeps you around."

"And why would that be?" Simms asked dryly.

Deliah hesitated, her mouth working as if she wanted to say something else, but had thought better of it. Then she said, "You have both a strong back and a complete inability to know when you ought to give up."

"I think I'll take that as a compliment." With a quiet groan, he sat down on the bank beside her. Before them, the Platte River flowed by, looking peaceful and shockingly clean. He'd never believe that again, having become intimately acquainted with just what the city dumped into that poor river.

Deliah laughed, the sound unsteady and exhausted. "That is how I meant it."

"Right. Well, I still don't like you either." Simms wiped muck away from his eyes, flicking the filth from his fingers and onto the ground with a series of disturbing plops. Then he cracked open the fallen pouch he'd retrieved, revealing a small cache of no doubt very valuable diamonds.

The diamonds Captain Ramos had wanted to steal from Lord Balthertate as a matter of fact. It seemed that Deliah *hadn't* just been after those papers.

He tilted the pouch toward Deliah. "I'll give these to the captain with your compliments, shall I?" He delivered the words as lightly as a man soaked with filth could, but he meant it earnestly enough. He didn't want to know how this bizarre relationship of theirs might work, and he most certainly didn't want to be caught in the middle of it, but…he could at least appreciate the depth of feeling there, now. "I hear ladies like diamonds when it comes to courting gifts."

And if he'd managed to survive an evening with Deliah, the captain certainly could as well.

Deliah, still breathing heavily, looked at the pouch, and away. "Do shut up, Mister Simms." One hand came up to draw something brown and perhaps mercifully unidentifiable from her hair. She dropped it onto the ground next to her with an unceremonious *plop*. But he could also see, under all that muck, her lips had turned up in an exhausted smile.

Simms answered with a tired smile of his own and tucked the pouch into his sodden pocket.

Wireless

ERIWETHER OCTAVIAN SIMMS, KNOWN by his own preferences as "Simms" to friend and foe alike, had never thought he'd live to see a day where he regretted his inclination for boredom. The promise of an ordinary, middle-class life, in which one had tea and read the paper and complained about one's tiresome profession—which no doubt had something to do with other sorts of papers, though what one would do with them escaped his imagination at that point—over the breakfast table had always seemed preferable to the sort of life that found one dangling off a fifty foot drop from a rail bridge by one foot whilst being shot at by angry men in uniforms, to pick an example completely at random from his current lifestyle.

And yet, here he was.

Life had been solidly boring for three months and Simms was *concerned*. No, he'd moved past concerned in the first few weeks, into *worried*, and was now headed straight for *anxious*. It was the sort of powerful emotion that had him tugging at his ginger muttonchops, which hadn't done his looks any good, and being unfairly snappy at his young daughter Dolly. And he wasn't the only one who felt as if things were definitely an unaccustomed sort of wrong. Amelia, driver for their vast raiding engine Diabola and former opera singer, had stopped singing. Gregory, the lookout, had taken to leaving knotted bits of string everywhere, to the point that Cook had started depositing them on his dinner plate every day. Lucius, a person of whom no one was yet certain if he was human or a shaved gorilla, had gone through all of the spare fabric in the Devil's Roost for sewing projects and had recently taken to stealing clothing out of the laundry to perform repairs or upgrades that involved things like lace edging and embroidery.

While it was relief that his anxiety took the form of something unexpectedly constructive, it had also caused several minor emergencies in which no one could find their trousers. Even the newest member of the crew, a mathematically gifted woman named Little Wren, intended to replace the still-sorely-missed navigator Elijah, had been cooling her heels for two months with nothing to do but start teaching Dolly her native tongue, and Simms felt a deep suspicion toward his daughter being given any power to call him names he couldn't understand.

The problem was simple to state and impossible to fix: something was wrong with Captain Ramos. While in Simms's opinion, something had been quite wrong with her in a delightfully right sort of way ever since they first met in a fetid jail cell, this was different. It was a wrongness that made of long silences with nothing clever and terrible hiding beneath. It was a lifeless sort of wrongness that seemed to have eaten the captain's words out from inside of her and left a hollow behind. And of course, she insisted that she was absolutely fine, in a sort of perfunctory way that didn't allow for argument.

Captain Ramos had told Simms the barest details of what had come to pass in the Dead Plains while she'd been away, but only after much prompting and stubborn insistence. It was increasingly obvious that something more than what she told him had happened up in the Black Hills, and she wasn't going to talk about it no matter how much Simms nattered at her.

So now he had his own plan. It wasn't a terribly complex one; in fact, it had only one step, which had been "see if Miss Nimowitz has any ideas." He felt a bit more at peace with Deliah now, which wasn't saying much, but Simms prided himself in knowing when he was overmatched and needed to retreat. He couldn't determine the cause of the captain's melancholy, let alone how to drag her out of it. Every other idea he'd had went nowhere, up to and including proposing ridiculous heists that at least would have made her laugh in happier days. But Deliah, he was not too proud to admit, was in an entirely different league from him. Her brain worked in the same disturbingly twisty way as the captain's, which he did his best to stand well clear of.

For weeks, he hadn't heard anything of use from Deliah, to the point he even checked to make certain that his letter had gone to her proper address—only to find her house shut up and the neighbors fairly certain that "lovely Miss Nimowitz" was "going for a bit of travel" and "maybe she'll find a nice husband while she's at it." (He'd bitten his lip rather hard at that last comment.) Simms had begun to fear that his letter had gone entirely astray and he was back where he'd started, with no hope.

Then he'd picked up the mail three days ago from their post office box and found in the bundle a heavy envelope of cream-colored paper addressed to him in the neatest handwriting he'd ever seen. All the letter inside had said was: *Make certain she reads the society page of the Tribune on November 12. Yours, DN.*

He didn't like Deliah being all mysterious, nor trust it, but he had no choice. Deliah had been his weapon of last resort, and he had to find faith that there was a reason for her to not have done something useful, like showing up in person to shake Captain Ramos until her teeth rattled.

Yet he found himself swimming in even deeper doubt, three days later, now that he had that particular issue of the *Tribune* in hand. He'd even re-folded it to the page Deliah had wanted. In the past, he wouldn't have dared interfere with Captain Ramos's newspapers, but as of late she didn't even seem to be bothering to read most of them—another deeply worrying sign. The society sheet at a glance hadn't looked at all interesting, and while he'd made an attempt to read the breezy gossip, he'd had to stop two paragraphs in, his concentration utterly destroyed by a combination of boredom and enraged contempt at the recounting of an unseemly squabble over an expensive cheese plate in a hotel restaurant.

Rich people. He wanted to drown them all in their own barrels of imported oysters.

With nothing but his questionable faith to sustain him, he now stood in front of the heavy iron door to the captain's lab. It was funny how the door, normally closed to prevent the escape of noxious smells or strange sounds into the rest of the Roost, had taken on a very unwelcoming air as of late, despite the fact that none of its looks had changed. Simms pounded on it with his fist. When there was no response, he let himself in, as he had hundreds of other times before.

The captain was engaged in some activity that involved hundreds of vials of what appeared to be sand arrayed on the worktop in front of her. She was in the process of examining the contents of one such vial spread over a piece of white paper with a hand lens.

"Got today's papers," Simms said, when she didn't acknowledge him. That, in itself, wasn't so strange.

"Drop them on the table," she said disinterestedly, without looking up. That was the strange and disturbing part and had been since she had come back. The papers had always been her window into the world; she could take the tiniest details from their pages and craft them into the foundation of some sort of scheme that might just get them all killed. She always devoured newspapers (as well as the far rarer scientific and engineering dispatches from various societies) like a starving dog that had been given a side of beef.

Simms noted yesterday's papers on the table, untouched. He frowned, an expression that would have made them sweat ink if they'd been alive. "Should I cancel the subscriptions?" he asked.

"Of course not." The captain still hadn't looked up. "I'll get to them."

"Might be some really interesting stuff in these."

"I'm sure."

He frowned at her turned back. Her shirtsleeves were smudged with brown dust; her curly black hair was pulled back from her brown face in a tight bun. Nothing out of the ordinary there. Simms frowned at the papers in his hands, then shrugged to himself and kicked over the table where the old papers sat. It went over with a satisfying crash, scattering a nearly geological cross-section of newspapers, from the new to ancient, across the floor.

The captain's head jerked up. "What the blazes?"

"Clumsy me," Simms said.

She looked at him through narrowed brown eyes. "You've never been the clumsy sort."

"Guess things are just odd these days," Simms said. He draped the new papers over one of the legs of the overturned table, where they wouldn't be lost on the floor. "I'll send Gregory along with your dinner in a few hours."

"I don't suppose he's been hit with this plague of clumsiness as well?"

"You can't ever know what'll happen when you aren't paying attention," Simms said. His dark thoughts made his footsteps slow as he retreated into the long hallway with its string of overhead electric lamps. Calling it a hallway was more a courtesy than anything; it was an old mineshaft, like every other part of the Roost. A faint breeze from the bellows that kept air circulating ruffled his muttonchops.

Just before he hit the intersection that lead to the main corridor, there was an almighty *SLAM*, the sound of a metal door crushing into the wall.

"Simms!" Captain Ramos bellowed.

Simms felt a flutter in his chest at that, though he wasn't certain if it was hope, or being half-startled out of his own skin by the loud noise. He turned. "Yes, Captain?"

The captain leaned in the doorway, a queer expression on her face. Like perhaps she'd caught some scent—but also that she was deeply upset. He'd never seen anything quite like it—and it gave him a sinking feeling in the pit of his stomach. "Get Mr. Kinzer now. I need to speak with him immediately."

"Will do." He rushed off, knowing he'd get his answer because he'd damn well plant himself in whatever conversation happened next and refuse to be moved. He didn't know what Deliah had done, but his money was dead on this being the result. He could only hope it wasn't anything permanent that he'd have to count himself responsible for.

"And you're certain I'm not in trouble?" Gregory asked anxiously. He half-trotted to keep up with Simms. The poor man had been cursed with a short stature, and Simms, whom Captain Ramos had often referred to in mostly affectionate terms as "a monstrosity," was in a bit of a hurry.

Simms made a noncommittal mumbling noise that he was happy to allow Gregory to interpret as a reassurance if he so chose.

"I wonder what she wants, then," Gregory said, still verbally fishing.

"I suspect she'll tell you that herself."

The door at the end of the long hallway still stood open, though the captain was nowhere in sight. Simms ushered Gregory through in front of him, assuring himself that he wasn't planning to use the younger man as a shield, truly.

In the few minutes he had been gone, the captain's lab had become a sea of strewn papers beyond those he'd overturned, ranging from clips taken from the various newspapers to sheets in a variety of handwritings, perhaps letters or notes of some sort.

Captain Ramos had repaired to one of her file cabinets and was digging through it frantically.

"Captain?" Gregory asked, his voice cracking.

She flung herself back toward them, brandishing the newspaper that Simms recognized as the one he'd so wanted her to look at. This, she thrust under Gregory's nose. "Nieman DeLuc," she said. "Does the utterly execrable sketch match?"

For a bare second, Simms thought she might be calling Gregory that strange name—then he recalled it had been in the gossip column he'd barely glanced at. Gregory looked down at the paper, then took it from the captain when she gave it an impatient snap. Without pause, she went back to her file cabinet and began digging again.

As he looked at the paper, Gregory's face went utterly sallow, only saved from a ghostly white by the natural dark tone of his skin.

"Well?" Captain Ramos demanded, still elbows-deep in her file cabinet.

"It's him," Gregory said. The color rushed back into his face. He shook the paper like he wished to tear it apart. "It's bloody well him!"

"Who?" Simms demanded. He intercepted the paper and looked at the sketched picture on the page, a gentleman and a lady, captioned: *Mr. Nieman DeLuc and Miss Evangeline Winterlong seemed to have reached an understanding at Lady Smith's ball.*

"You recall the Rail King, Simms?" Captain Ramos said.

"The utter ballsack that had our switch at the Spanish Peaks dynamited three bloody times?" Simms growled. "Of course I do."

In truth, anyone who had any interest in using the rails knew who the Rail King was, and most had a much shinier view of the man. Rail lines were the limitation on nearly all transit between the duchies; air ships, while luxurious, were far more costly to build and maintain. In the western duchies, travel was made even more difficult by the large swathes of rugged, Infected-infested terrain to be crossed, and the rails still had to be maintained in useable condition.

The Rail King had, at first—and before he'd given himself that title—seemed like a savior. Rumored to be the son of a wealthy but reclusive member of the nobility, he'd used his riches to fix and improve the rail lines most desperately in need of maintenance, to the relief of local dukes who had been skimming that money to fund their armies or their lifestyles—or hadn't been able to agree with their neighbors just who was responsible for fixing which bits of track. The Rail King had even built new lines, engineering marvels that had shortened travel times and made far-flung towns more accessible.

Which led to the other bit of the story, with the dynamite and the large men with crowbars and Simms's desire to find the bloke and at the least break his nose. The Rail King had quickly begun demanding large sums of money from the dukes and the train operators down to anyone who had the temerity to run their own little rail car, for transit on *his* lines. And begun to outfit them with ingenious devices that derailed unauthorized trains or destroyed track junctions if he didn't receive his proper due. Captain Ramos had, in years past, tried to dismantle a few of these devices for her own edification, and they had promptly destroyed themselves from within and become useless slag before she could get a proper look.

As independent operators, Captain Ramos's crew had told the Rail King's "toll collectors" to spin on it on more than one occasion. Which then meant they'd had to find their own way through the Rocky Mountains and beyond, using carefully-maintained maps of which bits of track were safe because dukes or other wealthy patrons were paying the Rail King off, and on a few occasions, they'd even had to build their own well-hidden bypasses and switches, which the Rail King's bully boys destroyed whenever they came across them. They'd never quite gotten to the point of all-out war, and if Simms was forced to be logical he had to admit that was for the best. The Rail King had a much bigger operation than their own, family-sized crew, not to mention powerful friends and technology Captain Ramos hadn't been able to crack.

"He's this Nieman DeLuc fellow?" Simms asked. His back twinged in reminder of just how much sweat that bastard had cost them all.

"No," Gregory said, his voice tight. "DeLuc's one of his enforcers."

"Oh." That didn't raise the man in Simms's estimation. He had no use for hired thugs. "Well, he can take his tolls and—"

"And," Captain Ramos interrupted, returning with a sheaf of papers in her hand, "Evangeline Winterlong is one of Miss Nimowitz's aliases. She thinks it's terribly funny."

"Of course she does," Simms said. Trust Deliah to find the most dangerous yet flush person possible to get mixed up with. He ought to have known better than to ask her for help.

"I don't know what he's doing in the Grand Duchy of Salt Lake, though," Gregory said. "He was out in the Missions before.

That was his area. Because he hates Mexicans and the King thought that was funny."

"That is something we will find out, if we catch him," the captain said. "Or Miss Nimowitz might already know."

"Got a keen nose for information to go with trouble, that one," Simms agreed. He cracked his knuckles. "I'd like to give him a message or two to send to his boss… if there's anything left of him after Deliah's had her way."

The second mention of Deliah seemed to shake Gregory from his reverie. "Miss—Deliah? But she's in a right mess, if she's in with him." He brandished the paper. "An understanding? She's courting a kidnapping, there. And I thought…" He trailed off as he looked at Captain Ramos's face.

"Steady on," Simms said. "Miss Nimowitz is clever as a weasel and more twisty than a snake. I don't think you need spare much worry for her." If anyone always landed on her feet more than Captain Ramos, it was Deliah. He'd borne witness to the fact of it himself.

"Terribly clever people are his favorite," Gregory said, his grimness unabated. If anything, there seemed a terrible note of self-awareness in his voice. "Because they've all sorts of lovely ideas, and think they can't be tricked, see? This sort of thing isn't some lark for them. It's part of the operation."

"Captain?" Simms asked, beginning to feel a bit queasy at Gregory's insistent concern.

"All hands, Mister Simms," the captain said firmly. "We depart for Salt Lake immediately."

"Yes, Captain. Taking Diabola?" There was more life to her than he'd seen in months, but he was starting to wonder just what he'd prodded Deliah into doing. If something terrible happened, how much of her blood might be on his hands? No, he dismissed the thought. The captain quivered like a bloodhound at scent. It would be all right.

"And every gun we've got," the captain said.

THE ATMOSPHERE IN DIABOLA was a strange one, as the great engine thundered through the Rocky Mountains. Amelia, Lucius, and Little Wren were positively jubilant to be out and about work. Being told that they were after one of the near-mythical Rail King's men only cranked their excitement to a higher pitch, like they were big game hunters in the long-ago days before the Infection and they'd just spotted the spoor of a lion. Captain Ramos moved up and down the engine as if this were to be a normal raid, checking that ammunition was properly racked and ready, that machetes were properly sharpened, that all the boarding equipment was in top shape.

(Of course it all was in top form. What else had any of them to do for the last few months but sharpen their knives into oblivion, Simms thought with a hint of annoyance. Yet the normalcy of it all was more than enough to cheer him, as much as he was ever cheered.)

Gregory alone seemed immune to all of this, sunk into a grim and melancholy silence. He ignored the cup of tea that Simms brought him, and the second to replace the first. No amount of cajoling got more than a one-word response.

But what truly bothered Simms and kept him worrying at Gregory like a terrier with a rat, now that there was nothing to do but sway along with the engine as they rode the rails, was how he had known about DeLuc. As a matter of course, no one asked too many questions about anyone's past…but also as a matter of course, people who lived in each other's pockets tended to absorb that knowledge by a kind of psychic osmosis. For example, Simms knew that Amelia had been a trained opera singer, even if she got a bit vague about why she'd decided to decamp in the middle of a performance and run off with pirates. Lucius had worked as a miner just long enough to decide that it wasn't for him and he'd much prefer to put his pickaxe skills toward hitting rich fellows and taking their money. Little Wren had been dragged about the country as a carnival curiosity—who would have thought, a woman who could do maths, and one considered "savage" at that?—and made her escape at a precisely calculated moment. Of Gregory, Simms knew that he'd been an overly rowdy farmer's son obsessed with astronomy and other natural sciences…and that did little to explain anything, now.

Obviously, there was some sort of connection, and it was one that Captain Ramos knew about—not that it was any surprise she was seven steps ahead of Simms.

As he brought a third cup of tea to Gregory's look out perch to replace the second, now gone cold and still untouched, Simms grew tired of being subtle. It never worked for him anyway. "How do you know this DeLuc fellow?" he said, as he handed the cup over.

It was a good thing he'd kept hold of it, because Gregory's grip went slack. His face twisted like he was chewing on something that tasted horrible but couldn't quite spit it out. Finally, he said, "I worked for him, for a short time. And then I got out."

Simms considered pressing for more detail, but the man looked about to explode, and now was probably not a good time for it. The way Gregory had been acting, he was no friend of the

Rail King's now, and nothing motivated a person quite like the searing desire for revenge—Simms had observed that magic at work twice now. It had kept Cook alive when she ought to have been died, and powered Lucius out of the wilderness he'd been abandoned in. He nodded and wrapped Gregory's fingers around the cup of tea so he could safely let it go. "Glad you landed in a better crew, then."

Gregory nodded, his expression softening to something a little less dire. "I am, too."

The bigger question that became more pressing as they barreled down the western slope of the Wasatch Range was where exactly they were going. Deliah might be anywhere within the Grand Duchy of Salt Lake, and just rolling into the rail station with guns blazing didn't seem to be the best idea to Simms. More anxious than he'd ever admit aloud, he sought the captain in the cockpit, where she stood over Amelia and Little Wren at the controls. Since she rarely bothered the pilots of the great engine when she was confident of their competence, Simms took this as a sign that something was afoot. "Stopping soon?" he asked.

"We can hardly take Diabola into the main station," the captain said, dryly. "I presume you have Deliah's correspondence address?"

He ought not to have been surprised that she'd figured that out once her brain started working again, but Simms did succumb to a minor cringe of guilt. "I do." He had the letter that had instructed him to find the paper still tucked in his pocket.

"That will do as a starting place, then. Mister Little Wren, calculate for the spur off mile marker seventeen. That ought to keep Diabola sufficiently out of sight whilst we are in the duchy proper."

The small, dark woman nodded, pulling up another page of the maps and noting their speed. "Be about thirty-two minutes," she said.

"That will do. I'll want Mister Kinzer and Mister Cavendesh with us. We'll take the rail car down into the valley—see to it that we won't waste even a minute, Mister Simms."

Relieved that once more, there was a plan directing his life, even if he hadn't been privy to it, Simms headed back to Diabola's aft, to pick up Lucius so the both of them could prepare the rail car for release from the larger engine.

THEY PARKED THE SMALL rail car in a private berth at the central station of Salt Lake. Captain Ramos had left her distinctive, piratical frock coat behind on Diabola, though Simms fancied that the great stone angel that watched over the station, the less angry twin of the one on the great temple at the city's center, still looked down on her disapprovingly.

The address on Deliah's letter lead them to a part of the city Simms had never been in, not far from the temple square. The curved roof of the Salt Lake Tabernacle was visible over the bare spikes of the trees like a giant, floating boiled egg. The streets were still eerily similar to every other street in the Grand Duchy of Salt Lake enormously wide and on a grid so precise that it made Simms feel nervous. The difference was in the houses. Rather than gray-boarded tenements, there were both neat row houses, and farther down the street, multi-storied mansions, faced with brick or carefully-hewn, pink granite. The lawns, winter dead, were still neat, and the merry shrieks of children echoed down the streets. It also, Simms noted ruefully, smelled much better than the sulfur, garbage, and dank water stink of the poorer areas.

Deliah's address took them to one of the stone-faced row houses, the sort a lady might rent a set of rooms in for a season if her family were so inclined. Captain Ramos paused and turned to consider their motley group; their rough clothing marked them all as working class—and male—which would have had them fitting right in to the parts of the city Simms knew. Here, they were very out of place. She pinched the bridge of her nose and muttered, "I ought to have thought of this."

Amelia wrinkled her nose. "Haven't been here before, have we," she offered, by way of an excuse. "Even rich people need sweeps and people to clean out the gutters, though."

It wasn't the best of cover stories without them carrying any tools, but Captain Ramos gave a sharp nod. "Well thought, Mister Cavendesh. Though I think we shall still attempt to go in the back way."

An alley led behind the row houses, separating them from a set of carriage houses. As they turned into the alley, a few dogs half-heartedly barked, low and echoing, though for a minute Simms thought he heard the muffled yipping of some well-bred lady's purse-sized dog as well. He shuddered at the thought of it, since those ones tended to have very sharp little teeth and not enough brains to know when to stop biting.

Mercifully, none of the barking seemed to be coming from behind their target door. Less mercifully, the lane had human occupants as well—a housekeeper hanging washing on a line strung between the carriage houses, and a set of maids with brooms, who'd paused in their sweeping, most likely to gossip. Captain Ramos walked past all of them, touching her cap politely, as if this was the most natural thing in the world. Simms followed suit, keeping his head ducked in a vain effort to look a bit smaller.

The maids ignored both him and the Captain in favor of giving Gregory and Amelia little, flirtatious waves. The housekeeper seemed much less impressed. She rested her hands on her hips, stepping out into the lane. "You got business here?" she demanded.

"House number seven," Captain Ramos said. "Drains have been acting up a fright."

"Lady at number seven left yesterday." The housekeeper's eyes narrowed. "This is a nice neighborhood, you mind, and we don't want any trouble or rough sorts hanging around. City watch checks in on us regular."

The housekeeper was obviously the local busybody; Simms knew her type and had long learned that it was best to be the good side of such ladies…which was tricky, at times. They knew everything and also considered everything to be their personal business, ruling over their little territories like empresses. The news she'd so casually dropped was even more worrisome, however, though he kept his face stoically blank. Perhaps it wasn't a cause for concern—Deliah might have just moved on to whatever step occurred next in her grift.

Captain Ramos continued on, unperturbed, "Best time to be working on the drains then, innit? No one around to be in-con-ven-ienced." The last, long word, she broke into its component syllables and strung out for emphasis.

"You got any tools?"

"Smith's got 'em in his pack. Wire scrubs and the like, all wrapped in oilcloth since they stink a fair do. You want to see 'em?" Marta asked, gesturing Simms forward.

For a moment, Simms thought the housekeeper might as the pinched look on her face only intensified. Then she grimaced and shook her head. "I just hope you're not going to be about it all day, if you'll be making a mess. My Mister Graham in number eight gets in a terrible temper if anything disturbs his luncheon."

Marta touched the brim of her cap. "We'll do our best. And if you like, give the wall a firm thump when his lordship's comin' home and we'll knock off for a few hours."

The older woman relaxed, though she didn't quite smile. "That's very…neighborly of you."

No one else moved to stop them as they clattered up the steps to the back door of number seven. Captain Ramos was thankfully a quick enough hand at lockpicking that she might as well have had a key. Keenly aware that they were still being watched, Simms ushered Gregory and Amelia into the house ahead of him.

They all paused inside once the door had shut and simply listened for a moment, held in place by a gesture from Captain Ramos. Other than the occasional snap and pop of a house fighting against the brisk breeze outside, there was no sound. If someone else was here, they were very good at not being heard.

"Mister Cavendesh and Kinzer, start at the attic and work down," Captain Ramos said. As the two clattered off to comply, with the ease of long practice, Simms and the captain began their own search. They'd start from the ground floor, as this was the more likely place for there to be something to find.

The small kitchen was as expected: very little evidence it had been used, though with a bit of stale bread and a wrapped-up cheese still in residence. The one room meant for a live-in servant smelled of dust and had clearly not been occupied for some time. They moved on to the front parlor; the row house was furnished, and from what Simms had seen of Deliah when she wasn't pretending to be someone else for her own twisted purposes, it was certainly not in her style. Everything was ostentatious and dark, whereas she tended to have more of an affection for watercolors and things that involved flowers.

Captain Ramos pulled a magnifying glass from her pocket and then threw herself down on the carpet, crawling around and looking for whatever grain of dust might lead her to some brilliant conclusion about Deliah's whereabouts.

Simms, not seeing anything else that really screamed *yes I'm a bloody great wad of useful evidence* at him, started poking at the grate. He'd found interesting and occasionally useful things in grates and fireplaces over the years, because people did like to try and burn the signs of their wrongdoing and were shockingly terrible at it. "Stone cold," he observed, then picked up the poker as still a slightly better tool than his own large hands.

"Consistent with her having left yesterday."

"Right." He stirred the ashes, and noticed a few bits came up paler—shredded papers. He fished these out as delicately as he could. Lines of ink were still visible, here and there. "Been burning papers. That's…"

"Not like Miss Nimowitz at all, no. Or at least not in such a sloppy fashion. Is anything intact enough to read?"

Simms set the crumbling bits on one of the end tables and carefully stirred them. "Only a letter here or there."

"Annoying." Captain Ramos had reached the carpet near the door to the front hallway. "Someone's tracked in a bit of dust from the street. I'm seeing two distinct shoe sizes…neither of which I think are Miss Nimowitz's."

"How so?"

"Too large." The captain straightened up. "And if she was going to be coming in through this door, she'd be wearing proper lady's shoes."

"I don't like this," Simms said.

"Neither do I," Captain Ramos agreed. "Let's find her writing desk."

"Captain!" Amelia called down the stairs. "Found her room. You ought to see this."

The bedroom in question was up two flights of steps, a third set beyond leading to the attic. Someone had pulled the room's curtains aside, letting the ample, warm light of the autumn sun in. The scene revealed was chaotic, though not violently so. Clothing was strewn about and the wardrobe doors left open, revealing a few abandoned items. Captain Ramos took in the sight and immediately went over to the room's vanity, examining the top. She gently touched a stray, curling hair left behind on the white-painted wood.

"Haven't found a valise or anything," Gregory said.

"She took her hairbrush, even if she packed in haste," the captain said, almost meditatively. "And then either met with the two men in her parlor or was intercepted by them as she was already leaving."

"What of the papers, then?" Simms asked.

"What papers?" Gregory asked.

"There's a little desk in the corner of the attic," Amelia offered.

The captain's head jerked up and she turned and strode from the room. By the time the little group had clattered up the stairs after her, Captain Ramos was already minutely examining the blotter on the desk, a rather scuffed affair, and muttering to herself. The attic room was quite bare; other than the desk and chair, there were a few chests and an old wardrobe shoved against the opposite wall. The room's window didn't even have curtains. Simms noted, "Good view of the street from here."

Gregory tried the lids on all the chests, something Simms grumpily noted that he should have done before, and revealed they were all locked. He opened the wardrobe doors, which made a hideous creaking sound, and began poking at the yellowing, lacy frocks hanging within in a desultory fashion. Then Amelia's eyes lit on one of the open doors, and she rushed forward to pull a scrap of paper from it. "Captain?"

"Hm?" the captain didn't look up until Amelia had shoved the paper under her nose. "Is this Miss Nimowitz's handwriting?"

Captain Ramos seized on the paper immediately. "Yes."

Simms and Gregory crushed in to look over (or in Gregory's case, around) her shoulder. The note, in Deliah's neat handwriting, said: *Telegram sent to C. MR at Grand Duchy of Denver at 11:34. Paid: $2.13.*

"We must have just missed that," Simms said. "Shit." There wasn't really a good way to find out what had been sent in good time.

"I can't believe she'd pay that much for a telegram," Gregory said.

Captain Ramos was frowning. "Neither do I. And she's addressed this directly to me. Which she certainly would not do."

"So it isn't a real telegram?" Simms asked. He'd never been good at puzzles that he couldn't solve with a smash of his fist once they became sufficiently frustrating.

"Why would she leave a note to herself about it if it was?" Captain Ramos asked.

A normal person might write themself a note in lieu of a receipt. Deliah, Simms knew, was no normal person. "Why can't she leave a clear note?" Simms complained. "Something like, help I'm being taken by two massive tossers in hobnails, please come rescue me at such-and-such track junction?"

"They weren't wearing hobnail boots," Captain Ramos said absently. "From what I could see of the impressions the soles made, they were actually quite fine."

Gregory jerked as if stung. He made as if to grab the note, nearly ripping it when Captain Ramos refused to let go. "Could be a measurement of longitude and latitude," he said.

"Aren't nearly enough numbers, are there?" Amelia asked.

"Not if they're merely additions or subtractions to a known value," Captain Ramos said. She spun on her heel, almost bowling the other three over in her haste. "We need to return to Diabola immediately."

As they left the house, they made one final, quick sweep for anything else they might find. Simms's eye caught sight of a little basket by one of the chairs in the parlor. There was a cushion in it, fuzzed with a slight halo of white fur. Had Deliah brought her deceased aunt's tiny dog, Chippy, with her? And if she'd been spirited away by a set of well-dressed goons, would they have let her take the little dog along? In Simms's long experience with toughs who ran the full spectrum of sartorial quality, none of them had been particularly keen on household pets.

He frowned as they exited the row house, only listening with half an ear as Captain Ramos talked them past another stern-faced woman who'd come to beat out a few rugs. Dogs were barking in the distance again, most of them low and deep and promising sharp teeth for anyone who thought a short cut through their garden would be a good idea. But he heard it again, that higher-pitched yelp.

Was it familiar?

Simms wasn't the sort of dedicated observationist that the captain was. He tended to just listen to his instincts, particularly when it came to his instincts suggesting someone needed a good thumping. He broke away from the group and headed in the direction he thought the yelp was coming from.

"Simms?" Amelia said, too startled to remember they weren't supposed to be using their real names.

"I'll catch up," Simms said.

He ignored the shouted demand from the housekeeper with the big stick—perhaps not his brightest idea—and dodged around the carriage houses. Yes, there was that muffled yip again. Still, he felt a bit foolish as he called, "Chippy?"

The muffled yipping became absolutely frantic. Simms followed the sound to the carriage house it seemed to be coming from. Of course when he tried the small side door, it was locked. He shrugged to himself and put his shoulder into it, bouncing off the wood with a deafening *CRACK* that he wasn't certain was the door or his bones. He was getting too old for this nonsense, really.

A woman's voice rang out from the alley: "What are you doing? I'll have the city watch on you!"

Simms gave the door another firm slam. He caught himself on the frame as the door sprang inward with a tearing *crunch*. Perhaps half a second later, a little ball of white fluff launched at his chest. He scrambled to catch the little dog, who proceeded to frantically lick his chin while whining. From the whiff of air that came out of the darkness inside the disused carriage house, Chippy must have been trapped in there since Deliah had gone missing.

"It's all right," Simms said, awkwardly petting the tiny dog as he cradled him against his chest. Another angry shout, "Are you stealing someone's dog? Thief!" from the back alley propelled his legs into a lumbering trot. He needed to catch up to Captain Ramos anyway. "We'll find your...uh...mummy."

For all that his rescue of Chippy had been only a brief distraction, Simms barely caught up to Captain Ramos in time. His flight toward the train station had been slowed by Chippy wiggling frantically and wanting to get down at every block. He cursed himself for not taking a moment to find the dog's lead as they'd left the house.

Captain Ramos had only greeted the sight of the squirming little ball of white fluff with a raised eyebrow before telling Simms to secure the both of them. Her intention to push the rail car as fast as it could handle was obvious, and having Amelia also at the controls wouldn't exactly calm the situation; she had a thing about high rates of speed that would best be described as "unholy," had Simms believed in the concept of holiness to begin with.

Simms had done his best to secure Chippy with a harness improvised from a bit of twine and some puzzled, but willing help, from Gregory. The journey back to Diabola was been one of tense silence, broken only by the occasional cheerful yip.

Once they had returned to the great raiding engine, Captain Ramos left the rest of them to deal with securing the rail car.

When Simms caught up with her, she and Little Wren were hunched over one of the rail charts, Little Wren quickly writing equations and calling out coordinates to the captain.

"That puts us near but not in the Duchy of Missoula," Captain Ramos said. She traced her finger over the map. "There is a rail route very near."

Little Wren tapped her pencil on the paper. "Seems like the most reasonable course then." She glanced up at Simms, and offered, "All of the other permutations landed in the middle of water, or where your people think to be waste lands."

Which generally meant lands controlled by the native tribes, Captain Ramos had once told Simms. "Should I get the boilers heating, then?" Simms asked. He did his best to hold on to Chippy, who was squirming toward Little Wren, frantic to make friends with her. The little dog went into paroxysms of delight as she patted his head and let him lick her hand.

"Yes," Captain Ramos said, stretching the word out. She was thinking. "Mister Little Wren…I require a new set of calculations. I want maximum speed to that site. We'll dump the rail car here…and I need to know precisely how much coal we'll need between each way station. Not one lump more."

"Sir? We don't want to get stranded." This time of year, it would be quite cold in the mountains—and even worse as they neared Missoula.

"We won't," Captain Ramos said. "Mister Kinzer has informed me our target travels in luxury, eschewing speed. We're at least twice as fast as him. We will catch up." She smiled, baring her teeth, "And when we do, we shall take all of his fuel, and anything else that might interest us."

Working on that kind of a razor's edge didn't appeal to Simms in the slightest—but he was used to that, now. The captain was the risk taker, and right now she was more alive than she'd been in months. He swallowed his protests happily. Besides, if he was going to trust anyone to figure out the numbers, it'd be Little Wren. "I'll start dumping the weight, then."

"See that you do. And send Mister Cavendesh to me."

Diabola, while big and sleek for an engine, was quite small when it came to its passenger occupancy. Simms found Amelia having a cup of tea with Lucius in the engine's cramped armory and sent her forward.

Lucius looked at the wiggling dog Simms was trying to stuff into his waistcoat and remarked, "Recruits keep getting' smaller 'n smaller."

"But their enthusiasm is boundless," Simms said. "Come on. We need to pack everything that isn't nailed down into the rail car."

"Feeling the need for speed?" Lucius threw back the last of his tea.

"We're on the chase."

"Good. Glad things 'r gettin' back to normal." Lucius gave Chippy another long look, then relented and scratched the yipping dog's ears. "Even more normal than ever was before."

"Captain Ramos! Captain Ramos!"

Marta tensed at the tinny sound of Gregory shouting down the lookout speaking tube. She had been hyper-focused on the darkness in front of Diabola as they barreled along at the highest speed the engine could handle, but it was questionable if the track itself could. The raiding engine's headlamp made a bright cutout ahead in the darkness, showing glittering track and a stretch of dirt and scrubby plants. The black blanket of the sky, spread with stars and the hanging sliver of moon, was interrupted only by the blacker cutouts of mountains that marched along on either side of the track.

Marta had decided they should best run with the lamp lit, the better to look like an ordinary passenger car to the casual observer—and to warn away any human that might be wandering about on the tracks in the wilderness. The small slice of rugged scenery it showed them wasn't useful to Amelia or Little Wren, navigating the train by precise timing and chart. At Diabola's speed and mass, it wasn't as if they'd be able to stop in time for an obstruction on the track anyway. Around her, Diabola hummed and clanked and rumbled like a beast of steel rather than flesh.

"Captain Ramos?"

She released the back of Amelia's chair, took half a step back, and received a look of gratitude from the woman in return. She hadn't even noticed her own actions, a disturbing thing. This, at least, was different from how out of sorts she had felt lately; this was the focus of the hunt, a relief after having been so directionless. She turned to address the tube. "Yes, Mister Kinzer?"

"Warning lamps up ahead. Three yellow, four red. Track diversion for repair works."

Of course there was. There were always interesting little bumps in the pursuit of answers or prey. "How far ahead?"

There was a pause as Gregory presumably consulted his telescope. He called down, "Eleven miles. It's the western junction."

"Understood, Mister Kinzer, thank you. We will deal with it." She turned to look at Amelia and Little Wren, manning the controls. "You heard?"

Little Wren unrolled the map that she'd used to plot their course and traced over the colored lines with one finger. "That's the track we need."

Marta had already known that, but the confirmation wasn't unwelcome. "Then we shall have to divert."

"How much travel is this going to add in?" Amelia said. "We're going to need to think of way stations for coal."

Little Wren's blunt fingers moved over the map, tracing out routes. "Probably two hundred miles," she said. "We'll have to circle around on the upper side."

It was far too long; distance was time, and from what Gregory had told her of his tenure with the Rail King, and what Marta herself knew, time was of the essence. They must catch the Nieman's engine before it reached its destination. While she trusted Deliah to take care of herself to a certain extent, anyone could be badly outnumbered. "Unacceptable. We can't be far behind them now. Show me again." She watched with hawkish intensity as Little Wren traced out the route again. Then she stabbed her finger down, almost striking the woman's hand. "Here. This line will take us back to our planned route. We'll only lose…twenty miles, I estimate."

The two rail lines crossed at nearly right angles. Amelia glanced over, dismay showing on her face. "That can't be a proper junction."

Little Wren shoved Marta's hand aside. "It's a bridge," she said flatly.

"And Diabola is made specifically to jump tracks," Captain Ramos said. That was what she had designed the engine to do, built her up from the ground to do: run for short distances with no track, and jump onto tracks with the use of a multitude of hydraulic pistons and stabilizing springs.

"We haven't ever jumped off a bridge," Amelia said. Her expression was a mixture of fear and excitement.

"Do the calculations for the jump, Mister Little Wren, and I shall check them." Marta tapped the map. "It's a low bridge, only twelve feet. I'll have Simms get the pistons charged to our specifications. We have…" Her finger traced the line down to their current location, "Thirty-six minutes."

"Simms is going to shit himself sideways," Amelia said.

"Simms isn't the only one," came Gregory's tinny voice.

Marta couldn't help but smile, the expression feeling odd and unpracticed. Had it been so long since she'd felt this alive? Since she'd had something to pursue? And this, she was determined, would end well. They would catch up to Deliah, and they would provide her rescue, and there would be no ambiguity to the successful conclusion of this challenge.

She leaned over the back of Little Wren's chair and watched as the woman began writing calculations in her curious shorthand, something that had provided a pleasant but short-lived distraction for Marta to learn. She checked the pages as Little Wren handed them off but could find no fault; that was why she had invited the woman into the company, a vague promise to herself of great raids that she hadn't overcome her own inertia to plan before now. As she worked, Little Wren relaxed slightly, like a master settling into a well-known piano piece that made the world fall away. They were both in their element now.

Marta snatched up the last of the pages as Little Wren finished, reading over the angles and necessary pressures to achieve them. "We'll have to fire twice, then," she said.

"The interchange is too extreme, otherwise. Will the shocks on the road wheels handle the impact?" Little Wren asked. She was a woman of numbers and vectors and forces, not one so acquainted with steel.

"Better them than the regular carriage wheels," Marta said. If the impact destroyed the shocks entirely, it would be annoying to fix later, but livable now. The rail wheels were indispensable for their continued pursuit.

Amelia tapped the glass on the clock fixed into the control panel. "Twelve minutes."

It would be tight, but it would be enough time. Marta strode aft into the crew section, ducking to avoid low cabinets, now emptied of anything unnecessary. "Mister Simms!" she roared. "Mister Lamburt!"

Simms, who had been stuffed into a corner and snoring lightly, rocketed to his feet. Only a hasty grab kept Chippy from being catapulted across the room from his place on Simms's chest. "What? What is it?"

Captain Ramos thrust one of the pages at him. "See that the starboard pistons are charged, each to this precise specification."

Simms, still bleary-eyed, took the paper and squinted at it. "We're jumping track?" With his other hand, he stuffed the sleepily protesting Chippy into his waistcoat.

Marta considered telling him the entirety of the plan, just for the pleasure of watching him shout at her—she'd missed out on that recently as well, hadn't she, because all his shouting had been the annoying variety where he kept asking her questions she didn't wish to answer—but decided not to. His attention needed to be precisely on the numbers.

"Yes," was her only answer. At which point Lucius lurched into view like a monster from a penny dreadful. "Ah, Mr. Lamburt. I need you to secure Diabola to jump track. You've got ten minutes."

Lucius grinned, showing an impressive display of yellow, square teeth. "My favorite bit, after the fighting."

"You'll particularly enjoy this one, I think," Captain Ramos said. Lucius was just delightful in certain ways. She turned and squeezed herself into the narrow space that gave access to the port pistons.

Dimly, she heard Simms curse as he did the same, followed by a yip from Chippy. "You stay here, fellow. No place for dogs," Simms said.

The piston access was a mass of copper pressure lines and signal wires, strung haphazardly, but with just enough space between them for a limber person to thread themselves through. Marta did precisely that to get to the most forward piston and then slowly work her way back, using the valves at the end of those copper lines to build up a precise amount of steam pressure in each of the piston cylinders, indicated by the dial at the top of each. She had to set half the pistons to fire secondarily as well, since usually they were all meant to fire at once.

A sharp rap sounded on the metal wall behind her as she contorted herself around another piston. "Yes?" she shouted.

Lucius's muffled voice came: "Five minutes, Captain. With compliments from Mister Cavendesh."

"Thank you. See that all hands not currently working are secured."

"Will do."

There were three pistons left. She'd get them done with a few seconds to spare. The problem with needing precise pressures was that filling the pistons too much would lead them to be overcharged; overcharging would lead to an uneven jump—normally not a problem, but they also didn't normally leap off a bridge whilst simultaneously changing their vector of travel off parallel. Marta turned another valve, eyes fixed on the little needle behind glass atop the piston. One more down, then another. She was cutting it close, she knew, as she filled the final piston.

The alarm bell rang through Diabola.

Marta kept her eyes on the needle as it slowly rose. She twisted the valve shut and squirmed her way out of the piston space with less care for her person, catching skin and hair on the wiring as she went. If she was still in there when the train jumped, she'd be pulped.

"Captain!" Simms shouted from forward.

"Nearly there," Marta called, lunging two sections ahead. Gregory, Lucius, and Simms were already strapped into their safety harnesses, Simms with a strange round lump showing in his jacket, which happened to be squirming—ah, Chippy.

The alarm sounded again. "Brace!" Amelia shouted from the front of the engine.

Marta shoved her arms into the nearest harness and fumbled for the buckle, then gave up and roughly knotted the lines. It would have to—

With a metallic SLAM, Diabola leaped up and sideways. Twelve feet wasn't so far to fall as that. For the crew, accustomed to much shorter hops, time stretched out into an infinity of falling. Marta felt limbs become weightless, her shoulders pressed up against the harness. Simms's eyes went wider and wider as they continued to fall, the engine beginning to tilt slightly toward its heavier rear. A much quieter series of *snaps* echoed through the engine, vibrating into Marta's bones as the road wheels snapped down past the rail wheels.

The CRASH that followed was the hardest impact she'd ever felt, sending metallic groans and shrieks echoing through Diabola. There was a loud hiss and a high-pitched alarm bell began to ring. The engine listed crazily back and forth as Amelia struggled with the controls, trying to pull her straight, then closer to parallel with the new track.

"What in the—" Simms began.

SLAM. The second set of pistons went and Diabola jumped again. Gregory screamed. There were more snaps, not so neat in series, not enough of them, and then an instant later, CRASH. Diabola came back down on the rails. There was another metallic groan, and Marta felt it, the engine pulling unevenly. At least one of the road wheels hadn't retracted. She felt Diabola begin to overbalance, and cursed herself, fumbling for the safety harness. She couldn't be fast enough—

Another metallic groan, louder and more terrible, the sound of something being torn apart. A rattle along the undercarriage. And suddenly Diabola rocked back, settling onto the rails fully. After a strange, coughing hesitation, the engine began to pull again, accelerating.

Lucius whooped. "That was bloody brilliant!"

Simms hung, panting, against his own harness. "What did you do?" he asked hoarsely. Chippy, in the vicinity of his stomach, voiced his own feelings with a gurgling howl. "I think the dog just vomited into my coat."

Marta pried apart her hasty—and now much tighter—knot. Her hands shook—from adrenalin, she assured herself. She'd been right to not question her own engineering brilliance. "We jumped track," she said.

"That wasn't the half of it."

"Twice."

"Marta…" growled Simms.

"Off a bridge." On slightly rubbery legs, she staggered aft. "I need to check on the boiler." And a thousand other things that might have given under the strain. But the sound of Simms cursing behind her did bring a smile to her face. It really had been too long.

"Lights sighted!" The call was a barely muffled shout, too distorted by metal and Marta's earplugs for her to be able to identify it immediately. She finished tightening a bolt on a makeshift new stabilizer for the boiler and slid back out into Diabola's living space. Sweat dripped off the end of her nose and stuck her shirtsleeves to her arms in broad patches. Marta felt, a bit incongruously considering being contorted in a sweltering, cramped space, better than she had been in months. There was a problem—a fixable one—to be had, liberally spiced with urgent seconds ticking away.

"Be more specific," she called, as she pulled the wadded gauze from her ears.

Simms ducked into view through the compartment's doorway. "Rear marker lanterns on the horizon. Green filtered. Some sort of engine ahead, though we're still too far to get a good idea of the size."

Marta felt a stir of excitement in her gut, though she did her best to throttle that down. It might be their quarry. It also might be another engine on the rails, traveling for its own purposes. But at least they were going in the same direction, so there'd be no time wasted on a pullout to avoid a collision. The green lanterns meant they were under power. "Douse the headlamp."

"Already done."

"Speed?"

"Mister Kinzer estimates we're going at least twice its speed. Mister Little Wren says it'll still be a well over an hour before we catch up."

Which could be a different sort of problem, but one that could be addressed once they had a better idea what they were dealing with. "Well done. Anything else?"

"There's also a city, not too distant," Simms said.

She mentally reviewed the map. "Probably Idaho Falls." A client city of the Duchy of Missoula, Idaho Falls mostly functioned as an outpost for Missoula to keep an eye on any incursions by the Grand Duchy of Salt Lake. "Will we intercept the other engine before we reach—"

At that point, the alarm bell began to clang frantically; Simms jerked as if he'd touched an electrified fence. They both rushed forward, Marta still holding her wrench in her hand. "Report, Mister Cavendesh!" she shouted, before she'd even gotten to the front.

"Red lanterns! The engine ahead is slowing down…a lot!" Amelia shouted back. "We'll be on them in minutes."

Marta and Simms leaned over the two seats, both squinting into the dark as if that would show them anything. The lights of their potential quarry were still far-off, ruddy dots, though growing rapidly. Marta frowned. "We'd best hope that is the engine we seek, or we'll waste a great deal of time pushing it to the next pull-out." It was a complication that only held the potential to be annoying.

"There's a great deal of steam coming out of it," Gregory's voice came tinny through the speaking tube. "Might have burst a boiler or something. And—wait, I see someone. On the back. I think…it's Miss Nimowitz. Oh, and there's someone coming out after her. And…oh, right in the bollocks. And…dirty pool. Another one got her from behind. Dragging her back in."

Marta hadn't realized how tight her grip on the back of Little Wren's seat had become until the woman shot her a sharp look. It was an irrational sort of reaction, as if she could pull them across the rapidly shortening distance. "Speed at your discretion, Mister Cavendesh," she said. "Sound all hands!"

Amelia obligingly slammed her fist down on one of the buttons on the far side of the panel, and the alarm bell began to ring again, a slightly different sequence this time. Marta hurried aft, flung her wrench into an empty cabinet, and grabbed her pistols and machete. Simms and Little Wren were close on her heels, Lucius coming in from further aft where he'd been tasked with checking the bolts on the starboard pistons. "Fight time?" Lucius asked.

Marta snatched up her scarlet frock coat from where she'd left it draped over one of the harnesses. "If Miss Nimowitz leaves anything for us to do."

"Sure she will," Lucius said. "She don't believe in starting small trouble, that one."

A hefty *thud* echoed through Diabola, the engine's metal walls vibrating around them: Gregory had fired the big grappling hook mounted to the roof at their quarry. Perhaps not strictly necessary if Deliah had somehow scuttled the engine ahead, but a precaution that Marta approved of nonetheless. A moment later another sequence rang out on the alarm bell and Diabola abruptly slowed, causing everyone to stagger forward a few steps to grab the nearest convenient handhold. Standard procedure; get the hook embedded in the other engine, brake down to force them to a slow crawl to keep the grapple taut long enough for a relatively safe boarding. Only now Diabola ground to a full halt, which felt odd indeed after so many hours of forward motion.

"This'll be an odd one," Simms commented as he offered a wickedly sharp metal hatchet over to Little Wren, who hung it on her belt. "Fighting at a standstill, I mean. Feet on the ground."

Ping ping ping—bullets bouncing off the raiding engine's heavily armored skin. "That's familiar at least," Marta said dryly. She considered the problem—they had a Gatling gun now, mounted next to the grapple. Gregory could lay down some suppressing fire, but if they had the freedom of that solid ground of Simms's, so would the enemy...but if they weren't moving at all, it also gave them far more time to complete their raid. There wouldn't need to be a rapid transit back and forth between the engines. Marta smiled.

Simms seemed to take her expression in with a great deal of trepidation, which was a pleasure all its own. "What." The word came out as a flat statement rather than a question.

"This is the opportunity I've been waiting for to test those sulfur flares."

A competing set of emotions fought for primacy in Simms's expression: confusion dismay, outrage, fear, annoyance. Annoyance ultimately won, as it usually did with him. "I thought you said you hadn't gotten them to stop exploding. And that we offloaded them when we dumped the rest of the excess weight."

"Yes and no to the first statement, no to the second," Marta said cheerfully. Life felt wonderfully normal. "I packed the latest iteration of the design. And if they do explode, they'll make an even better distraction."

A few minutes later, the flares were set, and the crew was ready, armed to the teeth and eager. The gunfire from the other engine had slowed to a few nearly random pings here and there, as their opposites settled down to conserve ammunition while keeping up a reminder that they were, indeed, armed.

"Goggles on," Marta said, and watched as the rest of the crew pulled on the sets she'd made for the occasion, with glass so smoked that it appeared black. It gave everyone a curious look of having round, bottomless pits in place of eyes, though even that semblance of humanity quickly disappeared as they wrapped their faces with leather scarves or hoods.

"Can't see a bleeding thing out of these," Gregory complained.

"You can flip those lenses up once you're on the engine and have discarded your flare," Marta said. Her own glass was still of the transparent sort, since she needed to be able to see to get them lighted. She sparked her portable welding torch into light and held it up. Lucius, ever eager to be in the fight—and probably the man most insensible to bullets—was the first in line, brandishing the hard paper tube of his flare.

"Count to ten," Marta said, and lit the fuse with her torch. "As soon as they get over the shock and start shooting near you, toss it away."

"Aye." The fuse caught with the spit of white sparks and Lucius lumbered past her sight range. She lit the next fuse quickly, and the next. When she'd gotten to the third—Gregory's—the room around her lit bright white as Lucius's flare spat into full life. She hastily pulled her dark lenses down, and still had to blink the glare from her eyes as she continued lighting fuses.

Behind her, there was a pause, followed by frantic firing from the light-blinded defenders. The rest of the crew piled out in absolute silence—no reason to risk giving their opponents sound to shoot at. The night filled with angry chemical hissing.

Marta lit her own fuse last and leaped out of Diabola. Her feet hit a railroad tie jarringly; her teeth snapped together, and she tasted blood. Bullets pinged off Diabola behind her; she saw in the illumination of the flares, cut down to a manageable level by the blackened lenses, that the rest of the crew had already discarded theirs on the ground. A bullet tore through the sleeve of her coat, scoring a hot line across her forearm, as Marta drew back to throw her own flare directly at the engine ahead. It struck the railing on the caboose and exploded in a flash of white fire that left the metal burning.

Sulfurous smoke stung the back of her throat as she sucked in a breath. Marta drew her saber and charged at the engine. The crew followed her, able to see in the now brightly-lit confusion thanks to their dark lenses. Wild shots cracked around them, throwing up gouts of sand and chips of rock. Marta saw the figures of men trying to put out the fire on the railing, beating at it with sacks that must not have been nearly damp enough. She leaped up and through the white flames, her saber taking one of the would-be fire fighters in the shoulder, the impact of it rattling up her arm. She drove her fist into the second man's face as she jerked her blade free. Screams joined the ongoing cacophony of the night.

Someone tried to close the door into the engine; she kicked it back open before the latch could engage and felt it rebound off yielding flesh. Simms brushed by her to slam his shoulder into the rebounding door, making doubly certain whoever was behind it would stay down.

They streamed into the narrow corridor of the engine, trailing dirt and ash on the plush carpet. Marta flipped her darkened lenses up so she could better see the brightly-lit interior, decorated in crimson and bronze. More men, none wearing any kind of uniform aside from a bronze-colored embroidered sash, stumbled in from the doors along the hall, another dropping from the hatchway above as they realized the engine had been breached. They reeled, squinting around them; in this, Marta's plans had worked perfectly, the bright light of the flares leaving horrible after-images in eyes that had already been widened against the dark.

The fight became the standard boarding fare, with the advantage that one side could see far better than the other—their only advantage, because they were far outnumbered. Marta plastered herself against the wall to let Simms and Lucius barrel through, trampling many of the defenders as they did. It cleared a path to allow the rest of the crew to move further in. While it strung out their line, it also prevented them from being bottlenecked at the door. Marta stayed hot on Lucius's heels even as Simms tackled a man coming from a door, sending them both sprawling into the room. A quick glance identified it as an armory—definitely good for Simms to take control of.

"Lucius, take the stairs to the upper deck and keep anyone there inside," Marta said, her voice made husky from smoke.

"Aye," he said again. He shoved his machete back into his belt and drew both his pistols, cutting across in the rather ostentatious—if still small—room that served as a lobby for a corkscrewing wooden staircase. Every possible surface that could receive gold leaf glittered, and there were lions and eagles rampant everywhere one looked. Marta kept running. Her destination was the front of the train. Whether Deliah would be there or not, taking control of the engine would ensure that she wasn't abducted a second time, and her rescuers with her.

Pistol shots rang out behind her, and she ignored them. The rest of the crew could take care of themselves, mostly, and needed to in this instance. Ahead, she heard the sound of metal thumping on metal. She slammed another dividing door open with her shoulder to see a rather Simms-sized man attacking the metal door that probably led to the control room with a wrench. He spun around, hefting the tool, and charged at Marta without pausing.

Marta parried a bone-cracker of a blow from the wrench and ducked aside from another swing. This man must not have been on the outside defense when the flares went up. He seemed able to see her just fine. She drew a pistol with her other hand and had it knocked stingingly from her grasp—when had she gotten so slow? Right, when she had spent such time closeted in her lab, escaping fresh air and exercise while failing to escape all her more internal conflicts. She cut at the man's knees, at least forcing him back a step, but then had to duck the wrench again. It left a sizeable dent in the wooden paneling where her head had been a second before. Glass from what had once been an electric lantern showered over her shoulders.

A metallic *CLANG* rang out, which seemed strange, since the man was hefting the wrench back up and had not yet swung… and he pitched down face first onto the carpet, revealing Deliah standing behind him, a long lever that trailed wires from one end held in her hands. Her hair was in wild disarray, half-fallen from its pins, her lips parted in a snarl and her eyes were shining.

She threw the lever down on top of the man and then stepped on top of him to reach Marta. Deliah's hands came out to grab her lapels and pull her in for a desperate, bruising kiss that sent a shock all the way to Marta's toes. Her saber fell from her hand so she could get an arm around Deliah's waist; she noted with a corner of her mind that wasn't engaged in a long and frantic kiss that Deliah was wearing only a night shift and her skin was quite warm beneath the fabric.

Deliah finally pushed her back and gulped air so she could demand, "What took you so bloody long?"

"Simms didn't get your message until you'd been gone from Salt Lake for nearly a day," Marta said, feeling slightly defensive. "I can hardly deduce there's a problem without any data."

"I did write to you before that," Deliah said with asperity, though her tone didn't quite match the kiss she pressed on Marta's jaw and then neck.

Marta swallowed against an uncharacteristic twist of shame and something darker that clogged the back of her throat. "I've had other distractions on my mind," she managed a bit hoarsely.

"Oh, am I only a distraction?" Deliah asked.

"That isn't—" Marta's clumsily forming excuse, too tangled in too many things that she hadn't even known how to put into the written word, was interrupted by a loud series of *thunk*s and *clang*s overhead. Then the ceiling began to move in a most curious fashion, rushing by. Marta ducked down out of instinct, taking Deliah with her and covering the woman's head with the questionable shield of her arms.

Something slammed down ahead of them, shaking the engine, and cool air rushed in from the night sky suddenly visible overhead.

"Uh… Captain?" Lucius called up the hallway. "I think they done a runner."

Marta straightened, Deliah coming to her feet with her, and peered forward to see lights beginning to accelerate away. The engine had separated into two pieces, with the top half apparently capable of independent motion and escape. "Damn. I hadn't thought to build something like that yet, myself," Marta said.

Deliah tugged insistently on Marta's coat and captured her for another kiss, enough to halt the schematics beginning to form in her mind and scatter them away entirely.

Without Marta's prompting, the crew went about their business efficiently. The remaining guards were rounded up, their hands and feet tied with loops of twine and rope and deposited in the various sleeping compartments. Another bit of rope tied all the door handles for those compartments together, just in case anyone proved ingenious or flexible enough to slip their bonds. The rest of the engine was quickly ransacked, anything marginally shiny and thus potentially of value taken back to Diabola and stowed in the empty cabinets. The remaining coal was also taken, managed by Gregory and Lucius, who rigged a temporary, but not badly engineered conveyor, to steal it as quickly as possible. Marta felt quite pleased at their level of initiative.

After checking on the progress of the raid, Marta closeted herself in what remained of the engine's control room, its roof gone and several panels smashed by the escape of the engine's top half. It was, she realized quickly, not even a proper control set up; the engine's functions must have been run from the now-missing second floor, with this as a backup. Still, it proved a rich trove of insight from the standpoint of engineering and considering the mind that had created this machine, showing a strict perfectionism very different from her own slapdash style. Marta made free to partially dismantle the remaining control panels so she could get a good look inside at the wiring and mechanical layout.

The person—presumably the Rail King himself—who had designed and overseen the construction of these devices had an ordered mind in a way at odds from her own. She didn't think this person, who layered all things so intricately, would feel as comfortable as her rigging changes or repairs on the fly. In fact, the existence of this backup set of controls, capable of driving the entire engine and not just the lower half, spoke volumes of both the resources available to her opponent, and a certain linearity of thinking. If something went wrong, his preference was not to effect emergency repair, but rather to switch to an entirely parallel and equally perfected system.

"Did you see this, darling?"

It took Marta a few seconds to process that Deliah must be speaking to her. She extracted her head from the guts of the control panel. "What?"

"This." Deliah tapped a part of the wooden paneling, which sounded suspiciously hollow. It popped open under her fingers.

Marta came over to inspect the contents: a telegraph of sorts, she realized after a moment. "Internal communication?" she said.

"Not that I ever saw in use. We shall have to look…" Deliah lifted the telegraph back, and its transmission wire ended in a box that, when opened, proved to be a series of wires and metal tubes secured to the substrate of the box, and a coil of wire that lacked the tension of a spring that disappeared up into the recesses of the wall. Deliah looked at Marta, one eyebrow arching up. "Seen its like before?"

It was familiar, in a vague way; she recalled seeing a paper that posited this sort of device, published a few years ago. "Wireless, perhaps."

"That much is apparent."

"No, I mean perhaps it transmits a signal through the air." After a moment of consideration, Marta used a pair of rubber-handled wire cutters to free the telegraph and its attached box from the cabinet, by severing the electrical wire and the much stiffer coil…perhaps its antenna, if she recalled correctly. She handed the device, which was about the size of a large bread box, to Deliah, who tucked it under her arm with an amused look.

In the device's absence, a cunningly-made little door in the already hidden compartment became apparent. Pried open with a knife, it revealed a leather-bound book.

"Nieman had a book like that in his personal belongings," Deliah remarked. "I'd stolen it and put it in my own chest, but it's…" She glanced up. "Out of reach now, I'm afraid."

"A good find then," Marta said. She flipped the book open, noting neat columns of numbers and strings of letters. "Do you know what it's for?"

"Not yet."

"So it isn't what you were after?"

"I'm not sure, honestly. You know that my greatest trade is in information. I intended to gather all I could, and then sort it out later."

Marta glanced up at Deliah's suddenly very neutral expression. She'd never realized how often Deliah let her amusement with the world show, even if only with her eyes, until now. "Didn't go as you planned?"

Deliah's lips thinned out. "I didn't intend to be abducted, if that is what you mean. Nieman said that the Rail King wanted to see me since he'd heard I had such a good head for puzzles, and apparently that isn't an invitation a lady ought to decline."

"Did they hurt you?" The question came out harsher than she'd intended. She was quite tired of people being hurt, sick with it, perhaps.

"Oh, he was working himself up to try. That's why I decided it was time to stop the engine and take my leave." Deliah reached over and closed the book, trapping one of Marta's fingers in the process. "Will you tell me what happened, while you were in the plains?"

"Now is hardly the time," Marta snapped. Such discussions were hardly useful at the best of times, and there were much better things to do now.

Deliah snorted. "Will it ever be the time?" She tugged the little book away and tucked it into a hidden pocket in her skirt. "Is it something to do with del Toro? It doesn't require much genius to realize that his supposed heroic death coincided with your time out there. Though I find it particularly confusing that idiot Douglas didn't try to pin it on you whether you were there or not."

Marta grimaced, wishing she had the solid barrier of that little book back. She could look at its still-indecipherable codes and perhaps that would chase away the images that sprang to mind instead: the smug look on del Toro's face, the sudden surprise when she'd pushed him, his solid form disappearing out of sight, down the cliff, and her own wild expression momentarily reflected in her old enemy Colonel Douglas's eyes.

Deliah touched her cheek. "Yes, I rather thought it was something to do with that."

Before Marta could formulate a response, caught between confusion and feeling quite insulted, Gregory shouted down from the truncated engine walls: "Running lights sighted! Big engine, probably military! Coming in from Idaho Springs."

"That didn't take them long," Deliah said.

"Money has a way of making the slowest bureaucracies move faster," Marta said dryly. "Good of Mister DeLuc to leave us such an excellent track blockade, however." Deliah's answer was a sharp laugh as she turned toward the rear of the engine. "Mister Kinzer! Sound the retreat!"

Simms made certain to count every nose present on Diabola twice before he gave Amelia the all-clear to take them away. They released the grapple, and with the sulfur flares still sputtering bright-white before them, went into rapid reverse. They wouldn't be able to change directions for quite some way, but that was a challenge for Amelia and Little Wren, he figured. The two women would have to navigate Diabola around the works that had shut down part of the track and safely back toward the Grand Duchy of Denver. After years of running the crew, he was finally getting the hang of delegating his authority and only feeling a little uncertain in the stomach about it.

He let Chippy out of the little storage cupboard he'd shut the dog up in during the raid—while it was no doubt claustrophobic and unpleasant, it was a better alternative to the poor animal getting shot or running off into the wilds, never to be seen again. Chippy just about threw himself into Simms's arms. "Still happy to see me," Simms said, as if the dog understood plain English. "Bet you'll be even happier in a minute."

He tucked the tiny dog under one arm and followed the sway of the engine as he made his aft, to where Captain Ramos and Deliah had retreated. As he'd expected, before he'd even reached the stripped-down workshop that sat between the spare bunk room and the throbbing heart that was Diabola's engine, Chippy began to squirm and yelp in his arms. It was all he could do to keep the animal contained until he got through the doorway.

Deliah looked up from the papers spread before her, pencil going loose in her fingers. She held out her arms; Chippy used Simms's chest as a springboard and launched himself directly into her bosom, where he immediately began to lick her chin and wag his entire body.

"There you are," Deliah murmured, using the special tone of voice that Simms recognized as one reserved for babies and particularly charming animals. "I'm so glad those mean, scary men didn't hurt you. And Uncle Simms took good care of you, didn't he?" She directed a look at him from under her lashes.

Simms crossed his arms and shrugged. He glanced over at Captain Ramos, who had a small, leather-bound book in her hands and hadn't been distracted in the slightest by the reunion going on next to her. "What are you up to, then?"

"As of yet, I'm not entirely certain," the captain said. "Divining a purpose for these codes, I suppose."

Deliah settled Chippy firmly on her lap and returned to her papers. Simms edged a little closer to see what looked like a web of rivers, perhaps, or…a rail line network. He didn't immediately recognize the shape of it, but navigation had never been his strongest suit. "We've got our own charts, if you want to see those."

"I'll want to compare them soon," Deliah said. "So if you wouldn't mind, that would be lovely."

Annoyed that he'd volunteered himself for the task when all he'd really wanted was to remind Deliah that he was capable of independent thought, Simms went to fetch the charts, which he then had to wait for until Little Wren was quite done with them. He returned expecting a snippy comment or two about getting lost in the engine, but Deliah only accepted the charts with a murmured, "Thank you."

He still wasn't sure how he felt about it, Deliah treating him like he might be a person instead of an occasionally useful bit of furniture.

"Yes, I think this is about right. I do remember the mile marker labels, even if I haven't gotten everything to perfect scale," Deliah said. She unrolled the charts, swaying with the motion of the particularly vicious curves—they must be in a canyon—that they were now traversing, and selected a particular one, which Simms recognized as the area around the Duchy of Missoula. She put one of her own sheets of paper next to it. A bit miniaturized, it did resemble the chart…but with quite a few extra lines. "I only regret I wasn't able to take Nieman's original charts, but I did get a good look at them."

Marta let the little book drop to her lap and leaned forward, the look on her face calculating. "That's quite a few unmarked lines."

Simms, not wanting to be left out of the conversation, reached out to not quite touch one of the lines that didn't appear on both charts. "These?"

"I shouldn't be surprised that the Rail King has private rail lines," Captain Ramos said. "We've built our own here and there, after all. But so many? How does he keep them hidden?"

"That, I don't know. I thought it might have something to do with the code book, but…"

Simms considered the chart. "We're not too far from one of the junctions, and Mister Kinzer says no one seems to be pursuing us. Could have a little look-see."

"What a lovely idea, Simms," Captain Ramos said. "I'm so glad I've at last instilled a sense of adventure into you."

It wasn't really that, he protested internally. It was that after months of Captain Ramos acting like a perturbed ghost of herself, things were finally back to normal, in all its terrifying glory. He rather wanted to keep it that way. But rather than voice those thoughts, he simply took Deliah's version of the chart page up to the control room to let Little Wren and Amelia know there'd been a slight change of plans.

THE JUNCTION WAS EXTREMELY well hidden—for a railroad junction. They were close to a set of black rock-topped hills on one side, a low valley filled with desert brush stretched out on the other. The hills were covered with scrubby pine trees, and a few of those trees had their branches artfully arranged in front of a piece of impressively well-painted canvas that gave the appearance of an empty gulch. Had they been passing by at full steam and not known precisely where to look, none of them would have been able to spot it…even if the effect was a bit comical at a standstill and up close. The private tracks themselves were quite visible where they met the public line, but easy for the mind to dismiss as a long-abandoned spur.

With no other engines in sight, and the sun creeping just above the horizon, Captain Ramos ordered Diabola stopped at the junction so that she could disembark and examine it. Simms, though no great engineer himself, joined her with Deliah, who still clutched Chippy to her chest. Gregory climbed down the side of Diabola and stood nervously nearby, his hat in his hands as Captain Ramos looked the track over.

"There isn't a switch to be seen," Captain Ramos commented. "So even if one knew of this junction, switching to the other track would be…difficult. I suppose it could be forced." She squatted down to examine the tracks more minutely, her goggles pulled over her eyes and the magnification loupes down. "Though it looks like it's been done before. There are tool marks on the tracks. Pry bar, most likely." She looked up at Gregory then. "What are you looking for, Mister Kinzer?"

Gregory was poking through the brush, his shoulders hunched. "Should be a box around here, somewhere," he answered.

"A box?"

"About the size of bread box, I think. Not sure where it would be. But it's the magic box that makes the tracks work." He shrugged. "That's what they always said."

Captain Ramos waved the rest of them forward. Simms moved the canvas aside—it was heavier than it looked—and they spread out to begin looking for the so-called magic box. Deliah set Chippy down to let him have a bit of a run around and take care of his business. Thin gold stripes glittered on the ties for the previously-hidden track as it disappeared between the rock walls.

Simms made the lucky discovery by grace of the direction he had gone and his friendship with Chippy. As he walked toward the canyon wall rather than along the tracks, Chippy trotted along next to him, feathery little tail waving happily. Simms noticed a line of exposed, black-wrapped wire cutting out of the earth and followed that to a gray-painted wooden box on a pole, which Chippy happily made a great deal of water on. As he opened his mouth to call to the captain, Deliah said, "There's a mechanism welded to the track, and a set of hydraulic rams concealed by the ties. Buried, but there must have been rain recently to wash them out."

"Might have something to do with this box," Simms called. "Got a wire running from it. To it. Whichever. Stop it, Chippy, you'll fry yourself like a sausage."

The rest of the group crowded around a moment later. Captain Ramos produced a small screwdriver and began to pry the box apart. Simms stood back to let her, under the principle that if someone was going to accidentally blow them all up, he'd much prefer it was the captain and not himself.

Inside, the box was crammed with more wires in a dizzying configuration that reminded Simms of nothing so much as a plate of spaghetti, or Xonghua black bean noodles. Captain Ramos poked around in it carefully, her expression intent. "I've no doubt this controls the mechanism. Probably to warp or disturb the track if someone who isn't of the Rail King's group attempts to use it. I saw some scarring on the opposite wall of the gulch and found some scattered metal debris. At least one engine has been derailed here, though long ago, perhaps scavenged after it had been downed."

"There's no buttons on the box or anything," Simms observed. If it was a trap, it had to be disarmed somehow.

"There don't need to be," Gregory said quietly.

"How is the trap sprung, Mister Kinzer?" Captain Ramos asked.

Gregory's words seemed to catch in his throat and he looked down at his shoes, shoulders hunching again. The captain directed a rather penetrating look at the top of his head, which was completely wasted on him.

"Wireless, perhaps," Deliah said. "That does seem to be the theme."

"Next you'll be saying it runs on fairies," Simms muttered.

"Unlike fairies, electricity exists and is invisible to the eye." Captain Ramos tapped the screwdriver against her lips. "Salt Lake," she finally said. "I recall the paper I read now, about a similar device. It was published there. I think speaking to the author might provide some insight."

"About what?" Gregory asked, sounding strangely alarmed. "We already rescued Miss Nimowitz—pardon me, miss, helped you finish rescuing yourself. Time we should be getting home, I think."

"This could prove a boon for us, should we figure out how these devices work," Captain Ramos said.

"Or could start a war with him," Gregory said. "Captain, I never…please. Please don't do this."

For all that his words were simple, his fear was obvious even to Simms. Captain Ramos regarded Gregory keenly, then gave a small nod. "Scientific inquiry only."

"For now," Deliah murmured, though everyone at least pretended to ignore her.

There was something quite wrong with Gregory's demeanor, Simms thought. But now was not the time to try to buck him up, not in front of Captain Ramos and Deliah. Those two together were enough to give any man the vapors, let alone one who already had something troubling him. "Give me a chance to telegraph Cook as well, I suppose, let her know we're late and not dead." He could recall some of the items the indomitable director of domestic details at the Roost always wanted from the Grand Duchy of Salt Lake; he'd do a bit of shopping for her while the captain had her incomprehensible conversation with a scientist who was no doubt stuffy, utterly mad, or both.

"That's the spirit," Captain Ramos said.

Simms scooped Chippy up in his arms; after a raised eyebrow from Deliah, he hastily handed the dog over and tucked his thumbs under his suspenders as if they'd always been there. "And I'll detail Lucius and Amelia to pick up all the weight we abandoned while we're at it, shall I? Keep them out of trouble."

Because of the present crew, other than Captain Ramos herself, those were the two most likely to end up in the gaol.

But Captain Ramos was already walking ahead, her attention fixed on the next step of her plan. Simms sighed and followed along.

A relatively brief visit to the scientific library at the austere yet angel-bedecked University of Deseret provided Marta with the paper she had remembered. The speed of the visit was mostly driven by Deliah, who had insisted on joining her. Marta had sufficient men's clothing of the right sort of dusty academic look to outfit both of them, which allowed them both into the library.

While Marta had been distracted by an unfamiliar volume of chemistry experiments, Deliah had taken it on herself to find the experimental treatise in the *Proceedings of the Academy of Natural Sciences of the Greater Western Duchies* from four years prior, going from Marta's recollection of the contents. The text itself was even more useful than she had recalled: a theoretical exploration of the possibility that electric waves might be generated and projected across air rather than wires. This was a well-known dream of all engineers; far more controversial was the author's proposal that electricity and magnetism were inextricably linked, and with that linkage the means for a wire-free communication could be achieved. The next several volumes of the *Proceedings* contained several letters in protest of this wild idea from other scientists who dismissed the author as an 'unknown hack.'

The treatise had a name on it—Dr. Javerle Smith-Ness—and an address that was merely a box at the central post office. Another change of costume and the acquisition of a few documents that

Deliah had hidden in a safe deposit box in the main bank saw to that difficulty. Under the guise of male postal inspector and assistant, they were able to access the ownership records for the postal boxes. The address provided led them on a merry chase through three other intermediaries. Whoever Dr. Javerle Smith-Ness might be, they obviously did not want to be found.

Simms and Gregory waited down the street from the last link in the chain of addresses, a solicitor's office that had required Marta to play distraction whilst Deliah slipped into the claustrophobic back room filled with files. The two men had, by some pure form of instinct, located a woman selling sausage rolls on a nearby street corner and acquired two each. They stood in a patch of sunlight shining down between the buildings; it was quite warm for a winter day, at least in the sun.

"What's the next step, then?" Gregory asked, gesturing with the half-eaten sausage roll he held in one hand. The other hand was still occupied by an as yet untouched sausage roll.

"Further out to the edge of the city," Deliah said, "If I'm remembering correctly." She pulled a slip of paper from the pocket of her skirt; she'd pulled on a coarse skirt and blouse after burgling the file room and blended in seamlessly with the working-class women going about their business.

Marta and the men leaned over to look at the address written thereon, Simms managing to dribble some crumbs from one of his sausage rolls on it as he did so. Deliah made a little moue of distaste and shook the paper clean.

"No idea," Gregory pronounced. "Never spent much time in this duchy. Just wanted to feel like I was helping."

"Nowhere I've been," Simms said. "Thank goodness."

Marta knew the city well; she'd spent enough time digging around in it for various bits of intelligence to do with hijack-ready shipments. And really, it was one of the easiest cities to know, as it was on a strict grid system. "Very much on the edge of the city," she agreed. But it was also toward the edges that some of the wealthiest denizens had their houses, since that was where the largest plots of land could be had. "Curious."

"Is that a good or bad 'curious?'" Simms asked suspiciously.

"We shall see," Marta answered.

Where the address took them earned its 'curious' and raised it by an 'interesting.' They found themselves in front of a manor house, one well-cared-for but obviously aging, its decorations at least fifty years out of date. Rather than the lush gardens the homes of the upper class normally sported—very much the same sort of status symbol here as they were in the Grand Duchy of Denver due to the low average rainfall of both—the grounds visible through the plain, wrought-iron fence were filled with carefully placed boulders of pink granite, black-red basalt, and creamy marble, as well as sculptures of carved stone, metal, glass, and fired clay.

Most of the visible sculptures were people, arranged in religious scenes, and a statue of the angel Moroni stood dutifully at the gate, his rather judgmental gaze directed toward the enormous form of the central temple, dimly visible in the distance. Red sandstone, familiar from their own side of the Rocky Mountains, made paths between beds of gravel and sand that seemed to have been carefully shaped and raked.

More interesting was the sign on the firmly-closed gate:

House for Unwed Sisters

Ring Bell for Service

Only Suitable Visitors, Please

Deliah made a rude noise as she took in the sign. "I always wondered what they did with the women who dared not marry and populate the duchy for the church."

"Seems peaceful up here at least," Simms offered.

Marta hummed under her breath, reserving her judgment for now. Considering the paper that had led them here, she had little doubt there was far more to the house than it appeared. The sign indicated a button to press rather than a rope to ring a bell; Marta did so and heard the muffled but still musical sound of chimes. "I don't see a wire going to the house from here," she remarked.

"It might be buried," Deliah offered.

"Perhaps."

After a few minutes of waiting, during which Simms and Gregory became increasingly anxious, the front door of the house opened and an impeccably—if shabbily—dressed man emerged. He took his time walking down the path; once he arrived at the gate, he regarded the small group through a set of spectacles perched on his nose before settling the bulk of his glowering suspicion on Simms and Gregory.

"Yes, what brings you to this simple home? If you…gentlemen are here to drop off this lady, I will need to see a properly signed letter of guardianship."

"What? We…no. Certainly not. I'd never…" Gregory said, stumbling over his words in his haste. Marta reflected that she ought to have primed him with a false story or two first. Simms clamped a hand on his arm to get him to quiet down.

"Then what do you want?" the man snapped. "This is a home for the unfortunate, not a place for gawkers."

Marta examined the man on the other side of the gate, part habit and part curiosity. Observations as to his handedness or eating habits weren't terribly useful at the moment. Observations as to the state of his neat mustache, as someone who had worn false facial hair on many an occasion, did give her more of a grasp of the potential situation. And his posture, that of defender rather than officious gaoler, sealed her approach.

"Javerle Smith-Ness," Marta said. She was pleased to see the man start slightly at the sound of her undisguised voice. "Not her real name, I presume. But nevertheless, I should like to speak with her, as an admirer of her theories."

The man blinked rapidly, lips pursing. "And what of the rest of you? Also admirers?"

"Dabbler, really," Deliah said.

"Just along for my good health," Simms said. "I wouldn't know a science if it bit me on the arse."

The man's lips twitched, the expression quickly suppressed. "You two can wait out here," he said to Simms and Gregory.

"No," Marta said firmly. "She'll want to talk to Mister Kinzer."

"And the big fellow?" the man asked, a bit desperately.

"Think of him as my shadow," Marta answered. "Only large and gingery and with a sweet tooth."

"Thanks for that," Simms muttered.

Reluctantly, the man let them in and led them around toward the back of the house. As soon as they were out of sight of the fence, behind a brick garden wall, the decoration scheme changed drastically. The subject of the sculptures shifted to be mostly of women, with a few animals or far more abstract and fluid pieces between. Marta caught Simms hastily averting his gaze from a rather accurate representation of a plump female form rendered in glazed red clay, the face of the figure smooth and blank.

Behind the wall there were also an array of small outbuildings, and an old carriage house and stable had been converted into an open-air blacksmithing workshop. And at last, there was more life visible than could have been imagined from the front. A multitude of women aged from youth to old age, dressed in plain and humble clothing that might have passed for nuns in a different context, filled the area. Some sat in small groups, sewing or spinning thread. Others moved around the workshop, their sleeves rolled up and dresses covered with leather aprons. One worked at a block of stone, while two others sat at potter's wheels, their hands red with clay to the elbow. The air was filled with merry chatter, which quickly died to a worried hum as the small group—but Marta was certain mostly Simms and Gregory— came into view. Only the ringing blows of the blacksmith's hammer continued without pause.

The man led them to one of the smaller buildings, past the curious and concerned faces of the women. The windows and door were open to let the fresh air and sunlight in fully. The man paused in the doorway. "Josephine? You have a…" He gave Marta a sharp glance "…fellow scientist who would like to speak with you."

A woman laughed inside, a low chuckle with no small amount of bitterness. "I somehow doubt that."

Stepping into the small building felt almost like entering her own home; the contents were so familiar to Marta. Wires and small welding tools and components for electrical devices were nearly arranged across several workbenches. One wall had been given over to mounted pieces of slate that made the entire thing a large blackboard. Equations, evolved from the ones Marta had read in Josephine's paper, covered the slates.

Josephine herself stood in front of the slates, her back as straight as a poker, a piece of chalk still held loosely in one hand. She half smiled at the sight of Deliah, but then her posture stiffened further as she took in the sight of Marta in her trousers, with Simms and Gregory at her back. Marta pointedly took off her hat and unknotted her hair, letting the deep brown curls cascade down her shoulders.

Josephine smiled faintly at that, though her worried gaze still stayed on the two men. Marta glanced back at them. Gregory had the oddest look on his face, as if he'd been struck in the stomach. Now was not the time for her to ascertain the cause, Marta decided. "Mister Simms, Mister Kinzer, do find an unobtrusive place to loom outside, if you please."

"Happy to," Simms said. "Maths give me hives." He turned, then grabbed Gregory by the shoulder when he didn't immediately follow. "Come along."

Only after the two men were well gone from the doorway did Josephine give herself a little shake, as if shedding cold water from her shoulders. "Forgive my surprise," she said. "I don't often have visitors from the outside. Unless…?"

"We shan't be taking up residence," Deliah said. "We are, thankfully, neither from this duchy, nor part of…gentle society."

"Rather, I came across a piece that I thought might have something to do with your work, and I would like to discuss it…" Marta took the stolen device from her satchel and laid it on the table. Josephine's reaction, after a moment of peering at the device, was unexpected—all of the color drained from her face, and she stepped unsteadily backwards to collapse down on a stool near the slate wall. "Or perhaps, this piece is in fact your work."

Josephine nodded mutely, one hand coming up to cover her mouth. Marta wasn't entirely certain if it was a sign of further shock, or an indication that she might be sick.

"Well," Deliah said firmly, clapping her hands. "I see there's much we shall be discussing. I'll go fetch a tea set."

Marta remained standing in silence; she turned her apparent attention to the slates on the wall to give Josephine time to compose herself, though she watched the process of the woman regathering her wits and emotional strength keenly from the corner of her eye. At long last, Josephine lightly touched the device, as if she expected it to bite her. "Did you take this from… *him?*"

"One of his lackeys, I'm afraid," Marta answered. She briefly outlined the escapade, during which time Deliah returned with a teapot and a few iced biscuits on a tray.

"I am glad you have such determined friends," Josephine said to Deliah.

"As am I," Deliah answered.

Josephine regarded the cup of tea Deliah handed to her as if it might hold the mysteries of the universe. "I did not have such friends, nor loyal family. Though I ultimately can blame only myself for my plight. I allowed myself to be charmed by Sylvester…yes, that's his name, no matter the self-aggrandizing title he's given himself since. Oh, he flattered my ego so! He listened to my theories and acted as if I had an intellect worth respect. I was so hungry for it, then. He told me he would see my inventions into reality, and that we would be full business partners, and I believed it. I believed it so fiercely that I accepted his abuse of my person as a necessary evil, that I let myself be ruined…" She put her face in one hand and took a deep breath. "Though perhaps that has been a blessing in disguise, because my family was more than happy to pack me off to this place, and little did they know what freedom it offered."

Marta well knew the freedom an escape from society offered, and the costs entailed. "It is a great evil all the same, that a man took such advantage of you, and that we live in such a cruel and unfair society that the power over you was his to take."

Josephine offered her a thin, sad smile. "It is why being among women…and others originally born to our sex…is my greatest comfort. I have my work, even if I cannot place my own name upon it."

That led to the discussion of her theories that Marta had been most interested in, one that lasted for the entire teapot. The longer they spoke of abstracts, the more relaxed and animated Josephine became, eventually rising to her feet to begin writing half equations with her chalk to illustrate her points.

Marta felt almost disappointed to circle the conversation back around to the more immediate business at hand. But while she understood the theory well enough, it would take her a great deal of time to try to develop her own answer to the Rail King's devices, and she'd begun to form other thoughts about what might be done there, fueled by the quiet seethe of her well-hidden anger at the layers of injustice that had been revealed. She reached out to tap one finger on the device again. "Can you make something like this now, perhaps one that could override the signals, or act as a sort of skeleton key?"

"Yes, of course, but…" The animation drained slowly away from Josephine as she contemplated this. "I cannot. I dare not. I live comfortably now because my family chose to hide my shame by keeping me at this sisterhood. Sylvester told me that if I broke my silence in any way, he would ruin me far more thoroughly in public, and have the law upon me. I can't bring that kind of attention to this place. It's not only my happiness and life at stake."

Next to her, Deliah raised an eyebrow. Not in surprise, but a gesture of inquiry, as if asking what part she should play. She had no reason to yet know what Marta intended; Marta herself hadn't quite decided. She was not, she reminded herself, a vigilante, nor the sort of person who did things for free. And yet this felt like a moment that had been waiting for her.

The Rail King had arguably ruined and hurt a great many people, even if his crimes didn't match the genocidal extent of the late and unlamented General del Toro. It felt like a chance where things might be done again, and right somehow—even if Marta still wasn't certain of the *how* of it, because she'd found no flaws in her own logic, and that was part of what had her chasing in circles for so many months. She opened her mouth to speak, only to be interrupted by a voice from the door.

"Unless we destroy him," Gregory Kinzer asked.

Simms had taken Gregory a short way around the back of the small building after Captain Ramos had dismissed them both. It took them out of sight of most of the women who seemed determined to either gawk or be overtly disturbed by their presence. He didn't much care for either of those options.

The shabby man who had answered the gate, after disappearing briefly into the house with Deliah, returned with a cup of tea for each of them. "I'd no idea she was Captain Ramos," he remarked. "Which must make you Mister Simms, correct?"

"Unfortunately," Simms said, though he couldn't help but smile a bit when he said it. "She isn't aiming to cause trouble here. My word on it."

"No," the shabby man said. "But I do hope she's aiming to cause trouble on behalf of Josephine."

"She doesn't work for free," Simms said. Though in truth, she'd done many things nearly so, because she wanted to. The words were enough to take the little man off, though, which saved Simms from any further uncomfortable questions.

A relative silence descended; there were still the sounds of the blacksmith shop, and the multitude of women talking quietly around the corner. But it felt like being on a different sort of planet, an oddly uncomfortable one where he—and Gregory—were the odd and unwelcome strangers. The only other time Simms had felt like this was when infiltrating high society functions with the captain, but that was far different because he was there to play a role and ultimately steal or cause other mayhem. That wasn't the intent here and he had no marrow-deep reason to dislike these women, so he simply felt…alien.

Simms turned to see if Gregory felt the same, only to find the young man pacing furiously, the tea spilling over the sides of his cup as his steps accelerated yet further. But then Gregory had been acting a bit off this entire time, with the quiet—and that right there was odd enough, since Gregory tended to be a merry fellow—strangeness coming to a head the moment they'd stepped into that woman's little building.

"It's a personal thing, ain't it," Simms said, a statement, not a question. "Lot more personal than just being on a bad crew."

Gregory stopped in his tracks and gave him a stricken look.

"You know that lady, in there."

"Only by name," Gregory said quietly. "I heard the…king… mocking her often."

"You laugh?" Simms asked.

"I did, then. Because it was the thing to do." Gregory scrubbed his face with one hand. "Because I was glad it wasn't me, you see. Only it was me, too. You get lured in with this thought of having money and power and…even a place of your own. And then you think that to get it, you'd best never say *no*…" Utter shame crushed his expression.

"We've all done damn fool things before, Gregory," Simms said gently, unsure what else he even could say.

But Gregory didn't even seem to be listening as he continued, like the words were pus from a boil that simply had to be drained away now that it had been lanced, "And then you find out that saying *no* doesn't matter at all anyway." He looked at Simms despairingly. "Women can be ruined, but men…"

Simms let out his breath carefully. Depending upon the duchy, such as the one they stood in at this moment, men could hang. He cleared his throat. "I'm sure it isn't much comfort, but you've got at least twelve other hanging offenses on your head now, in four different duchies."

Gregory stared at him, and then burst out laughing, though it was a horrible kind of laugh that sounded more like sobs than anything. Simms carefully put his arm around the man's shoulders, and Gregory briefly pressed his face against his jacket.

"You've been scared this whole time?" Simms asked.

Gregory nodded mutely.

"Horrible thing, to be afraid so long. But you're part of a good crew. You said it yourself. And Captain Ramos won't let anyone go after her crew, and you know that too."

"I do," Gregory said, his voice muffled against Simms's buckskin.

"So ask yourself…if you don't have to be afraid of this bastard any more, what would you do? What do you think the lady in there would like to do? You both have the same problem, I'd say." Simms already saw where his question led, and it wasn't to a cautious place. But he had his own temper, and the more he learned about the underbelly of what the Rail King did, the more apt he found the entire title of 'King.' He'd like to put the man on the chopping block himself.

Gregory pushed away from Simms, his eyes red but his back straight. He turned and walked around the building to the doorway. Simms followed, hearing the tail end of the conversation the ladies were having. And Gregory said, strong even if his voice was a bit scratchy, "Unless we destroy him."

As Gregory painfully told his story a second time, Josephine rose to take both of his hands before he'd even gone through the first two halting sentences. After he'd finished speaking, Josephine said, "We are far too alike. Even our scars match. But…I wish I shared your final conviction. Sylvester has too much power now."

"He only has power because no one can challenge his control of the rails," Deliah said. "Because no one has been able to challenge *your* inventions. Captain Ramos has a stalwart crew and her own armaments. If you give her the means, she will prove equal to this task."

She meant the *crew* would prove equal to the task, Simms thought. And for once he did not qualify the thought with an acknowledgment of his own allergy to adventure. This was no longer an adventure; it was a vendetta. He eyed Captain Ramos, waiting for her to demand some price, some kind of fig leaf to cover their involvement, as she had in the past for such cases. She'd always been very firm that they did not do charity, though at this point, Simms was ready to dip into his own hard-earned savings from shares of plunder to finance the whole mess.

But as Captain Ramos seemed to be chewing over some bit of mental gristle, Deliah stepped in. She looked at the captain as she spoke, a warm glitter in her tawny eyes. "If Josephine gives you means to thwart the traps of the Rail King, you will have complete freedom of the hidden rails. That seems a suitable price."

Captain Ramos smiled. "It does sound a lovely adventure, to break the monopolistic stranglehold of a self-described king."

Deliah's lips crimped with amusement. "You never have had any use for the monarchy as anything but ready sources of cash."

"And neither have you," Captain Ramos returned.

"They throw lovely parties, too."

"Good sausages," Simms remarked, then cleared his throat. "I'll send a telegram to let Cook know we'll have another delay then, shall I?"

Josephine still held on to Gregory's hands with a white-knuckled grip. Simms saw Gregory squeeze her hands in return as he said, "I no longer wish to be afraid. Will you join me?"

"I have far more to lose than you," Josephine said.

"I will place my life between you and that threat," Gregory said. "I give you my word."

That seemed a bit much, Simms thought, considering Gregory was the second most junior member of the crew. But a glance at Captain Ramos showed that she had no objection. And maybe that was how it should be.

"The word of men means little," Josephine said.

"What about the word of a pirate?" Simms said, catching a startled glance from both of them—and an approving nod from Captain Ramos.

Josephine's expression became uncertain with both fear and a spark of hope. She squeezed Gregory's hands tightly. "It will take a few days."

As an undertaking, the design and building of a new transmitter, one that Josephine assured Marta would "override" any other device, took four days. Marta's crew, once collected by Simms, made good use of that time with the House of Unwed Sisters serving as a home base of sorts. Marta and Little Wren worked to translate the codebook with a small amount of guidance from Josephine and updated their charts using the information from Deliah and older intelligence from Gregory's memory.

Lucius and Amelia, after setting Diabola to rights, went about effecting all necessary repairs on weapons and clothing as well as a full resupply of the engine. Then, when Lucius found himself idle, rather than repairing to a gambling hell that he'd have to be fished from later, he joined the endless sewing circle at the house to the initial trepidation and then unbridled enjoyment of the ladies.

The most difficult question was one that neither Marta nor Little Wren with their combined mathematical prowess, could hope to solve—where the Rail King might be found at this time of year. After spending another of the days gathering all known information about his appearances over the last five years, they could find no useful pattern in timing or location.

"Searching without a logical place to start will be a waste of time," Little Wren remarked, after another unsuccessful pass through the data. "Chance does not treat us kindly."

Marta, having calculated the odds in her head, couldn't help but agree. One in a million chances happened far more regularly than people understood, but on the other hand, they also could not be relied upon. "I suppose we could station ourselves centrally and wait for a sighting."

Little Wren frowned at the papers scattered before them. "Almost as bad of a way to hunt. It's better to know where your quarry will be and wait for them to pass by."

While true, that ran them against the lack of information again in a neat circle. "I don't have enough data about the man," Marta said. Deliah had a quite thorough read on one of his flunkies, but that would be of limited use; DeLuc wasn't the one calling the shots. But she did have access to two people who knew the Rail King much more intimately. And while she did not wish to disturb Josephine's work, Gregory was currently busying himself helping the ladies re-roof one of the out buildings.

Gregory's face, thoroughly sheened with sweat thanks to the bright sun warming the clear day, went sallow when Little Wren put the blunt question of the Rail King's whereabouts to him. "I don't know," he said. "I wasn't even close to as important as DeLuc. He certainly never told me about his…style of navigation."

Marta held up a hand. "Tell us about the man himself, Mister Kinzer, if you please. His interests or habits, anything of that nature."

Gregory rubbed at the stubble that was starting to show on his chin, grimacing. "You always do some sort of witchcraft with that sort of thing. Sir."

"Deduction," Marta answered. "Please proceed."

"I don't know…he likes games of chance. Gambling. But not with money, as such. He wasn't big into going into casinos, and he never played for real money with his crew. More that he liked the numbers." Gregory grimaced. "Ah…can't stand peaches because of the fuzz."

"I don't see how that is relevant," Little Wren remarked.

"The captain did say *anything*." Gregory shrugged. He continued on with a random assortment of likes and dislikes that built a certain picture of the man to which they attached but offered no other answers.

"What about music?" Marta asked. There was much musical preference might say about someone's personality and upbringing, she'd found.

"He loved opera, but only if translated properly into English," Gregory said. "Or preferably the home-grown stuff."

"Ghastly," Marta remarked. Most new opera was commissioned directly by the nobility, which meant it leaned toward bombastic praise of its patrons. Composers needed to eat, after all.

"Wasn't even so much about the music itself," Gregory said. "The sound. He's really interested in sound, and how things echo, and…you know that trick, where a lady who sings soprano can shatter a glass with her voice?"

"I'm familiar," Marta said dryly. It was something Amelia had used multiple times to earn herself free drinks in the little mining towns that snugged up against the mountains.

"He has this idea, about trying to take sound and make it into a weapon. To explode things with it. Always looking for more ways to study how sound works."

That was it, Marta realized. The detail that might give them direction. "Thank you, Mister Kinzer. You may go now. Please do send Mister Cavendesh to us before you return to your work."

Gregory departed with a little half bow, obviously relieved he'd been of some service. Little Wren raised one eyebrow, to which Captain Ramos answered, "If you wish to truly understand the destructive capabilities of a human voice, there's no one better to ask than Mister Cavendesh."

Amelia indeed provided the last piece of the puzzle; she knew of all the best natural amphitheaters in the west of the continent, sheepishly admitting that she'd sung at most of them, one time or another. She even had a general idea of when most might be in use for large concerts or small private recitals. She marked each out with a circle in pencil on the chart, so their position relative to the main rail lines and the Rail King's private lines would be evident, all the while adding detail such as, "Can't do this one in the winter…too high up and the snow gets far too deep on the passes. And this one… Not in the summer. You'd drown in your own tit sweat."

Armed with the few possibilities that would be unoccupied around this time of year, Marta repaired to the university's library again to find more particular information about each. One, called the Abo Amphitheater after its native rock formation, was located not far north from the gateway to the Mexican Empire, the Mesilla Valley, which had been experiencing unusually violent and frequent thunderstorms in the late autumn and early winter over the last several years.

They had found their logical place to start.

While they covered most of the distance to their destination at speed, they switched to a much more cautious approach as they neared the San Andres Mountains. They moved only at night with no headlamp and shaded lanterns—thankfully the lonely rails of this buffer zone between the duchies and the empire were not overly occupied with night travelers—and scouted out their best vantage on foot by day. There were a shocking number of hidden rail spurs in the area of the amphitheater, all of them guarded by traps that Marta was able to disarm with Josephine's new transmission device, which doubled as a comforting field test of its capabilities.

After they had found their place of best advantage, a combination of quick access to the main lines that the Rail King would be most likely to use and a good view of the amphitheater for their lookouts, there was little to do but wait and see if the Rail King would show up at all. Marta set the crew to camouflaging Diabola with pine boughs and other bits of brush, things that would break up their outline while also falling easily away without interfering with the operation of the engine once they were on the move. But that was a task for only a day.

Gregory became quieter and more withdrawn the longer they waited, a situation Marta was happy to leave to Simms. He'd always been better at dealing with the emotional vagaries of the crew than she, and it gave him a project to keep him busy as well. Amelia, Little Wren, and Lucius all seemed quite relaxed, treating this as a sunbathing holiday and a chance to catch up on their reading or practice at cards. Marta found herself increasingly restless, for all Deliah tried to distract her most pleasantly. There was only so much physical pleasure could distract an unquiet mind, however.

Marta found herself more and more often drawn to a cliff face overlooking the amphitheater. It was really nothing like the precipice that had been the denouement in the Black Hills, yet it haunted her all the same. She could all too easily imagine herself shoving a faceless figure over this edge and watch it pinwheel down to be lost in the branches of the trees below. Because really, how was the coming situation any different from what she'd faced before? The Rail King had enough wealth and power that he could no doubt pull the same sort of strings as General del Toro, and many would be all too eager to protect him to save their own reputations if nothing else.

"It is a lovely view," Deliah said, from behind her.

"Indeed," Marta agreed. The dark shapes of thunderheads boiled across the horizon to the north. They'd need to take shelter soon.

Deliah moved to stand next to her, one arm slipping around her waist. Marta allowed herself to lean a bit against the other woman's soft form. "Not really your style though," Deliah remarked. "Will you not tell me what's been eating at you since… oh, since no doubt long before Simms stirred himself to tell me he was concerned about you?"

"Oh, I'd wondered about that." She felt a small prick of annoyance at the thought, but Simms had always been the mother hen sort. Marta sighed. Keeping her concerns to herself had only put her in a logical loop with no escape. Perhaps it was time to try a different tactic. "You know that I consider cold-blooded murder to be the worst sort of crime?"

"Yes. Your list of acceptable moral outrages is one of your charms."

Marta couldn't help but snort. She rested her hand over Deliah's. "I murdered General del Toro in the Black Hills, rather than let him be brought back to the duchy for trial."

Deliah was silent for a long moment, as if deep in thought. She leaned her cheek against Marta's arm. "I see. Well, the man was a pig."

Marta wasn't certain if she wished to lean into the touch or jerk away and rub the sensation off of her skin. "It wasn't so simple."

"What was the complication, then?"

"He was willfully trying to spread infection among the tribes of the plains. For glory and all," Marta said bitterly.

"That seems even more simple a situation."

Intellectually, yes. The man had done incalculable harm and had been very clear about his intention to do more, because he knew he would not face justice of any sort. And it wasn't as if he was the first man Marta had ever killed—though it was also true that all previous times had been in the heat of engine-to-engine battle. It was somehow different, when someone was shooting at her; what choice did she have then but to shoot back? Del Toro had been of no immediate threat, even if he posed a greater danger to so many more people than herself than just a few decently-aimed bullets. "It isn't," she finally said.

"Then explain why."

Marta stepped back. "I'm a pirate, Deliah. I'm no one's savior, and I'm certainly no one's executioner." Or at least she wasn't supposed to be. She had no legal high ground, though it was of course up for debate if there was much use to the concept of legality as it currently existed; she spent her life stealing, though she took pride in the thought that she didn't steal from those who couldn't afford it. But it had always been much easier to wash her hands of the more difficult criminal questions and leave the execution of justice of the morally degenerate to the law. That was one thing Colonel Douglas had been good for: if she left him a murderer on a string, she knew damn well he'd deal with it, because that was his job and he had no imagination.

But this last time, she—and he, she'd seen that in his face— had known that there was nothing justice-shaped under the so-called legal system for someone of del Toro's power. It had been a stark reminder of the sort of gross unfairness that had driven her into the wilds of the Rocky Mountains years ago—which she normally managed to ignore *because* she had nothing to do with "normal" society.

"Are you sorry that he's dead?" Deliah asked.

"Goodness, no." Marta felt her lips twist. Because this was the true quandary that haunted her. "I'm sorry that it was me."

"We all must grow up some time," Deliah remarked, gently touching her nose.

"I don't know what I shall do when we apprehend the Rail King," Marta said. The wind, cold and picking up speed ahead of the coming storm, tugged at a few stray locks of her hair.

"If we're all lucky, he'll get himself shot in the melee, and then no one will have to search their soul," Deliah said dryly. "But I think you also ask the wrong question. You are not the law for the lawless, Marta Ramos. And the person here who has suffered is not you."

"Engine sighted!" Gregory shouted, his voice faint in the distance. He did not ring the alarm bell; Amelia had been concerned it would echo enough off the rock surrounding them that it would alert their quarry.

Deliah squeezed her arm. "Do what is best for your crew and yourself. That is all any of us might ask."

When Deliah had begun to be counted among their number was another question, to be addressed later. For now, Marta would simply be grateful for her presence.

Marta joined Gregory on the top of Diabola as Simms went about gathering and readying the rest of the crew. They passed the small, sturdy spyglass back and forth as they tracked the progress of the new engine coming up to the amphitheater along the winding track.

"Is this the one we want?" Marta asked.

Gregory nodded grimly as he passed her the spyglass. "It's one of his design. And look on the side of it. He's got a griffin in gold paint. That's his, all right."

"Ostentatious," Marta remarked, after examining the distant glint of the paint.

"Aye."

"Will he stay in the engine, or be getting out to run whatever experiments he has?" Marta asked.

"Could be either," Gregory said. He glanced at the thunderstorm darkening the horizon. "But I'd put my money on the former. Doesn't like being uncomfortable, though he might send some of his men out."

"And he'll likely be intending to stay here for several days?" Marta asked. Their greatest difficulty was the configuration of the tracks for the area. There was only a single track that wended through the mountains; they had to cut off the spur that led into the amphitheater, or there would be an open avenue for escape in one direction.

"Yeah," Gregory said.

"Then we'll go in at dark," Marta said. "We ought to be able to use the flares again, I—"

"I don't think you will," Deliah interrupted. "He's just reversed course."

"Bloody hell!" Gregory shouted, snatching the spyglass back. "Shit. Shit, sir. We've been pinched. How..."

"Does it matter?" Deliah asked.

Even at this distance, Marta could plainly see the steam beginning to roil from the distant engine's stack. She stared at it, as if her gaze alone might explode the boilers. "Is it faster than Diabola?"

"I don't know," Gregory said. "Perhaps?"

Marta thought back over the winding tracks they'd used to get here, the sharp curves necessitated by private construction that hadn't wanted to make itself obvious by blasting. "It doesn't matter," she concluded. "And I know he doesn't have a better navigator." She leaped into Diabola and rang the alarm bell. It no longer mattered if they were heard; only speed mattered now.

"Mister Cavendesh! Mister Little Wren!" she shouted as the two women came sprinting up to Diabola. "Hot pursuit. All speed short of jumping the track. Do you understand?"

Amelia grinned. When she answered, the single syllable was a pure, musical note that echoed piercingly from the high rock walls. "Sir!"

The crew scrambled and secured themselves as Marta brought Diabola's own boilers up to a roar. The only saving grace they had for the mad chase they were about to embark on was that the Rail King's engine had to reverse through the first twenty miles. Few drivers were as confident as Amelia and willing to go full speed when they could not see where they were going, particularly not on such difficult track. Diabola leapt into forward motion, caroming down the first curve in a way that had Simms shouting he'd felt half the wheels come off the track. Marta hastily got herself strapped in safely, out of range of Simms should he lose his lunch as he was threatening to do.

Rolling thunder grew louder and louder overhead as Diabola leaped and shuddered, swaying like a mad thing. "He's stopped at the junction," Gregory informed them through the speaking tube. "Now forward the other way…yeah, got himself turned." It was a move that lost him some time, at the least; Marta could only hope that her faith in Amelia and Little Wren was well-founded, because now the chase had begun in earnest.

With an unholy crash that shook Diabola and left sharp after-images in Marta's eyes, the storm announced itself fully as they reached the junction. Not even the deluge of rain that followed caused Gregory to abandon his post. The afternoon went black around them, visible through the small windows of the crew compartment, and the torrential rain pulsing with flashes of purple-white lightning.

Unable to stand it any longer, Marta unstrapped herself, ignoring the alarmed looks directed at her by Deliah and Simms. She staggered up the aisle to the cockpit, Diabola tilting drunkenly beneath her as they took another sharp turn at a speed that left her feeling light-headed.

The Rail King's engine was a barely-discernable smudge in the rain-lashed distance; it was impossible to tell if they were gaining or falling behind.

"It isn't really safe up here," Little Wren said, as Marta clutched at the back of her seat.

"I'll accept the risk," Marta said. "Can we take them?"

"In a fair chase, no," Amelia said, her gaze never wavering. "But we've got a plan."

"Open stretch in twenty seconds," Little Wren said, and began counting down.

Amelia lifted one hand up to hang over a button Marta knew well; she'd placed it on the control panel herself as an experiment. It was an overdrive of sorts, a secondary pressure vessel waiting to be drained to provide a temporary burst of speed.

Marta dug her fingers into the back of Little Wren's chair as the count reached zero. Amelia's fist came down on the button. A horrific shrieking sound echoed up the engine and Diabola leaped forward like a scalded cat.

"How long until the turn?" Amelia asked.

"Three minutes, two seconds until maximum brake," Little Wren answered.

Not long at all, but the burst of speed had them gaining precipitously on the engine ahead—but what was the use, if they'd have to lose it all in braking at the curve?

Marta squinted into the rain, and…yes, she was certain that there was more steam billowing from the three stacks of the engine ahead. It all became clear. "Clever," she commented.

"Tell me that once we're on the other side of that turn and not dead," Amelia said.

But it was plain that the driver ahead of them, hearing that they'd gained, had panicked and poured on far more speed than he should. And he did not have Little Wren, with all of her uncanny precision, to tell him when he ought to stop.

"Five seconds until brake," Little Wren counted down calmly. "Four… three… two… one… brake."

As Amelia slammed on Diabola's brakes, almost sending Marta tumbling into the control panel, the Rail King's train had only just begun to slow for the turn. It wasn't enough. The three-stacked, gaudy engine tilted crazily and began to tumble into the canyon far below.

Suddenly a familiar *THUNK* resounded through Diabola— the grappling gun being fired. It struck the engine ahead true, and as Amelia cursed and applied more emergency braking, as

Diabola herself tilted horribly to the side as the line went taut… Marta reached ahead and trigged the emergency release on the starboard side pistons.

A confused, horrible moment later, she picked herself up off the floor. Her head and nose ached, and she definitely had blood running all down her chin. But Diabola was now leaned the other way, propped up by the released pistons, and holding steady. And as Marta looked out into the wild storm, she saw illuminated in flashes of lightning: the Rail King's engine stopped, half-dangling into the canyon.

"Boarding party," Marta said thickly through swollen lips. But Amelia got the hint and hit the alarm.

The entire crew scrambled out into the soaking black of the storm. No one was quite steady on their feet, but they had to strike first and quickly. Lucius surged ahead of the group, an enormous maul in his hands that he used to break the rear door of the engine in two.

Marta followed on Lucius's heels into the narrow corridor of the engine, which if anything was more sumptuously decorated than the previous one. The sharp downward angle of the engine leant everything an extra feeling of vertigo. Marta dashed rainwater from her eyes and ducked to avoid a door as someone burst into the corridor ahead of her. She cut at his legs with her machete and felt the blade bite. "Up the stairs first!" she shouted.

Behind her, Simms roared, and Marta let go of her machete to press herself against the wall. He went barreling after Lucius, with Gregory and Deliah at his heels. A hand grabbed at Marta's ankle, and she swiftly kicked it off, then aimed another kick at the person who had grabbed her. The carpet squished unpleasantly under foot, soaked already with rain and blood. Marta yanked her machete free from the leg of the enemy crewman and followed the rest of her people.

It was a melee, with the Rail King's compliment already injured from their derailment, and everyone confused by the strange angle of the battlefield. There was too much light and sound from the storm above them. Amelia and Little Wren played tag team, each wielding hand axes as they chased disoriented crewmen back into their quarters. Lucius took two bullets in the shoulder, which didn't slow him down at all but only made him rage about the ruin done to his handmade jacket, while Simms put the man who had shot him through a second-floor window and out into the canyon below.

Deliah and Gregory made it to the upper control room at the same time, with Marta at their heels. Panting and soaked, they both still held their pistols steady, Deliah's pointed at Niemen DeLuc, and Gregory's pointed at a tall, older man whom Marta could only assume was the Rail King himself. His ostentatious clothing, all gold and brocade with more of the eagles, lions, and griffins, said as much. The rest of him was unremarkable, washed out by his finery—plain face, shaggy hair, pale gray eyes.

"Hello, darling," Deliah said to DeLuc. "Did you miss me?"

"I know you haven't missed me," Gregory said to the Rail King.

"Of course I have," the Rail King said. He had his hands half up, but he was smiling, as if he couldn't believe any of this was serious. And yet he leaned back against the control panel, showing ease against the downward pull of gravity. "I'd never forget you, Gregory. You were such a hard worker. You still could be, you know."

At each word, Marta saw Gregory tense a bit further, like it was a key winding him up. "He already is," she said quietly. She saw his finger tense on the trigger and knew how this might play out: another sheer cliff, another tumbling body. And yet... She looked at Gregory's face in profile, his eyes wide and wild, and remembered the anguish he'd shown when speaking with Josephine—and what Deliah had said to her much more recently. This frozen moment in time with its ridiculous horror-show thunder and blood, was not about her. Marta carefully took Gregory's shoulder and squeezed to gain his attention. Into his ear, she murmured. "I killed a man recently, out of...moral efficiency, I suppose you could say. It did not make me feel any better about my situation."

His eyes widened slightly. "I didn't know that. Why are you telling me?"

"I don't believe I have a right to make this decision for you, because I cannot possibly imagine what it is like to stand where you are," she said, after a long moment. "I simply want you to know that I've already trusted you with my life on every job we have done. So, I shall trust you in this as well."

Gregory swallowed hard, his Adam's apple bobbing. "Thank you, sir." He turned his attention back to the Rail King's pale face and faintly smug smile. "It's over. I know where you keep your charts in here. We know how to disable all the traps. No one's going to give you a bloody cent anymore."

"Come on, Gregory. I know you. You're not going to shoot me. Let's get back to working together. There are a lot of ugly things no one needs to ever know about—"

Even over the thunder, the bark of Gregory's pistol was almost deafening in the confined space. The Rail King crumpled to the floor, blood running from the distinct hole in his head. Marta's stomach clenched sickly at the sight and she felt no satisfaction at it.

Deliah, next to him, smiled as she tipped her pistol slightly toward the wet stain beginning to spread down the front of Nieman's trousers. "Oh dear, I'd forgotten how delicate your nerves are," she said sweetly.

Gregory seemed steadier on his feet than ever as he lowered his hand to his side, his eyes still fixed on the Rail King's corpse. "Josephine and the other ladies send their regards. I'll be certain to convey your lack of regret in return."

They abandoned Nieman DeLuc and the other survivors of the Rail King's engine in the mountains to fend for themselves, which was a kinder fate than Gregory felt they deserved—though his personal thirst for vengeance seemed to have been slaked by the Rail King's death. They cannibalized the Rail King's engine for parts, along with the charts and other interesting devices he had aboard. Diabola required a few field repairs to the pistons, which between this abrupt use and the earlier double jump they'd taken in pursuit of DeLuc, were having trouble holding sufficient pressure for Marta's comfort. The remains of the Rail King's engine, Gregory cut loose to fall into the canyon with a crash that even Marta found quite satisfying.

From there, they spent the next month traveling the rails—and breaking the snow on quite a few passes as they did—to find all of the private rail lines and disable the Rail King's traps, as well as making note of what repairs might be necessary. Their last stop was in the Grand Duchy of Salt Lake where Marta, Deliah, and Gregory once more paid a visit to the unwed sisters. Josephine's face was quite still as Gregory told her of the Rail King's fate, though her posture shifted as if a great weight had been lifted away.

"I feel strange," she said. "It's a wicked thing to wish to celebrate someone's death, and yet I do."

"You have a friend in wickedness, at the least," Gregory said.

Marta, feeling a bit as if she was intruding on a private moment, and not the sort she might have fun spying on, said, "As a pirate, I find myself unprepared to make such moral judgments." It seemed best to give the two a bit of privacy for any further discussion they might have; it wasn't long past breakfast, so there was time. "And with that, I shall take my leave. Mister Kinzer, we shall depart at five o'clock from the main station."

Gregory offered her a small, but grateful smile. "I'll be there sharpish, captain."

"Thank you, Captain Ramos," Josephine said.

Marta acknowledged the words with a small wave as she headed for the door. Deliah caught her other hand and squeezed it, and they walked together into the warm sunlight.

It was cold on the mountainside that concealed Devil's Roost. The mountain snow was covered with a thin crust of ice, just enough for Marta to not break through it as she walked out beneath the pine trees. It had been a long time since she'd viewed the dawn from its right side. Deliah, a disturbingly early riser, seemed to be having an effect on her. She'd had her first truly restful sleep in ages down in the depths of the abandoned mine, with Deliah's arms wrapped around her and Chippy nestled between them.

Behind her, she heard the door to the Roost open, and then Simms cursing as he tried to come out onto the snow—and ended up sinking to mid-thigh. "You're a monstrosity," Marta observed.

"This monstrosity has your tea, so you'd best watch yourself," Simms grumbled. A minute of crunching and cursing later, he found a secure enough patch of snow to stand next to her. And indeed, he had a teacup steaming in each hand.

Marta took the one he offered and simply held it, warming her fingers. "I suppose I ought to feel more satisfied," she said.

"Did some good work," Simms observed.

"And the churches do so like to tell us that good work is a path to redemption."

Simms made a rude noise. "Think most of 'em would say it was donating money and praying, actually. But I don't believe for one second you've ever been to a proper church and paid attention to anything but the state of their silver." He sighed. "If this is the first time you've hit a decision you couldn't shake, you're luckier than I've ever been."

She glanced at him. "So what do you do then, Simms?"

"If you're an idiot, you drink too much. If you're lucky, you get a friend to give you a hand out of the hole, and then…you just keep going, I guess." He shrugged. "At least that's what's worked for me. Life isn't a neat thing. Or if it is, I suppose it'd be fair boring."

"I thought you liked boredom." In his own way, Marta reflected, Simms was quite the philosopher. And if she ever pointed that out, he'd no doubt be properly horrified. She transferred her teacup to one hand. With the other, she took a bemused Simms's hand in a firm shake.

"What's that for?" he asked.

"You aren't thanked very often."

He regarded her suspiciously. "If you start now, I'll know you've been drinking."

Marta laughed. She gave his hand one more squeeze and let go. "Did you know that Josephine has been corresponding with Mister Kinzer, and she recently passed along the news that there's to be quite the wedding in the Grand Duchy of Salt Lake? One of the Grand Duke's nieces, and all we'd have to do is sneak into the temple…"

Simms groaned theatrically. But his eyes were smiling as he did it, and so were Marta's.

About the Author

Alex Acks is an award-winning writer, Book Riot contributor, geologist, and sharp-dressed sir. Angry Robot Books has published their novels *Hunger Makes the Wolf* (winner of the 2017 Kitschies Golden Tentacle award) and *Blood Binds the Pack* under the pen name Alex Wells. A collection of their steampunk novellas, *Murder on the Titania and Other Steam-Powered Adventures*, is available from Queen of Swords Press. They've had short fiction in Tor.com, Strange Horizons, Giganotosaurus, Daily Science Fiction, Lightspeed and more, and are a regular contributor at Book Riot. They've also written several episodes of Six to Start's Superhero Workout game and races for their RaceLink project. Alex lives in Denver (where they bicycle, drink tea, and twirl their ever-so-dapper mustache) with their two furry little bastards.

For more information, see **http://www.alexacks.com**

About

QUEEN OF SWORDS PRESS

Queen of Swords is an independent small press, specializing in swashbuckling tales of derring-do, bold new adventures in time and space, mysterious stories of the occult and arcane and fantastical tales of people and lands far and near. Visit us online at **www.queenofswordspress.com** and sign up for our mailing list to get notified about upcoming releases and offers. Or follow us on Facebook at the Queen of Swords Press page so you don't miss any press news.

If you have a moment, the author would appreciate you taking the time to leave a review for this book at Goodreads, your blog or on the site you purchased it from.

Thank you for your assistance and your support of our authors.